Charles G. D. Roberts

Around the Camp-Fire

Charles G. D. Roberts

Around the Camp-Fire

ISBN/EAN: 9783337255480

Printed in Europe, USA, Canada, Australia, Japan

Cover: Foto ©Andreas Hilbeck / pixelio.de

More available books at **www.hansebooks.com**

AROUND THE CAMP-FIRE

BY

CHARLES G. D. ROBERTS, M.A., F.R.S.C.

ILLUSTRATED

BY

CHARLES COPELAND

NEW YORK: 46 EAST FOURTEENTH STREET

THOMAS Y. CROWELL & COMPANY

BOSTON: 100 PURCHASE STREET

CONTENTS.

iii

iv   *CONTENTS.*

CHAPTER VII.

CHAPTER VIII.

CHAPTER IX.

LIST OF ILLUSTRATIONS.

AROUND THE CAMP-FIRE.

CHAPTER I.

OFF TO THE SQUATOOKS. — THE PANTHER AT THE
PARSONAGE. — BEAR VS. BIRCH-BARK.

IT was toward the end of July, and Fredericton, the little New Brunswick capital, had grown
hot beyond endurance, when six devoted canoe-
ists — Stranion, Magnus, Queerman, Sam, Ranolf,
and myself — heard simultaneously the voices of
wild rapids calling to them from afar. The desire
of the woods awoke in us. The vagrant blood
that lurks in the veins of our race sprang up and
refused to be still. The very next day we fled
from the city and starched collars, seeking freedom and the cool of the wilderness.

It was toward Lake Temiscouata and the wilds
of the Squatooks that we set our eager faces. In
shirt-sleeves and moccasins we went. For conven-
ience we had our clothes stitched full of pockets.
Our three good birch canoes and our other *impedi-
menta* we put on board a flat-car at the station.
And that same evening found us at the village of

Edmundston, where the Madawaska flows into the St. John at a point about one hundred and fifty miles above Fredericton.

Unless you are an experienced canoeman, skilled not only with the paddle but with the pole, and expert to run the roughest rapids, you should take a guide with you on the Squatook trip. You should go in the bow of your canoe, with a trusty Indian in the stern; one Indian and one canoe for each man of the party. The art of poling a birch-bark against a stiff current is no easy one to acquire, and needs both aptitude and practice. Your Indian will teach you in the gentler waters; and the rest of the time you may lounge at your ease, casting a fly from side to side, and ever climbing on between the changing shores. But as for us, we needed no Indians. We were all six masters of canoe-craft. Each took his turn at the white spruce pole; and we conquered the currents rejoicing.

Temiscouata is a long, narrow lake just outside the boundaries of New Brunswick. It lies in the Province of Quebec; but its outlet is the Madawaska River, a New Brunswick stream. Our plan of proceeding was to take to the canoes at Edmundston, and pole fifteen miles up the Madawaska, make a portage of five miles across country to Mud Lake, follow Beardsley Brook, the outlet of Mud Lake, to its junction with the Squatook River, and then slip down this swift stream, with its chain of placid expansions, till we should float out upon the waters of Toledi Lake. Toledi River would then receive us among its angry rapids and cascades, to eject us forcibly at last upon the great bosom of Temiscouata, whence we should find plain paddling back to Edmundston. This would make a round trip of, say one hundred and forty miles; and all of them, save the first fifteen, with the current.

At Edmundston that evening we pitched our tent beside the stream; and next morning, though it was raw and threatening, we made an early start. In one canoe went Stranion and Queerman; in the second, Sam and Ranolf; in the third, Magnus and myself. The bedding, extra clothing, etc., laced up snugly in squares of oiled canvas, made luxurious seats, while the eatables were stowed in light, strong boxes built to fit the canoes.

The first day out is usually uneventful, and this was no exception. When adventures are looked for they pretty certainly fail to arrive. We reached the portage with an hour of daylight to spare, and there found an old log cabin, which saved us the necessity of pitching our tent. It was dry, well-ventilated, abundantly uncivilized. What a supper Stranion cooked for us! And then what a swarm of mosquitoes and midges flocked in to bid us welcome! We hedged ourselves about with a cordon of slow fires of cedar bark, the smoke of which proved most distasteful to them, and almost equally so to us. And then with a clear blaze crackling before the open door, and our blankets spread on armfuls of spruce boughs, we disposed ourselves luxuriously for pipes and yarns.

Queerman drew a long, blissful whiff through his corn-cob, blew a succession of rings, and murmured like a great bumblebee, —

> "The world is Vagabondia
> To him who is a vagabond."

"Who'll tell us the first yarn?" inquired Sam, as his pipe drew freely.

"Stranion begins," said Magnus quietly. Magnus was a man of few words; but when he opened his mouth, what he said went. He was apt to do more and say less than any one else in the party.

"Well, boys," said Stranion, "if Magnus says so, here goes. What shall I talk about?"

"Who ever heard of Stranion talking about anything but panthers?" jeered Ranolf.

"Well," assented Stranion, "there's something in what you say. The other night I was thinking over the various adventures which have befallen me in my devotion to birch and paddle. It surprises me to find what a lot of scrapes I've got into with the panthers. The brutes seem to fairly haunt me. Of course fellows who every year go into the Squatook woods are bound to have adventures, more or less. You get cornered maybe by an old bull-moose, or have a close shave with some excited bear, or strike an unusually ugly lynx, or get spilled out of the canoe when you're trying to run Toledi Falls ; but in my case it is a panther every time. Whenever I go into the woods there is sure to be one of these creatures sneaking around. I declare it makes me quite uneasy to think of it, though I've always got the best of them so far. I'll bet you a trout there are one or two spotting me now from those black thickets on the mountain ; and one of these days, if I don't look sharp, they'll be getting even with me for all the members of their family that I have cut off in their sins."

"Oh, you go along !" exclaimed Sam. "You're getting sentimental. I can tell you, I have killed more trout than you have panthers, and there's no old patriarch of a trout going to get even with me !"

Sam's practical remark went unheeded ; and in a few moments Stranion resumed, —

" You see, boys, the beasts began to haunt me in my very cradle so to speak. Did any of you ever hear mother tell that story ? "

" I have !" ejaculated Queerman ; but the rest of us hastened to declare our ignorance.

" Very well," said Stranion. " Queerman shall see that I stick to the facts."

" Oh, boys, I've a heavy contract on hand then," cried Queerman.

But Stranion blandly ignored him, and continued, —

"I'll call this tale —

'THE PANTHER AT THE PARSONAGE.'

"You have all seen the old parsonage at the mouth of the Keswick River. That's a historic edifice for you! Therein was I born. There were more trees around it then than now.

"At the mature age of ten months I moved away from that neighborhood, but not before the Indian devil, as the panther is called in that region, had found me out and marked me as a foreordained antagonist.

"One bright June morning, when I was about five months old, and not yet able to be much protection to my young mother, my father set out on one of his long parochial drives, and we were left alone, — no, not quite alone; there was Susan, the kitchen-girl, for company. That constituted the garrison of the parsonage on that eventful morning, — mother, Susan, and myself.

"I cannot say I *remember* what took place, but I have so often been told it that I feel as if I had taken an active part. Mother and I were sitting by an open window, down-stairs, looking out on the front yard, when suddenly mother called out sharply, —

"'Susan, Susan! Come here and see what sort of a creature this is coming through the grove!'

" There was a frightened ring in my mother's voice which brought Susan promptly to her side.

" Just then the 'creature,' which was long and low and stealthy, reached the garden fence. It mounted the fence gracefully, and paused to look about.

" With a horrified gasp, mother caught me to her bosom, and whispered, —

" ' It's a tiger ! '

" ' No'm,' cried Susan, ' it ain't no tiger ; but it's an Injun devil, which is pretty nigh as bad.' And she ran and slammed down the window.

" The noise attracted the brute's attention. He glanced our way, dropped to the ground, and crept stealthily toward the house.

" ' The attic ! ' cried mother wildly. ' All the windows down-stairs are wide open.'

" I need hardly assure you, boys, it didn't take those two women and me very long to get up-stairs. As we reached the top we heard a crash in the parlor, and mother nearly squeezed me to death in her terror for me ; but Susan exclaimed almost gleefully, —

" ' I declare, if he ain't got in the wrong winder ! Parlor door's shut ! '

" By this time we were on the attic stairs ; and the door at the foot of the stairs — a solid, old-fashioned country door — was safely bolted behind us.

"That door was the only means of access to the attic; and on the head of the stairs we all sat down to take breath. Then in mother the anxious housewife began to reappear.

"'What *was* that the horrid brute broke in the parlor, Susan?' she queried.

"'Must a' been them dishes on the little table by the winder, ma'am,' responded the girl.

"And then we heard a clatter again, as the beast, in springing out of the window, knocked the fragments of pottery aside.

"In a few moments he found another entrance. The soft *pat, pat* of his great furry feet could be heard on the lower stairs. He was evidently hungry, and much puzzled at our sudden disappearance.

"We could hear him sniffing around, in and out of the bedrooms, and at last that soft, persistent tread found its way to the attic door.

"How he did sniff about the bottom of that door till the blood of his prisoners ran cold with horror! Then he began to scratch, which was more than they could stand.

"Terror lent them invention, and mother put me into a basket of old clothes, while she helped Susan drag a heavy bedstead to the head of the stairs. This bedstead effectually blocked the narrow stairway, and when they had piled a chest of drawers on top of it they once more felt secure.

"All this trouble was unneeded, however, as

that door, opening outward, was an insurmountable barrier to the panther.

"In a few minutes he stole away restlessly. Then we heard some flower-pots, which stood on the window-ledge of the front bedroom, go crash on the steps below. The Indian devil was getting out of the window.

"Now, the attic in which we had taken refuge was lighted by two windows, — a small one in the gable, looking out upon the barnyard, and the other, a very small skylight, reached by a sort of fixed step-ladder from the attic floor.

"As soon as mother heard the animal's claws on the side of the house, she thought of the skylight, and cried to Susan to shut it.

"The skylight had an outer shutter of wood, which was closed in winter-time to keep the heavy snowfall from breaking the glass.

"This shutter was now thrown back upon the roof, and the inner sash was raised a few inches for the sake of ventilation. Susan fairly flew up the ladder, and pulled out the little stick that supported the sash.

"She had barely got the hook slipped into the staple when the panther's round head and big light eyes appeared within a foot of her face. She gave a startled shriek, and fell down the ladder.

"At this juncture the two women gave themselves up for lost; and mother, seizing an old curtain-pole, which lay among the attic lumber, prepared to sell my infant life at a pretty high figure.

"All escape from the attic was blocked by the articles they had so carefully wedged into the stairway. This it would take them some time to clear.

" They never imagined that so fierce a brute as the panther could be stopped by an ordinary sash and glass, however strong.

" But the Indian devil is wary, and this one was suspicious of the glass. When, on attempting to put his head down through the skylight, he met with an obstacle where he did not see any, he thought he detected a trap.

" He sniffed all over each pane, stopping every moment to eye us angrily. Then he scratched, but very gingerly, at the sash, and only tore away some splinters. The sash was stout and new.

" At last he thrust his muzzle over roughly against the pane, and his nose went through the glass. Susan sank in a heap, while mother, with deadly purpose, grasped her curtain-pole, expecting instant attack.

" It was not to be so, however; for which the world is much to be congratulated. The panther cut his nose pretty severely on the broken glass, and shrank back, snarling viciously.

" He was more than ever convinced that the skylight was a trap, and would not trust his muzzle again in the opening.

" Observing the beast's caution, mother plucked up new hope. She remembered having read that lions and tigers were afraid of fire, and forthwith she hit on a truly brilliant expedient.

"' Get up, Susan,' she commanded, 'and be of some use. Go and light that lamp on your washstand, and bring it to me.'

" Susan obeyed with alacrity, cheered by the thought that there was anything left to do. When the lamp was brought, mother laid the chimney aside, and turned up the wick so as to give a flaring, smoky blaze. Then she handed the lamp back to Susan.

"' Take it,' she said, 'and set it on the top of the ladder, right under the broken pane.'

" This was too much for poor Susan.

"'Oh, I dasn't — never!' she whimpered, backing hastily out of her mistress's reach.

" Mother regarded her with withering scorn, then turned and looked at me, where I lay close behind her in a basket of old clothes.

" Assuring herself that the panther could not get me in her absence, she seized the lamp and marched up the ladder with it. The panther growled most menacingly, and thrust his face down to the opening ; but as the smoke and flame came under his nose, he snarled and drew back.

" On the very topmost step did mother deposit the lamp, where it blazed right up through the broken pane. As she turned down the ladder, the panther's claws were heard along the shingles, beating a reluctant retreat.

" In a moment or two he was heard on the shed, and then mother opened the skylight, reached out, and clapped down the wooden shutter. Susan's courage revived.

" Now that the danger was over, mother picked me out of the basket, and gathered me again to her bosom, while Susan began to speculate on what the panther would be up to next. On this point she was not long left in doubt.

" In the corner of the barnyard was a pig-pen, inhabited at the time by a pig three months old. Presently the poor little pig set up a terrific squealing, and mother and Susan rushed to the gable window.

" As I have said before, this window commanded a view of the barnyard. The panther was on the roof of the pen, peering down through the cracks, and scratching vigorously to gain an entrance. Baby had been denied him, but pork he was determined to have.

" The pig squealed in a way that mother trusted would alarm the neighborhood, and tried to hide himself in the straw from the reach of those pale, cruel eyes. At last the panther quitted the roof, and found the pen door. Here he paused a moment or two, suspecting another trap. Then, finding nothing suspicious, in he glided. There was one terrific squeal, and all was still.

"I fancy mother and Susan both wept, think-ing how well the fate of poor piggie might have been their own — and mine.

"For a long while the two women kept watch at the window. At last the panther reappeared, walking very lazily, and licking his chops. He glanced at the house in a good-natured fashion, as if he bore us no grudge; cleaned his great face with one paw, sniffed the air thoughtfully in vari-ous directions, and then made off towards the woods: and we knew that our pig went with him.

"When he was well out of sight, mother and Susan removed the barricades and forsook the attic. You may be sure they fastened every win-dow, kept a keen outlook, and went about their work in fear and trembling.

"When my father got home, in the middle of the afternoon, he heard the story before he could unharness the horse. Straightway he set out again, and organized a hunting-party among the neighbors. The party was armed with all sorts and conditions of weapons; but it bagged that panther before sundown, whereby was my mother much consoled. And now, have I stuck to the facts?" said Stranion, turning to Queerman.

"To my surprise, you have!" responded the latter.

"Well," went on Stranion, unruffled, "since the panthers got after me so early, it's not much cause for wonder if they've kept it up."

At this moment a strange, unearthly, gurgling cry broke the night's stillness, and we started involuntarily.

"There is one of mine ancient enemies now," said Stranion. "I'm sure to fall foul of him to-morrow, and one or the other of us will rue the day!"

"Well," said Sam, "we all know it won't be Stranion!"

The story done, I rose and replenished the fire, while Magnus passed around a tin of hot coffee. A whippoorwill, —

> "Threshing the summer dusk
> With his gold flail of song,"

was heard in a hillside thicket, and Queerman cried, —

"Listen to him, boys!"

"No," said Stranion; "we'll now give our very best attention while Sam tells us one of his old bear stories."

"Indeed," said Sam with an indignant sniff; "I'll tell you one I never told before, and a true one at that. Now don't interrupt, for I intend to do it up in a somewhat literary fashion, to save the Old Man trouble in writing it down."

"Thank you kindly," said I. I was the official scribe of the party, and familiarly known as the Old Man, or simply O. M., for short.

"BEAR VS. BIRCH-BARK,"

continued Sam, "is the title of my narrative. It was on the upper waters of the Oromocto River that the case of Bear *vs.* Birch-bark was decided. Thither had Alec Hammond and I betaken ourselves in our canoe to kill some Oromocto trout.

"The Oromocto is for the most part much less rapid than other trout rivers of New Brunswick; in fact, for long distances its current is quite sluggish, a characteristic finely suited to our indolence of mood. Paddling quietly, or poling when the water was swift, we soon left behind us all traces of civilization. Instead of beautiful open meadow shores shaded with here and there a mighty elm or ash, we entered the ruggedest parts of the original wilderness, where the soil was too barren and stony to tempt even a squatter, and where the banks were clothed with dark hemlocks to the water's edge. Sometimes these sombre woods gave back a space, and a wild confusion of many kinds of trees took their place, — pines, ash. birch, basswood, larch, and beech, mixed with fallen trunks and staring white bowlders. Sometimes. again, in the midst of the most impenetrable forest a delightful little patch of interval, or dry waterside meadow. would open up before us, inviting us to pitch our tent amid its deep, soft grasses. Scattered through the grass were clumps of tall wild lilies, their orange blossoms glowing amid the green ; and around the stately heads of the wild-parsnips, which made the air heavy with rich perfume, fluttered and clung the silver-throated bobolinks. What wonder we rested when we came to these wilderness gardens whose possession there was none to dispute with us ! We found that as a rule we might count upon an ice-cold brook near by. Wherever such brooks flowed in, there would be a deep pool, or an eddy covered with foam-clusters, or a pebbly, musical rapid, which meant a day of activity for our rods and reels and flies.

" One day, after such a morning with the trout as had left our wrists well tired, we were inclined to give our rods a resting-spell. The afternoon was sultry and drowsy, — it was toward the close of July, — and Alec's highest ambition was to take a long siesta in the tent-door, where an over-hanging beech-tree kept off the sun, and a sweet breeze seemed to have established its headquarters. There was no wind elsewhere that I could perceive, yet round our tent a soft breath of it was wandering all the day.

" For my own part I didn't feel like loafing or lotus-eating. The fever for specimens was upon me. I have an intermittent passion, as you know, for the various branches of natural history, and am given at times to collecting birds and plants and insects. This afternoon I had visions of gorgeous butterflies, rare feathered fowl, and various other strangely lovely things thronging my brain, so I put into the canoe my gauze net and double-barrelled breech-loader, and set off up stream in a vague search after some novelty.

" Let me confess it, my taste was destined to be gratified beyond my hopes.

" Above our camping-ground the river for some distance was swift and deep. Beyond this it widened out, and became almost as motionless as a lake. Along these still reaches the shores were comparatively low, and less heavily wooded, with here and there a little corner of meadow, a bit of wet marsh covered with cat-tail flags, or a dense fragrant thicket of Indian willow. There were water-lily leaves in broad patches right across the stream ; and the air was gay with green and purple dragon-flies, which lit on my gunwale, and glittered in the sun like jewels. There was not even a rustle of leaves to break the silence.

" At last, as I noiselessly rounded a low bushy point. right ahead I saw a splendid blue heron. which was watching intently for minnows in the shallow water. He spread his broad wings and rose instantly. I had just time to let him have one barrel as he disappeared over a thicket of alders, flying so low that his long legs swept their tops. I felt certain I had hit him. for straightway arose a great crackling and struggling among the bushes beyond. In my haste I failed to notice that this disturbance was rather too violent to be proceeding from any wounded bird, unless it were a dodo.

"Running my birch ashore alongside of a mouldering trunk which had fallen with half its length in the stream, I made my way, gun in hand, through the underwood, without stopping to load my empty barrel. There was no sign of blue herons where my bird was supposed to have fallen; but to my unlimited astonishment I beheld a black bear cub making off at his very best speed, badly scared.

"At my sudden appearance he gave a curious bleat of alarm, and redoubled his efforts to escape. He had little cause for alarm, however, as I did not want him for a specimen; and had I wanted him ever so much I could not well have bagged him with no heavier ammunition than bird-shot. I was watching his flight with a sort of sympathetic amusement when, with a most disagreeable suddenness and completeness, the tables were turned upon me. In the underbrush behind me I heard a mighty crashing; and there to my dismay was the old she-bear, in a fine rage, rushing to the rescue of her offspring. Considering that the offspring's peril was not immediate, I thought she need not have been in such a tremendous hurry.

"She had cut off my retreat. She was directly in the line of my sole refuge, my faithful and tried birch-bark. There was no time left for medita-

"I COULD HEAR THE ANIMAL PLUNGING IN PURSUIT."   Page 19.

tion. I darted straight toward the enemy. Undaunted by this boldness she rose upon her hind-legs to give me a fitting reception. When almost within her reach I fired my charge of bird-shot right in her face, which, not unnaturally, seemed somewhat to confuse her for a moment. It was a moment's diversion in my favor. I made the most of it. I dashed past, and had gained some paces toward the canoe, when my adversary was again in full chase, more furious than ever. As I reached the canoe she sprang upon the other end of the log, and was almost aboard of me ere I could seize the paddle and thrust out.

" Fortunately I had headed down stream, for the mad brute took to the water without hesitation. Had the stream been deep I should merely have laughed at this, but in these shallows it was no laughing matter. The channel was deep enough to impede the bear's running, but by no means to make running impossible. I felt that the question of speed between us was now a painfully doubtful one. My back bent to the paddle. The broad blade flashed through the water with all the force and swiftness I was master of. Close behind, though I could not spare time to look back, I could hear the animal plunging in pursuit, and I was drenched with the spray of her splashings. I was a skilful canoeist; I have won many races; but never was another canoe-race I was so bent upon winning as this one.

" At last, snatching a glance over my shoulder, I saw that I had gained, though but slightly. It was well I had, for the tremendous pace was one which I could keep up no longer. I knew the deep water was still far ahead, and I knew, too, the obstinacy and tireless strength of my pursuer. There was, therefore, a grave uncertainty in my mind as to whether I could succeed in holding the lead much longer. I slackened a little, saving my strength all I could; but the bear at once made up her lost ground, and my breathing-space was brief. At a little short of my best, but still at a killing pace enough, I found I could keep out of reach. But if a shoal should come in the way, or a sunken log, or any like obstruction, the game was up. With this chance in view I had little leisure for watching my pursuer's progress. I could hear, however, and feel, quite too much of it.

" After what seemed an age of this desperate racing, we came to a part of the stream where I expected a change in my favor. For a quarter of a mile I would have a fair current, in a narrower and deeper channel. Here I gained ground at once. I relaxed my efforts a good deal, gave my aching arms a moment's rest, and watched the angry bear wallowing clumsily after me, able now neither to run nor swim. This ended the matter, I fondly imagined, and I drew a long sigh of relief.

"But I was far yet from being out of the wood! I had begun to 'holloa' too soon! When the bear saw that I was about to escape she took to the land, which just here was fairly open and unobstructed; and to my horror she came bounding after me, along the water's edge, at a rate which I could not hope to rival. But in the pause I had recovered my breath and my strength. I shot onward, and my antagonist had a hard gallop before she overhauled me. I could mark now every bound of her great black form. The sharp chattering laugh of a kingfisher startled me, and I noticed the bird fly off down stream indignant. How I wished I might borrow his wings! Just then the bear, having got a little in advance of me, sprang for mid-stream, so sagaciously timing her effort that had I kept on she must inevitably have seized or upset me. But it was this I was on the watch for. In the nick of time I backed water with all my might, swerved aside, and darted past close behind her — so close that I could have clutched her shaggy hind-quarters. I had no special reason for attempting this feat, however, so I sped on.

"And now began a second stretch of shoals. For the next half-mile it was much the same old story, save that I had gained a better start. There was one little variation, however, which came near making an end of the whole affair. In rounding a sharp turn I did just what I had been dreading,

— ran aground. It was only on the skirts of a sloping shoal, and I was off again before I had time to think; but the distance twixt pursuer and pursued had grown painfully less in that moment. I could all but feel the animal's hot breath upon the back of my neck. The strain was terrible; but soon I began to take heart again. I thought to myself that surely I could hold out till clear of these last shallows; and after that I knew the shores were such as might be expected to baffle even this most indomitable of bears. When again we reached deep water I was paddling a splendid stroke, and the bear, apparently as fresh and as wrathful as ever, was floundering along perhaps two canoe-lengths in the rear.

"By this time the camp was in sight, a good half-mile off. I saw Alec come lazily out of the tent, take a glance at the situation, and dart back again. Gun in hand he re-appeared, and ran up the shore to meet us. Feeling that now I had matters pretty well my own way, I waved him back. So he took his stand on the summit of a precipitous bluff, and awaited his chance for a shot.

"As soon as the bear found herself again compelled to swim, with a snort and a growl she turned shoreward to repeat her former manœuvre. She took the opposite shore to that occupied by Alec. The banks were steep and crumbly, clothed along top with bushes and fallen trees and rocks, and a tangle of wild vines. Yet the unwearied brute managed to overcome these difficulties by her stupendous strength, and actually outstripped me once more. It was all she could accomplish, however; and just as she sprang for the canoe the edge of the bank gave way beneath her weight, and in an avalanche of stones and loose earth she rolled head over heels into the river. I was far away before she could recover herself. I saw she was utterly disgusted with the whole thing. She clambered ashore, and on the top of the bank stood stupidly gazing after me. Then I laughed and laughed till my over-strained sides were near bursting. I could hear peals of mirth from Alec at his post on the bluff, and was calmed at last by a fear lest his convulsions might do him some injury.

"Reaching the landing-place, I only waited to pull the canoe's nose up onto the grass, then threw myself down quite exhausted. A moment later the bear gave herself a mighty shaking, and, accepting her defeat, moved sullenly back up stream."

As Sam concluded, Stranion rose and gravely shook him by the hand.

"I congratulate you on winning your case!" said he. "And now, being first night out, let's all turn in, or we'll be fagged to-morrow."

It is hard to get to sleep the first night in camp, and I was awake for an hour after all the rest were snoring. I lay listening to the soft confusion of night sounds, till at last the liquid gabble of a shallow below the camp faded into an echo of cathedral bells ; and while I was yet wondering at the change, I found the morning sun in my face, and saw Stranion holding out a tin of hot coffee. I sprang up, and found myself the laggard of the crowd.

"Come to breakfast," cried Stranion. "Lynch is here, and it's time we were over the portage."

Tom Lynch was a lumberman whom we had engaged by letter to come with his team and drag, and haul our canoes over to Mud Lake. His team was a yoke of half-wild brindle steers. The portage was five miles long, the way an unvarying succession of ruts, mud-holes, and stumps, and Mr. Lynch's vocabulary, like his temper, was exceedingly vivacious. Yet the journey was accomplished by the middle of the afternoon, and with no bones broken. The flies and mosquitoes were swarming, but we inflicted upon them a crushing defeat by the potent aid of "slitheroo." This magic fluid consists of Stockholm tar and tallow spiced with pennyroyal, and boiled to about the consistency of treacle. It will almost keep a grizzly at bay.

By half-past three in the afternoon we were launched upon the unenchanting bosom of Mud Lake, a pond perhaps three miles in circumference, weedy, and swarming with leeches. It hardly exceeds two feet in apparent depth, but its bottom is a fathomless slime, stirred up vilely at every dip of the paddle. Its low, marshy shores, fringed here and there with dead bushes and tall, charred trunks, afforded us but one little bit of beauty, — the green and living corner where Beardsley Brook flows out. At this season the brook was very shallow, so that we had often to wade beside the canoes and ease them over the shallows. And now Sam did a heroic thing. He volunteered to let the rest of us do the work, while he waded on ahead to catch some trout for supper.

It was by no means unpleasant wading down this bright and rippling stream, whose banks were lovely with overhanging trees through which the sunlight came deliciously tempered. Time slipped by as sweetly as the stream. But a little surprise was in store for us. We were descending a beautiful alder-fringed reach. when around a bend below us appeared Sam with undignified impetuosity. He struggled toward us knee-deep in the current, dashing up the spray before him, his eyes as wide as saucers. " A bear ! A bear ! " he gasped ; and hurling down his rod and fish in the canoe he seized a heavy revolver. We had grasped our weapons precipitately, and halted. But Sam urged us on, leading the way. As thus full-armed we pressed forward down stream, he told us in a suppressed voice how, as he angled and meditated, and there was no sound save the hushed tumult of a little rapid or the recurrent swish of his line, suddenly from the bank behind him rose the angry, blatant growl which he knew for the utterance of a she-bear with cubs. At this he had felt indignant and startled; and, with a terrific yell, had hurled a stone into the bushes as a hint that he was a bad man and not to be trifled with. Thereupon had arisen a roar which put his yell to shame. The undergrowth had rocked and crashed with the swift approach of the monster; and, filled with penitential misgivings, he had made haste to flee. When we reached the scene of the possible tragedy, however, the bear, or bears, had disappeared. We grieved not greatly for their absence.

CHAPTER II.

THE CAMP ON BEARDSLEY BROOK.

By this time the stream, having taken in two or three small tributaries, had grown deep enough to float us in comfort. A little before dusk we reached a spot where some previous party had encamped, and had left behind a goodly store of elastic hemlock boughs for bedding. We took the hint and pitched tent.

Sam's trout were a dainty item on our bill of fare that night. Our camp was in a dry but gloomy grove, and we piled the camp-fire high. When the pipes were well going, I remarked, —

"It's time Magnus gave us a story now."

"Hear! Hear!" cried every one but Magnus.

"One of your own adventures, Magnus," urged Queerman. "Be content to be your own hero for once."

"I'll tell you a story my uncle told me," said Magnus with a quiet smile. "And the O. M. can enter it in his note-book as —

'A TIGER'S PLAYTHING.'

"My uncle, Colonel Jack Anderson, a retired officer of the English army, was a reticent man.

He had never explained to me the cause of a certain long red scar, which, starting from the grizzled locks behind his ear, ran diagonally down his ruddy neck, and was lost beneath his ever-immaculate shirt-collar. But one night an accidental circumstance led him to tell the story.

" We were sitting coseyly over his study fire, when his cat came stalking in with sanguinary elation, holding a mouse in her mouth. She stood growling beside my chair till I applauded her and patted her for her prowess. Then she withdrew to the middle of the room, and began to play with her half-dazed victim, till Colonel Jack got up and gently put her outside in order to conclude the exhibition.

" On his return my uncle surprised me by remarking that he could not look without a shudder upon a cat tormenting a mouse. As I knew that he had looked quite calmly, on occasion, into the cannon's mouth, I asked for an explanation.

" 'Do you see this?' asked the colonel, touching the scar with his lean, brown finger. I nodded attentively, whereupon he began his story : —

" 'In India once I went out on a hot, dusty plain near the Ganges, with my rifle and one native servant, to see what I could shoot. It was a dismal place. Here and there were clumps of tall grass and bamboos, with now and then a tamarisk-tree. Parrots screamed in the trees, and the startled caw of some Indian crows made me pause and look around to see what had disturbed them.

"'The crows almost at once settled down again into silence; and as I saw no sign of danger, I went on carelessly. I was alone, for I had sent back my servant to find my match-box, which I had left at the place of my last halt; but I had no apprehensions, for I was near the post, and the district was one from which, as was supposed, the tigers had been cleared out some years before.

"'Just as I was musing upon this fact, with a tinge of regret because I had come too late to have a hand in the clearance, I was crushed to the ground by a huge mass which seemed to have been hurled upon me from behind. My head felt as if it had been dashed with icy or scalding water, and then everything turned black.

"'If I was stunned by the shock, it was only for an instant. When I opened my eyes I was lying with my face in the sand. Not knowing where I was or what had happened, I started to rise, when instantly a huge paw turned me over on my back, and I saw the great yellow-green eyes of a tiger looking down upon me through their narrow black slits.

"'I did not feel horror-stricken; in fact, so far as I can remember. I felt only a dim sense of resignation to the inevitable. I also remember that I noticed with curious interest that the animal looked rather gratified than ferocious.

"'I don't know how long I lay there, stupidly gazing up into the brute's eyes; but presently I made a movement to sit up, and then I saw that I still held my rifle in my hand. While I was looking at the weapon, with a vague, harassing sense that there was something I ought to do with it, the tiger picked me up by the left shoulder and made off with me into the jungle; and still I clung to the rifle, though I had forgotten what use I should put it to.

"'The grip of the tiger's teeth upon my shoulder I felt but numbly; and yet, as I found afterwards, it was so far from gentle as to have shattered the bone.

"'Having carried me perhaps half a mile, the brute dropped me, and raising her head uttered a peculiar, soft cry. Two cubs appeared at once in answer to the summons, and bounded up to meet her. At the first glimpse of me, however, they sheered off in alarm; and their dam had to coax them for some minutes, rolling me over softly with her paw, or picking me up and laying me down in front of them, before she could convince them that I was harmless.

"'At last the youngsters suffered themselves to be persuaded. They threw themselves upon me with eager though not very dangerous ferocity, and began to maul and worry me. Their claws and teeth seemed to awaken me for the first time to a sense of pain. I threw off the snarling little animals roughly, and started to crawl away. In vain the cubs tried to hold me. The mother lay watching the game with satisfaction.

" ' Instinctively I crept toward a tree, and little by little the desire for escape began to stir in my dazed brain. When I was within a foot or two of the tree the tiger made a great bound, seized me in her jaws, and carried me back to the spot whence I had started.

" ' " Why," ' thought I to myself, ' " this is just exactly the way a cat plays with a mouse ! "

" ' At the same moment a cloud seemed to roll off my brain. No words of mine, my boy, can describe the measureless and sickening horror of that moment, when realization was thus suddenly flashed upon me.

" ' At the shock my rifle slipped from my re-laxing fingers ; but I recovered it desperately, with a sensation as if I had been falling over a precipice.

" ' I knew now what I wanted to do with it. The suddenness of my gesture, however, appeared to warn the tiger that I had yet a little too much life in me. She growled and shook me roughly. I took the hint, you may be sure, and resumed my former attitude of stupidity ; but my faculties were now alert enough, and at the cruelest ten-sion.

" ' Again the cubs began mauling me. I re-pelled them gently, at the same time looking to my rifle. I saw that there was a cartridge ready to be projected into the chamber. I remembered that the magazine was not more than half empty.

"'I started once more to crawl away, with the cubs snarling over me and trying to hold me; and it was at this point I realized that my left shoulder was broken.

"'Having crawled four or five feet, I let the cubs turn me about, whereupon I crawled back toward the old tiger, who lay blinking and actually purring. It was plain that she had made a good meal not long before, and was, therefore, in no hurry to despatch me.

"'Within about three feet of the beast's striped foreshoulder I stopped and fell over on my side, as if all but exhausted. My rifle-barrel rested on a little tussock. The beast moved her head to watch me, but evidently considered me past all possibility of escape, for her eyes rested as much upon her cubs as upon me.

"'The creatures were tearing at my legs, but in this supreme moment I never thought of them. I had now thoroughly regained my self-control.

"'Laboriously, very deliberately, I got my sight, and covered a spot right behind the old tigress's foreshoulder, low down. From the position I was in, I knew this would carry the bullet diagonally upward through the heart. I should have preferred to put a bullet in the brain, but in my disabled condition and awkward posture I could not safely try it.

"LABORIOUSLY, VERY DELIBERATELY, I GOT MY SIGHT" — Page 82.

" ' Just as I was ready, one of the cubs got in the way, and my heart sank. The old tiger gave the cub a playful cuff, which sent it rolling to one side. The next instant I pulled the trigger — and my heart stood still.

" ' My aim had not wavered a hair's breadth. The snap of the rifle was mingled with a fierce yell from the tiger; and the long, barred body straightened itself up into the air, and fell over almost on top of me. The cubs sheered off in great consternation.

" ' I sat up and drew a long breath of thankful relief. The tiger lay beside me, stone dead.

" ' I was too weak to walk at once, so I leaned against the body of my vanquished foe and rested. My shoulder was by this time setting up an anguish that made me think little of my other injuries. Nevertheless, the scene about me took on a glow of exquisite color. So great was the reaction that the very sunlight seemed transfigured.

" ' I know I fairly smiled as I rapped the cubs on the mouth with my rifle-barrel. I felt no inclination to shoot the youngsters, but I would have no more of their over-ardent attentions. The animals soon realized this, and lay down in the sand beyond my reach, evidently waiting for their mother to reduce me to proper submission.

" ' I must have lain there half an hour, and my elation was rapidly subsiding before the agony in my shoulder, when at last my man, Gunjeet, appeared, tracking the tiger's traces with stealthy caution.

"'He had not waited to go for help, but had followed up the beast without delay, vowing to save me or avenge me ere he slept. His delight was so sincere, and his courage in tracking the tiger alone was so unquestionable, that I doubled his wages on the spot.

"'The cubs, on his approach, had run off into covert, so we set out at once for the post. When I got there I was in a raging fever which, with my wounds, kept me laid up for three months.

"'On my recovery I found that Gunjeet had gone the next day and captured the two cubs, which he had sent down the river to Benares, while the skin of the old tiger was spread luxuriously on my lounge.

"'So you will not wonder,' concluded the colonel, 'that the sight of a cat playing with a mouse has become somewhat distasteful to me since that experience, I have acquired so keen a sympathy for the mouse!'"

While Magnus was speaking, a heavy rain had begun. It had little by little beaten down our fire; and now, as the wind was abroad in the hemlocks and the forest world was gloomy, we laced the tent-doors and lit our candles. It was announced by some one that Queerman's turn was come to speak. He grumbled an acquiescence, and then dreamed a while; and in the expectant stillness the rush of rain, the clamor of currents, and the lonely murmur of the tree-tops, crept into our very souls. We thought of the sea; and when Queerman spoke, there was a vibration in his voice as of changing tides and the awe of mighty shores.

"Magnus," said he, "your tale was most dusty and hot, though not *too* dusty, if I may be allowed to say so. It was of the earth earthy; mine shall be of the water watery. It may be entered in the O. M.'s log as —

"A FIGHT WITH THE HOUNDS OF THE SEA."

"It was just before daybreak on a dewy June morning of 1887, when a party of four set out to drift for shad. There was the rector (whom you know), my cousin B—— (whom you don't know), and myself (whom you think you know). We went to learn how the business of drifting was conducted. There was also the old fisherman, Chris, the owner of the shad-boat. He went for fish.

"By the time the long fathoms of brown net were unwound from the great creaking reel and coiled in the stern of the boat, the tide had turned, and a current had begun to set outward from the little creek in which our boat was moored. Our rusty mainsail was soon hoisted to catch the gentle catspaws from the shore, and we were underway.

"A word of explanation here. The shad-fishing of the Bay of Fundy is carried on, for the most part, by 'drifting.' The boats employed are roomy, heavy, single-masted craft, with a 'cuddy,' or forward cabin, in which two men may sleep with comfort. These craft, when loaded, draw several feet of water, and are hard to float off when they chance to run aground. They carry a deep keel, and are stanch sea-boats — as all boats need to be that navigate the rude waters of Fundy.

" When we had gained a few cable-lengths from shore the breeze freshened slightly. It was a mere zephyr, but it drove the boat too fast for us to pay out the net. We furled the sail, and thrust the boat along slowly with our heavy sweeps, while Chris paid out the net over the stern.

" These Fundy boats sometimes stay out several tides, making a haul with each tide ; but it was our intention merely to drift out with this ebb, and return by the next flood.

" It was slow work for a while. We ate, told stories, speculated as to how many fish were entangling themselves in our meshes, and at about nine o'clock appealed to Chris to haul in.

" The tremendous tide had drifted us in five hours over twenty miles. We decided to run the boat into the mouth of a small river on our right to take a good swim before we started on the return trip. The plan was accepted by Chris, and we set ourselves to haul in the net.

" In the centre of the boat stood two huge tubs, into which we threw the silvery shad as we took them from the meshes. When we found a stray skate, squid, or sculpin, we returned it to its native element; but a small salmon we welcomed as a special prize, and laid it away in a wrapping of sail-cloth.

"The catch proved to be rather a light one, though Chris averred it was as good as any he had made that year.

"'Why, what has become of the shad?' asked the rector. 'It seems to me that in former years one could sometimes fill these tubs in a single trip.'

"'Ay, ay,' growled Chris, 'that's true enough, sir! But the fishin' ain't now what it used to be; and it's all along o' them blamed dogfish.'

"'What do the dogfish have to do with it?' I asked.

"'Do with it!' answered Chris. 'Why, they eat 'em. They eat everything they kin clap ther eye onto. They're thicker'n bees in these here waters the last year er two back.'

"'They are a kind of small shark, I believe?' put in the rector in a tone of inquiry.

"'Well, I reckon as how they be. An' they're worse nor any other kind as I've heern tell of, because they kinder hunt in packs like, an' nothin' ain't a-goin' to escape them, once they git onto it. I've caught 'em nigh onto four foot long, but mostly they run from two to three foot. They're spry, I tell you, an' with a mouth onto 'em like a fox-trap. They're the worst varmin that swims; an' good fer nothin' but to make ile out of ther livers.'

" ' I've heard them called the "hounds of the sea," ' said B——. 'Are they bold enough to attack a man ? '

" ' They'd attack an elephant, if they could git him in the water. An' they'd eat him too,' said Chris.

" ' I hope they won't put in an appearance while we're taking our swim,' remarked the rector. 'I don't think we had better swim far out.'

" By this time we were near the mouth of the stream, a broad, shallow estuary three or four hundred yards wide. In the middle was a gravelly shoal which was barely uncovered at low water, and was then marked by a line of seaweed and small stones. We bore up the northern channel, and saw that the shores were stony and likely to afford us a firm landing; but the channel was unfamiliar to Chris, and suddenly, with a soft thud, we found ourselves aground in a mud-bank, a hundred yards from shore. The tide had yet a few inches to fall, and we knew that we were fast for an hour or so.

" When we had got ourselves out of our clothes, the surface of the shoal in mid-channel was bare. It was about fifty yards from the boat, and we decided to swim over to it and look for anemones and starfish. B——, who was an indifferent swimmer, took an oar along with him to rest on if he should get tired. We laughed at him for the precaution as the distance was so short; but he retorted, —

" 'If any of those sea-dogs should turn up, you'll find that said oar will come in pretty handy.'

" The water was of a delicious temperature; and we swam, floated, and basked in a leisurely fashion. When we had reached the bar the tide was about to turn. The Fundy tides may be said to have practically no slack; they have to travel so fast and so far that they waste no time in idleness. We hailed Chris, whom we had left in the boat, and told him the tide had turned.

" Chris rose from his lounging attitude in the stern, and took a look at the water. The next moment he was on his feet, yelling, ' All aboard ! all aboard ! Here's the dogfish a-comin' ! '

" B—— and I took the water at once, but the rector stopped us. ' Back ! ' he commanded. ' They're upon us already, and our only chance is here in the shoal water till Chris can get the boat over to us.'

" Even as he spoke we noted some small black fins cutting the water between the boat and our shoal. We turned back with alacrity.

" The first thing Chris did was to empty both barrels of my fowling-piece among the advancing fins. At once a great turmoil ensued, caused by the struggles of two or three wounded dogfish. The next moment their struggles were brought to an end. Their companions tore them to pieces in a twinkling.

" The rector shouted to Chris to try to throw us the boat-hook. It was a long throw, but Chris's sinews rose to the emergency, and the boat-hook landed nearly at our feet. The boat-hook was followed by a broken gaff, which struck the sand at the farther side of the shoal.

" Meanwhile between us and the boat the water had become alive with dogfish. Our shoal sloped so abruptly that already they could swim up to within two or three feet of us. We knew that the tide would soon bring them upon us, and we turned cold as we thought what our fate would be unless Chris could reach us in time. Then the battle began.

"B—— and I, with our awkward weapons, managed to stun a couple of our assailants. The rector's boat-hook did more deadly execution; it tore the throat out of the first fish it struck. At once the pack scented their comrade's blood, darted on the wounded fish, devoured it, and crowded after us for more.

" Our blows with the oar and gaff served temporarily to disable our assailants, but not gash their tough skin. But the moment blood was started on one of our enemies his comrades finished the work for us. Almost every stroke of the boat-hook tore a fish, which straightway became food for its fellows. The most I could do with my gaff was to tap a dogfish on the head when I could, and stun him for a while.

" During these exciting minutes the tide was rising with terrible speed. The water that now came washing over our toes was a lather of foam and blood, through which sharp, dark fins and long keen bodies darted and crowded and snapped.

" Suddenly one fish, fiercer than the rest, made a dart at B——'s leg, and its sharp snout just grazed his skin, causing him to yell with horror. We tried to get our feet out of the water by standing on the highest stones we could find. Our arms were weary from wielding the oar and the gaff, but the rector's boat-hook kept up its deadly lunges.

" Chris had been firing among our assailants; but now, beholding our strait, he threw down the gun, and strained furiously upon his one oar in the endeavor to shove off the boat. She would not budge.

" ' Boys, brace up! brace up!' cried the rector. ' She'll float in another minute or two. We can give these chaps all they want.' As he spoke, his boat-hook ripped another fish open. He had caught the knack of so using his weapon that he raked his opponents from underneath without wasting an ounce of effort.

" The fight was getting too hot to last. A big

fish, with a most appalling array of fangs, snatched at my foot. Just in time I thrust the broken end of the gaff through his throat and turned him on his back. His neighbors took charge of him, and he vanished in bloody fragments.

" As I watched this an idea struck me.

" 'Chris!' I yelled, 'the shad! the shad! Throw them overboard, a dozen at a time!'

" 'Splendid!' cried the rector; and B—— panted approvingly, 'That's the talk! That'll call 'em off.'

" Down came his oar with fresh vigor upon the head of a dogfish, which turned at once on its side. Then the shad began to go overboard.

" At first the throwing of the shad produced no visible effect, and the attack on us continued in unabated fury. Then the water began to foam and twist where the shad were dropping, and on a sudden we were left alone.

" The whole pack forsook us to attack the shad. How they fought and lashed and sprang and tore in one mad turmoil of foam and fish!

" 'Spread them a bit!' B—— cried. 'Give them all a chance, or they'll come back at us.'

" 'She's afloat! she's afloat!' he yelled the next moment, in frantic delight.

" Chris threw out another dozen of fish. Then he thrust his oar over the stern, and the big boat moved slowly toward us. At intervals Chris stopped and threw out more shad. As we eagerly watched his approach the thought occurred to us that when the boat should reach us it would be with the whole pack surrounding it. The ravenous creatures seemed almost ready to leap aboard.

" ' We can use these oars and things as leaping-poles,' suggested B——.

" ' That's what we'll have to do,' agreed the rector. Then he cried to Chris, ' Bring her side onto the shoal, so we can all jump aboard at the same time.'

" As the boat drew nearer, Chris paused again, and threw a score of shad far astern. Away darted the dogfish; and the boat rounded up close before us.

" The agility with which we sprang aboard was remarkable, and Chris almost hugged us in his joy.

" ' Not another shad'll they git out er me!' he declared triumphantly.

" ' Well, I should rather think not," remarked the rector. ' But they might as well have some more dogfish.'

" With these words he put his foot upon the gunwale, and his unwearying boat-hook went back jubilantly into the battle.

" Rapidly loading and firing my shotgun, I picked off as many of our enemies as I comfortably could; and B——, by lashing the boat's hatchet on the end of the gaff, made a weapon with which he played havoc among our foes.

" But the fray lasted not much longer. Innumerable as were yet the survivors, their hunger was becoming appeased, and their ferocity diminished. In a little while they sheered off to a safer distance.

"When we had time to think of our own condition, we found that our backs were painfully scorched by the blazing June sun. As with pain we struggled into our clothes, Chris trimmed our course toward home.

"'I reckon you know now 'bout all you'll wanter know 'bout the ways o' dogfish,' he suggested.

"'They are certainly very bloodthirsty,' said the rector; 'but at the same time they are interesting. That they gave us a noble contest you can't deny.'"

When Queerman relapsed into silence, Ranolf took up the parable without waiting to be called upon.

"Queerman's story," said he, "reminds me of an adventure of my own, which befell me in that same tide-region which he has just been talking of. You know, I spent much of my illustrious boyhood about the Tantramar marshes, and overlooking the yellow head-waters of the Bay of Fundy. The name of my story is, 'The Bull and the Leaping-Pole,' and the scene of it is within a mile of the spot whence Queerman and his crowd set out for shad. It will serve to show what agility I am capable of on a suitable occasion.

THE BULL AND THE LEAPING-POLE.

" Out on the Tantramar marshes the wind, as usual, was racing with superfluous energy, bowing all one way the purple timothy-tops, and rolling up long green waves of grass that shimmered like the sea under the steady afternoon sun. I revelled in the fresh and breezy loneliness, which nevertheless at times gave me a sort of thrill, as the bobolinks, stopping their song for a moment, left no sound in my ears save the confused ' swish ' of the wind. Men talk at times of the loneliness of the dark, but to my mind there is no more utter solitude than may be found in a broad white glare of sunshine.

" Here on the marsh, two miles from the skirt of the uplands, perhaps half a mile from the nearest incurve of the dike, on a twisted, sweet-smelling bed of purple vetch, I lay pretending to read, and deliciously dreaming. My bed of vetch sloped gently toward the sun, being on the bank of a little winding creek which idled through the long grasses on its way to the Tantramar. Once a tidal stream, the creek had been brought into subjection by what the country people call a ' bito,' built across its mouth to shut out the tides ; and now it was little more than a rivulet at the bottom of the deep gash which it had cut for itself through the flats in its days of freedom. From my resting-place I could see in the distance a marsh-hawk noiselessly skimming the tops of the grass, peering for field-mice; or a white gull wandering aimlessly in from the sea. Beyond the dike rose the gaunt skeletons of three or four empty net-reels; and a little way off towards the uplands stood an old barn used for storing hay.

" Beside me among the vetch-blossoms, hummed about by the great bumblebees and flickered over by white and yellow butterflies, lay my faithful leaping-pole, — a straight young spruce trimmed and peeled, light and white and tough. Some years before, fired by reading in *Hereward* of the feats of 'Wulfric the Heron,' I had bent myself to learn to leap with the pole, and had become no less skilful in the exercise than eagerly devoted thereto. It gave me, indeed, a most fascinating sense of freedom. Ditches, dikes, and fences were of small concern to me, and I went craning it over the country like a huge meadow-hen.

"On this particular afternoon, which I am not likely soon to forget, when the bobolinks had hushed for so long that the whispering stillness grew oppressive, I became ashamed of the weird apprehension which kept stealing across me; and springing to my feet with a shout, I seized my leaping-pole, and went sailing over the creek hilariously. It was a good leap, and I contemplated the distance with satisfaction, marred only by the fact that I had no spectators.

"Then I shouted again, from full lungs; and

turning instinctively for applause toward the far-off uplands, I became aware that I was not so much alone, as I had fancied.

"From behind the old barn, at the sound of my voice, appeared a head and shoulders which I recognized, and at the sight of which my satisfaction vanished. They belonged to Atkinson's bull, a notoriously dangerous brute, which only the week before had gored a man fatally, and which had thereupon been shut up and condemned to the knife. As was evident, he had broken out of his pen, and wandering hither to the marshes, had been luxuriating in such plenty of clover as well might have rendered him mild-mannered. I thought of this for a moment; but the faint hope — it was very faint — was at once and emphatically dispelled.

"Slowly, and with an ugly bellow, he walked his whole black-and-white length into view, took a survey of the situation, and then, after a moment's pawing, and some insulting challenges which I did not feel in a position to accept, he launched himself toward me with a sort of horrid grunt.

"After the first chill I had quite recovered my nerve, and realized at once that my chances lay altogether in my pole.

"The creek was in many places too wide for me to jump it in a clear leap from brink to brink of the gully, but at other points it was well within my powers. To the bull, however, I perceived that it would be at all points a serious obstacle, only to be passed by clambering first down and then up the steep sides.

"Without waiting for close parley with my assailant, I took a short run, and placed myself once more amongst the vetch-blossoms whence I had started. I had but time to cast my eye along, and notice that about a stone's throw farther down, toward the dike, the creek narrowed somewhat so as to afford me an easier leap, when the hot brute reached the edge opposite, and, unable to check himself, plunged headlong into the gully.

" As he rolled and snorted in the water I could scarcely help laughing ; but my triumph was not for long. The overthrow seemed to sting him into tenfold fury. With a nimbleness that appalled me he charged straight up the bank, and barely had I taken to my heels ere he had reached the top and was after me. So close was he that I failed to make the point aimed at. I was forced to leap desperately, and under such disadvantage that only by a hair's-breadth did I gain the opposite side. Somewhat shaken by the effort, I ran on straightway to where I could command a less trying jump.

" The bull made no halt whatever, but plunged right into the gully, rolled over, and all covered with mud and streaming weeds was up the slope again like a cat.

"I WAS FORCED TO LEAP DESPERATELY." — Page 48.

" But this performance delayed him, and gave me a second or two, so that I was enabled to make my leap with more deliberation and less effort. As I did so, I noticed with gratitude that the banks of the creek had here become much steeper. The bull noticed it too, and paused, bellowing vindictively; while as for me, I leaned on my trusty pole to regain my breath. With more circumspection this time the brute attempted the crossing, but losing his foothold he came to the bottom, as before, all in a heap.

" As he gathered himself up again for the ascent I held my ground, resolved to move but a yard or two aside when compelled, and not lightly to quit a position so much to my advantage. But here my foaming adversary found the slope too steep for him, and after every charge he fell back ignominiously into the water. It did not take him long, however, to realize the situation, and dashing up stream to his former crossing-place he was at the top in a twinkling, and once more bearing down upon me like a whirlwind of furies. The respite had given me time to recover my breath, and now with perfect coolness I transferred myself once more to the other side. Upon this my pursuer wheeled round, retraced his steps without a pause, crossed over, and in a moment I found my position again rendered untenable.

" Of course, there was nothing else for it but to make another jump; and in the result there was no perceptible variation. The inexorable brute left me no leisure to sit down and plan a diversion. I was conscious of a burning anxiety to get home, and I tried to calculate how much of this sort of thing it would take to discourage my tireless foe. Not arriving at any satisfactory conclusion, I continued to make a shuttle-cock of myself for some minutes longer.

"Immediately below me I saw that the sides of the gully retained their steepness, but so widened apart as to make the leap a doubtful one. At a considerable distance beyond, however, they drew together again, and at last I convinced myself that a change of base would be justified. By such a change, supposing it safely accomplished, it was evident that I would gain much longer breathing-spells, while my antagonist would be forced to such detours as would surely soon dishearten him.

"At the next chance, therefore, I broke at the top of my speed for the new position. I had but a scant moment to spare, for the bull was closing upon me with his terrific gallop. I made my jump, nevertheless, with deliberation. But, alas for the 'best laid schemes o' mice an' men'! I had planted my pole in a spot of sticky clay, and after a slow sprawl through the air I landed helplessly on hands and knees about half-way up the opposite bank.

"Seeing my mishap, the bull forgot his late-learned caution, and, charging headlong, brought

-up not a couple of yards below me. Without waiting to pull my pole out of the mud I scrambled desperately to the top. It was a sick moment for me as the brute recovered his footing, and made up the steep so impetuously that he almost conquered it; but I threw myself flat on my face and reached for the pole, knowing well that without it the game was pretty well up for me. As I succeeded in wrenching it from the clay, my pursuer's rush brought him so close that I could almost touch his snorting and miry nostrils. But this was his best effort, and he could come no nearer. Realizing this, he did just what I expected him to do, — gave his tail an extra twist of relentless malice, and swept off up the bed of the creek to his former place of transit. I now breathed more freely; and having prodded the bottom till I found a firm foundation for my pole, I began to feel secure.

"When the bull had gained my side of the creek, and had come so far as to insure his coming all the way, I sprang across; and a moment later saw him tearing up the soil on the very spot my feet had just forsaken. This time he shirked the plunge, and stood on the bank bellowing his challenge. I patted my good spruce pole. Then I threw some sods across at him, which resulted in a fresh tempest, a new rush to the old crossing, and another 'over' for my leaping-pole and me.

" Meanwhile I had concocted a plan for checkmating my antagonist. I saw that from this point forward to the dike the gully became more and more impassable, and I thought if I could lure the bull into following me but for a little way down the opposite bank, I could gain such a start upon him that to reach the dike would be an easy matter. With this design then, when the bull again repeated his angry challenge, I shouted, threw another sod, and started on a trot down the creek. But the cunning brute was not to be deceived in such fashion. He turned at once to repeat his former tactics, and I was fain to retrace my steps precipitately.

"The brute now resolved, apparently, upon a waiting game. After pawing his defiance afresh, he proceeded to walk around and eat a little, ever and anon raising his head to eye me with a sullen and obstinate hatred. For my own part, now that time had ceased to be an object, I sat down and racked my brains over the problem. Would the brute keep up this guard all through the night? I felt as if there was a sleuth-hound on my trail. That now silent presence across the creek began to weigh upon me like a nightmare. At last, in desperation, I resolved upon a straight-away race for the dike. As I pondered on the chances, they seemed to grow more and more favorable. I was a good runner, and though handicapped with the pole, would have a fair start on my enemy. Having made up my mind to the venture I rose to my feet, ready to seize the smallest advantage.

"As I rose, the bull wheeled sharply, and sprang to the edge of the bank with a muffled roar. But seeing that I stood leaning idly on my pole and made no motion to depart, he soon tossed away in the sulks and resumed his grazing. In a few moments a succulent streak of clover so engrossed him that he turned his back fairly upon me — and like a flash I was off, speeding noiselessly over the grass.

"Not till several seconds had been gained did I hear the angry bellow which told of the detection of my stratagem. I did not stop to look back, and I certainly made some very pretty running; but the dike seemed still most dismally remote when I heard that heavy gallop plunging behind me. Nearer, nearer it drew, with terrible swiftness; and nearer and nearer drew the dike. I reached it where it was perhaps about seven feet high. Slackening up to plant my pole squarely, I sprang, and had barely time to steady myself on the summit when the beast brought up with a roar at my very feet. It was a narrow, a very narrow escape.

"With a sigh of relief and gratitude I sat me down to rest, and took some satisfaction in poking the ribs of the baffled brute below. Then, lightly balancing my pole in one hand, I turned my face toward the 'bito,' and made my way thoughtfully homeward. It was altogether too literally a 'hair's-breadth' adventure."

When Ranolf concluded there was a general stir. Pipes were refilled, and a " snack " (of biscuits, cheese, and liquids to taste) was passed around. Then Stranion said, —

" It's your turn, O. M."

" But it's bedtime," pleaded I ; " and besides, as I have the writing to do, let others do the speaking ! "

My arguments were received with a stony stare, so I made haste to begin.

" Like Magnus," said I, " modesty forbids me to be my own hero. I'll tell you a story which I picked up last fall, when I was alleged to be pigeon-shooting twenty miles above Fredericton. We will call the yarn —

'SAVED BY THE CATTLE.'

" I was talking to an old farmer whom I had chanced to come across, and who had passed me a cheery good-day. After I had spoken of the crops, and he had praised my new gun, I broached a subject of much interest to myself.

" How do you account for the fact, if it is a fact," said I, slipping a cartridge into my right barrel, " that the caribou are getting yearly more numerous in the interior of New Brunswick, while other game seems to be disappearing. As for the wild pigeons, you may say they are all gone. Here I have been on the go since before sunrise, and that bird is the only sign of a pigeon I have so much as got a glimpse of."

"'Well,' replied my companion, 'as for the pigeons, I can't say how it is. In old times I've seen them so plenty round here you could knock them down with a stick; that is, if you were any-ways handy with a stick. But they do say that caribou are increasing because the wolves have disappeared. You see, the wolves used to be the worst enemy of the caribou, because they could run them down nice and handy in winter, when the snow was deep and the crust so thin that the caribou were bound to break through it at every step. However, I don't believe there has been a wolf seen in this part of the country for fifty years, and it's only within the last ten years or so that the caribou have got more plenty."

" We had seated ourselves, the old farmer and I, on a ragged snake-fence that bounded a buck-wheat-field overlooking the river. The field was a new clearing, and the ripened buckwheat reared its brown heads among a host of blackened and distorted stumps. It was a crisp and delicious autumn morning, and the solitary pigeon that had rewarded my long tramp over the uplands was one that I had surprised at its breakfast in the buckwheat. Now, finding that my new acquaint-ance was likely to prove interesting, I dropped my gun gently into the fence corner, loosened my belt a couple of holes, and asked the farmer if he had himself ever seen any wolves in New Brunswick.

"'Not to say many,' was the old man's reply; 'but they say that troubles never come single, and so, what wolves I *have* seen, I saw them all in a heap, so to speak.'

"As he spoke, the old man fixed his eyes on a hilltop across the river, with a far-off look that seemed to promise a story. I settled into an attitude of encouraging attention, and waited for him to go on. His hand stole deep into the pocket of his gray homespun trousers, and brought to view a fig of 'black-jack,' from which he gnawed a thoughtful bite.

"Instinctively he passed the tobacco to me; and on my declining it, which I did with grave politeness, he began the following story: —

"When I was a little shaver about thirteen years old, I was living on a farm across the river, some ten miles up. It was a new farm, which father was cutting out of the woods; but it had a good big bit of 'interval,' so we were able to keep a lot of stock.

"One afternoon late in the fall, father sent me down to the interval, which was a good two miles from the house, to bring the cattle home. They were pasturing on the aftermath; but the weather was getting bad, and the grass was about done, and father thought the 'critters,' as we called them, would be much better in the barn. My little ten-year-old brother went with me, to help me drive them. That was the time I found out there were wolves in New Brunswick.

"The feed being scarce, the cattle were scattered badly; and it was supper-time before we got them together, at the lower end of the interval, maybe three miles and a half from home. We didn't mind the lateness of the hour, however, though we were getting pretty hungry, for we knew the moon would be up right after sundown. The cattle after a bit appeared to catch on to the fact that they were going home to snug quarters and good feed, and then they drove easy and hung together. When we had gone about half-way up the interval, keeping along by the river, the moon got up and looked at us over the hills, very sharp and thin. 'Ugh!' says Teddy to me in half a whisper, 'don't she make the shadows black?' He hadn't got the words more than out of his mouth when we heard a long, queer, howling sound from away over the other side of the interval; and the little fellow grabbed me by the arm, with his eyes fairly popping out of his head. I can see his startled face now; but he was a plucky lad for his size as ever walked.

"'What's that?' he whispered.

"'Sounds mighty like the wind,' said I, though I knew it wasn't the wind, for there wasn't a breath about to stir a feather.

" The sound came from a wooded valley winding down between the hills. It *was* something like the wind, high and thin, but by and by getting loud and fierce and awful, as if a lot more voices were joining in; and I just tell you my heart stopped beating for a minute. The cattle heard it, you'd better believe, and bunched together, kind of shivering. Then two or three young heifers started to bolt; but the old ones knew better, and hooked them back into the crowd. Then it flashed over me all at once. You see, I was quite a reader, having plenty of time in the long winters. Says I to Teddy, with a kind of sob in my throat, 'I guess it must be wolves.' — 'I guess so,' says Teddy, getting brave after his first start. And then, not a quarter of a mile away, we saw a little pack of gray brutes dart out of the woods into the moonlight. I grabbed Teddy by the hand, and edged in among the cattle.

" ' Let's get up a tree ! ' said Teddy.

" ' Of course we will,' said I, with a new hope rising in my heart. We looked about for a suitable tree in which we might take refuge, but our hopes sank when we saw there was not a decent-sized tree in reach. Father had cleared off everything along the river-bank except some Indian willow scrub not six feet high.

" If the cattle, now, had scattered for home, I guess it would have been all up with Teddy and me, and father and mother would have been mighty lonesome on the farm. But what do you suppose the 'critters' did ? When they saw those gray things just lengthening themselves out across the meadow, the old cows and the steers made a regular circle, putting the calves — with me and Teddy — in the centre. They backed in onto us pretty tight, and stood with their heads out and horns down, for all the world like a company of militia forming square to receive a charge of cavalry. And right good bayonets they made, those long, fine horns of our cattle.

"To keep from being trodden on, Teddy and I got onto the backs of a couple of yearlings, who didn't like it any too well, but were packed in so tight they couldn't help themselves. As the wolves came streaking along through the moonlight, they set up again that awful, shrill, wind-like, swelling howl, and I thought of all the stories I had read of the wolves of Russia and Norway, and such countries; and the thought didn't comfort me much. I didn't know what I learned afterward, that the common wolf of North America is much better fed than his cousin in the Old World, and consequently far less bloodthirsty. I seemed to see fire flashing from the eyes of the pack that were rushing upon us; and I thought their white fangs, glistening in the moonlight, were dripping with the blood of human victims.

" 'I expect father'll hear that noise,' whispered Ted, 'and he and Bill ' (that was the hired man) ' will come with their guns and save us.'

" ' Yes,' said I scornfully; 'I suppose you d like them to come along now, and get eaten up by the wolves !'

"I was mighty sorry afterward for speaking that way, for it near broke Teddy's heart. However, sobbing a bit, the little fellow urged in self-defence, ' Why, there's only five wolves anyway, and father and Bill could easily kill them !'

"It was true. There were just five of the brutes, though my excited eyes had been seeing about fifty — just such a pack as I had been used to reading about. However, these five seemed mighty hungry, and now they were right onto us.

"I guess they weren't used to cattle like ours. Father's old black-and-white bull was running the affair that night, and he stood facing the attack. The wolves never halted; but with their red tongues hanging out, and their narrow jaws snapping like fox-traps, they gave a queer, nasty gasp that it makes my blood run cold to think of, and sprang right onto the circle of horns.

" We heard the old bull mumble something away down in his throat, and he sort of heaved up his hind-quarters and pitched forward, without leaving the ranks. The next thing we saw, one of his long horns was through the belly of the leader wolf, and the animal was tossed up into the air, yelping like a kicked dog. He came down with a thud, and lay snapping at the grass and kicking; while the other four, who had been re-

pulsed more or less roughly, drew back and eyed
their fallen comrade with an air of disapproval. I
expected to see them jump upon him and eat
him at once, but they didn't; and I began to distrust the stories I had read about wolves. It appeared, however, that it was not from any sense
of decency that they held back, but only that they
wanted beef rather than wolf meat, as we found a
little later.

"Presently one of the four slouched forward, and
sniffed at his dying comrade. The brute was still
lively, however, and snapped his teeth viciously at
the other's legs, who thereupon slouched back to
the pack. After a moment of hesitation, the four
stole silently, in single file, round and round the
circle. turning their heads so as to glare at us all
the time, and looking for a weak spot to attack.
They must have gone round us half a dozen times,
and then they sat down on their tails, and stuck
their noses into the air, and howled and howled
for maybe five minutes steady. Teddy and I,
who were now feeling sure our 'critters' could
lick any number of wolves, came to the conclusion
the brutes thought they had too big a job on
their hands and were signalling for more forces.
'Let 'em come,' exclaimed Teddy. But we were
getting altogether too confident, as we soon found
out.

"After howling for a while. the wolves stopped
and listened. Then they howled again, and again

they stopped and listened; but still no answer came. At this they got up and once more began prowling round the circle, and everywhere they went you could see the long horns of the cattle pointing in their direction. I can tell you cattle know a thing or two more than they get credit for.

"Well, when the wolves came round to their comrade's body, they saw it was no longer kicking, and one of them took a bite out of it as if by way of an experiment. He didn't seem to care for wolf, and turned away discontentedly. The idea struck Teddy as so funny that he laughed aloud. The laugh sounded out of place, and fairly frightened me. The cattle stirred uneasily; and as for Teddy, he wished he had held his tongue, for the wolf turned and fixed his eye upon him, and drew nearer and nearer, till I thought he was going to spring over the cattle's heads and seize us. But in a minute I heard the old bull mumbling again in his throat; and the wolf sprang back just in time to keep from being gored. How I felt like hugging that bull!

"I cheered Teddy up, and told him not to laugh or make a noise again. As the little fellow lifted his eyes he looked over my shoulder, and, instantly forgetting what I had been saying, shouted, 'Here come father and Bill!' I looked in the same direction and saw them, sure enough, riding furiously towards us. But the wolves didn't notice them, and resumed their prowling.

" On the other side of the circle from our champion, the black-and-white bull, there stood a nervous young cow ; and just at this time the wolf who had got his eye on Teddy seemed to detect this weak spot in the defence. Suddenly he dashed like lightning on the timid cow, who shrank aside wildly, and opened a passage by which the wolf darted into the very centre of the circle. The brute made straight for Teddy, whom I snatched from his perch and dragged over against the flank of the old bull. Instantly the herd was in confusion. The young cow had bounded into the open and was rushing wildly up the interval, and three of the wolves were at her flanks in a moment. The wolf who had marked Teddy for his prey leaped lightly over a calf or two, and was almost upon us, when a red 'moolley' cow, the mother of one of these calves, butted him so fiercely as to throw him several feet to one side. Before he could reach us a second time the old bull had spotted him. Wheeling in his tracks, as nimble as a squirrel, he knocked me and Teddy over like a couple of ninepins, and was onto the wolf in a flash. How he did mumble and grumble way down in his stomach ; but he fixed the wolf. He pinned the brute down and smashed him with his forehead, and then amused himself tossing the body in the air ; and just at this moment father and Bill rode up and snatched us two youngsters onto their saddles.

"'Are you hurt?' questioned father breathlessly. But he saw in a moment we were not, for we were flushed with pride at the triumph of our old bull.

"'And be they any more wolves, so's I kin git a shot at 'em?' queried Bill.

"'Old Spot has fixed two of 'em,' said I.

"'And there's the other two eating poor Whitey over there,' exclaimed Teddy, pointing at a snarling knot of creatures two or three hundred yards across the interval.

"Sure enough, they had dragged down poor Whitey and were making a fine meal off her carcass. But Bill rode over and spoiled their fun. He shot two of them, while the other left like a gray streak. And that's the last *I've* seen of wolves in this part of the country!"

"'That was a close shave,' said I; 'and the cattle showed great grit. I've heard of them adopting tactics like that.'

"'Well,' said the old farmer, getting down from the fence rail and picking up his tin can. 'I must be moving. Good-day to you.' Before he had taken half a dozen steps he turned round and remarked, 'I suppose, now, if those had been Norway wolves or Roossian wolves, the "critters" would have had no show?'

"'Very little, I imagine,' was my answer."

Whether it was that my story had gone far toward putting every one to sleep, I know not.

The fact remains, to be interpreted as one will, that no longer was there any objection raised when I proposed that we should turn in. That night, I think, no one of us lay awake over long. Before I dropped asleep I heard two owls hooting hollowly to each other through the wet woods. The sound changed gradually to a clamor of wolves over their slain victim, and then to the drums and trumpets of an army on the march; and then I awoke to find it broad daylight, and Stranion beating a tin pan just over my head.

CHAPTER III.

AT CAMP DE SQUATOOK.

THE next morning we got off at a good hour. For the last half mile of its course we found Beardsley Brook so overgrown with alders that we had to chop and haul our way through it with infinite labor. Here we wasted some time fishing for Sam's pipe, which had fallen overboard among the alders. The pipe was black, with crooked stem, plethoric in build, and so heavy that we all thought it would sink where it fell. As soon as the catastrophe occurred we halted till the water, here about two feet deep, had become clear. Then, peering down among the alder-stems, Ranolf spied the pipe on the sandy bottom, looking blurred and distorted through the writhing current. Long we grappled for it, poking at it with pole and paddle. We would cautiously raise it a little way towards the surface; but even as we began to triumph it would wriggle off again as if actually alive, and settle languidly back upon the sand. We all knew, without Ranolf's elaborate explanations, that its lifelike movement was due to its being so little heavier than the water it displaced, or to the uneven refraction of the

light through the moving fluid, or to some other
equally satisfactory and scientific cause. Finally
Sam, getting impatient, plunged in arm and shoulder, and grasped the pipe victoriously. He came
up empty-handed ; and we beheld a huge tadpole,
now thoroughly aroused, flaunting off down stream
in high dudgeon. Ranolf remarked that the laws
of refraction were to him obscure; and we continued our journey. The real pipe we overtook
farther down stream, floating along jauntily as a
cork.

Once out upon the Squatook River our course
was rapid, for the current was swift and the
channel clear. There were some wild rapids, but
we ran them victoriously. By noon we were on
the bosom of Big Squatook Lake. By six o'clock
we had traversed this beautiful and solitary water,
and were pitching our tent near the outlet, on
a soft brown carpet of pine-needles. Here was
a circular opening amid the huge trunks. Between the lake and our encampment hung a
screen of alder and wild-cherry, whence a white
beach of pebbles slanted broadly to the waves.
While Stranion and Queerman made preparations
for supper, the rest of us whipped the ripples of
the outlet for trout. The shores of the lake at
this spot draw together in two grand curves, and
at the apex flows out the Squatook River, about
waist-deep and a stone's throw broad. It mur-
murs pleasantly on for the first few rods, and then

begins to dart and chafe, and lift an angry voice. Hither the Indians come to spear whitefish in their season. To assist their spearing they had the outlet fenced part way across with a double row of stakes. All but the smallest fish were thus compelled to descend through a narrow passage, wherein they were at the mercy of the spearman. This fence we now found very convenient. Letting the canoe drift against it, we perched on top of the stakes, a couple of feet above water, and cast our flies unimpeded in every direction. The trout were abundant, and took the flies freely. For an hour we had most exciting sport. It was in itself, for all true fishermen, worth the whole journey. The Squatook trout are of a good average size, and very game. Of the twenty odd fish we killed that evening, there were two that passed the one and one-half pound scratch upon our scales, and several that cleared the pound.

Deciding to spend some days in this fair spot, we named it Camp de Squatook. Lopping the lower branches of the trees, we made ourselves pegs on which to hang our tins and other utensils; while a dry cedar log, split skilfully by Stranion, furnished us with slabs for a table. Our commissariat was well supplied with campers' necessities and luxuries, but it was upon trout above all that we feasted. Sometimes we boiled them; sometimes we broiled them; more often we fried them in the fragrant, yellow corn-meal. The delicate richness of the hot, pink, luscious flakes is only to be realized by those who feast on the spoils of their own rods, with the relish of free air and vigor and out-door appetites.

Campers prate much of early hours, and of seeking their blankets with sunset; but we held to no such doctrine. Night in these wilds is rich with a mysterious beauty, an immensity of solitude such as day cannot dream of. Supper over, we stretched ourselves out between tent-door and camp-fire, pillowing our heads on the folded bedding. Across the yellow, fire-lit circle, through the trunks and hanging branches, we watched the still, gleaming level of the lake, whence at intervals would ring out startlingly clear the goblin laughter of the loon.

We were not so tired as on the previous evening, and it took us longer to settle down into the mood for story-telling. At last Stranion was called upon. He was ready, and speech flowed from him at once, as if his mouth had been just uncorked.

A NIGHT ENCOUNTER.

"I'll tell you a tale," said he, "of this very spot, on this very Big Squatook; and, of course, with me and the panther both in it.

"Once upon a time — that is to say in the summer of 1886 — I fished over these waters with Tom Allison. You remember he was visiting

Fredericton nearly all that year. We camped right here two days, and then went on to the Little Lake, or Second Squatook, just below.

" One moonlight night, when the windless little lake before our camp was like a shield of silver, and the woody mountains enclosing us seemed to hold their breath for delight, I was seized with an overwhelming impulse to launch the canoe and pole myself up here to Big Squatook. The distance between the two lakes is about a mile and a half, with rapid water almost all the way; and Allison, who had been amusing himself laboriously all day, was too much in love with his pipe and blankets by the camp-fire to think of accompanying me. All my persuasions were wasted upon him, so I went alone.

"Of course I had an excuse. I wanted to set night-lines for the gray trout, or *togue*, which haunt the waters of Big Squatook. A favorite feeding-ground of theirs is just where the water begins to shoal toward the outlet yonder. Strange as it may seem, the togue are never taken in Second Lake, or in any other of the Squatook chain.

" It was a weird journey up-stream, I can tell you. The narrow river, full of rapids, but so free from rocks in this part of its course that its voice seldom rises above a loud, purring whisper, was overhung by many ancient trees. Through the spaces between their tops fell the moonlight in

sharp white patches. As the long slow thrusts
of my pole forced the canoe stealthily upward
against the current, the creeping panorama of the
banks seemed full of elvish and noiseless life.
White trunks slipped into shadow, and black
stumps caught gleams of sudden radiance, till
the strangeness of it all began to impress me
more than its beauty, and I felt a curious and
growing sense of danger. I even cast a longing
thought backward toward the camp-fire's cheer
and my lazier comrade ; and when at length, slipping out upon the open bosom of the lake, I put
aside my pole and grasped my paddle, I drew a
breath of distinct relief.

" It took but a few minutes to place my three
night-lines. This done, I paddled with slow
strokes toward that big rock far out yonder.

" The broad surface was as unrippled as a mir-
ror, like it is now, save where my paddle and the
gliding prow disturbed it. When I floated motionless, and the canoe drifted softly beyond the
petty turmoil of my paddle. it seemed as if I were
hanging suspended in the centre of a blue and
starry sphere. The magic of the water so persuaded me, that presently I hauled up my canoe
on the rock, took off my clothes, and swam far
out into the liquid stillness. The water was cold.
but of a life-giving freshness ; and when I had
dressed and resumed my paddle I felt full of
spirit for the wild dash home to camp, through

the purring rapids and the spectral woods. Little did I dream just how wild that dash was to be!

"You know the whitefish barrier where you fellows were fishing this evening. Well, at the time of my visit the barrier extended only to mid-channel, one-half having been carried away, probably by logs, in the spring freshets. For this accident, doubtless very annoying to the Indians, I soon had every reason to be grateful.

"As I paddled noiselessly into the funnel, and began to feel the current gathering speed beneath me, and noted again the confused, mysterious glimmer and gloom of the forest into which I was drifting, I once more felt that unwonted sense of danger stealing over me. With a word of vexation I shook it off, and began to paddle fiercely. At the same instant my eyes, grown keen and alert, detected something strange about the bit of Indian fence which I was presently to pass. It was surely very high and massive in its outer section! I stayed my paddle, yet kept slipping quickly nearer. Then suddenly I arrested my progress with a few mighty backward strokes. Lying crouched flat along the tops of the stakes, its head low down, its eyes fixed upon me, was a huge panther.

"I was completely at a loss, and for a minute or two remained just where I was, backing water to resist the current, and trying to decide what was best to be done. As long as I kept to the open water, of course I was quite safe; but I didn't relish the idea of spending the night on the lake. I knew enough of the habits and characteristics of the panther to be aware the brute would keep his eye on me as long as I remained alone. But what I *didn't* know was how far a panther could jump! Could I safely paddle past that fence by hugging the farther shore? I felt little inclined to test the question practically; so I turned about and paddled out upon the lake.

" Then I drifted and shouted songs and stirred up the echoes for a good round hour. I hoped, rather faintly, that the panther would follow me up the shore. This. in truth, he may have done; but when I paddled back to the outlet, there he was awaiting me in exactly the same position as when I first discovered him.

" By this time I had persuaded myself that there was ample room for me to pass the barrier without coming in range of the animal's spring. I knew that close to the farther shore the water was deep. When I was about thirty yards from the stakes, I put on speed. heading for just about the middle of the opening. My purpose was to let the panther fancy that I was coming within his range. and then to change my course at the last moment so suddenly that he would not have time to alter his plan of attack. It is quite possible that this carefully planned scheme was unnecesary, and that I rated the brute's intelligence and forethought quite too high. But owever that may be, I thought it safer not to take any risks with so cunning an adversary.

"The panther lay in the sharp black shadow, so that it was impossible for me to note his movements accurately; but just as an instinct warned me that he was about to spring, I swerved smartly toward him, and hurled the light canoe forward with the mightiest stroke I was capable of. The manœuvre was well executed, for just before I came fairly opposite the grim figure on the stake-tops, the panther sprang.

"Instinctively I threw myself forward, level with the cross-bars; and in the same breath there came a snarl and a splash close beside me. The brute had miscalculated my speed, and got himself a ducking. I chuckled a little as I straightened up; but the sigh of relief which I drew at the same time was profound in its sincerity. I had lamentably underestimated the reach of the panther's spring. He had alighted close to the water's edge, just where I imagined the canoe would be out of reach. I looked around again. He was climbing alertly out of the hated bath. Giving himself one mighty shake, he started after me down along the bank, uttering a series of harsh and piercing screams. With a sweep of the paddle I darted across current, and placed almost the full breadth of the river between my enemy and myself.

"I have paddled many a canoe-race, but never one that my heart was so set upon winning as this strange one in which I now found myself straining every nerve. The current of the Squatook varies greatly in speed, though nowhere is it otherwise than brisk. At first I gained rapidly on my pursuer; but presently we reached a spot where the banks were comparatively level and open; and here the panther caught up and kept abreast of me with ease. With a sudden sinking at the heart I called to mind a narrow gorge a quarter of a mile ahead, from the sides of which several drooping trunks hung over the water. From one of these, I thought the panther might easily reach me, running out and dropping into the canoe as I darted beneath. The idea was a blood-curdling one, and spurred me to more desperate effort; but before we neared the perilous pass the banks grew so uneven and the underbrush so dense that my pursuer was much delayed, and consequently fell behind. The current quickening its speed at the same time, I was a good ten yards in the lead, as my canoe slid through the gorge and out into the white moonlight of one of the wider reaches of the stream.

" Here I slackened my pace in order to recover my wind; and the panther made up his lost ground. For the time, I was out of his reach, and all he could do was to scream savagely. This, I supposed, was to summon his mate to the noble hunting he had provided for her; but to my inexpressible satisfaction no mate came. The beauty and the weirdness of the moonlit woods were now quite lost upon me. I saw only that long, fierce, light-bounding figure which so inexorably kept pace with me.

"To save my powers for some possible emergency, I resolved to content myself, for the time, with a very moderate degree of haste. The panther was in no way pressed to keep up with me. Suddenly he darted forward at his utmost speed. For a moment this did not trouble me; but then I awoke to its possible meaning. He was planning, evidently, an ambuscade, and I must keep an eye upon him.

"The order of the chase was promptly reversed, and I set out at once in a desperate pursuit. The obstructed shores and the increasing current favored me, so that he found it hard to shake me off. For the next half mile I just managed to keep up with him. Then came another of those quieter reaches, and my pursued pursuer at last got out of sight.

"Again I paused, not only to take breath, but to try and discover the brute's purpose in leaving me. All at once it flashed into my mind. Just before the river widens into Second Lake, there occurs a lively and somewhat broken rapid. As there was moonlight, and I knew the channels well, I had no dread of this rapid till suddenly

I remembered three large bowlders crossing the stream like stepping-stones.

" It was plain to me that this was the point my adversary was anxious to reach ahead of me. These bowlders were so placed that he could easily spring from one to the other dry-shod, and his chance of intercepting me would be excellent. I almost lost courage. The best thing I could do under the circumstances was to save my strength to the utmost ; so for a time I did little more than steer the canoe. When at last I rounded a turn, and saw just ahead of me the white, thin-crested, singing ripples of the rapid, I was not at all surprised to see also the panther, crouched on one of the rocks in mid-stream.

" At this point the river was somewhat spread out, and the banks were low, so the moonlight showed me the channel quite clearly. You'll understand better when we run through in a day or two. I laid aside my paddle and took up the more trusty white spruce pole. With it I "snubbed" the canoe firmly, letting her drop down the slope inch by inch, while I took a cool and thorough survey of the ripples and cross-currents.

" From the sloping shoulder of the rock lying nearest to the left-hand bank a strong cross-current took a slant sharply over toward the middle channel. I decided to stake my fate on the assistance of this cross-current. Gradually I snubbed the canoe over to the left bank, and then gave her

her head. The shores slipped past. The rocks, with that crouching sentinel on the central one, seemed to glide up-stream to meet me. I was almost in the passage when, with a superb bound, the panther shot through the moonlight and lit upon the rock I was approaching! As he poised himself, gaining his balance with some difficulty on the narrow foothold, a strong lunge with my pole twisted the canoe into the swirl of that cross-current; and with the next thrust I slid like lightning down the middle channel before my adversary had more than got himself fairly turned around! With a shout of exultation I raced down the rest of the incline and into widening reaches, safe from pursuit. The panther, screaming angrily, followed me for a time; but soon the receding shores placed such a distance between us that I ceased to regard him. Presently I bade him a final farewell, and headed across the lake for the spot where the camp-fire was waving me a ruddy welcome."

"That's getting pretty near home," remarked Ranolf, glancing apprehensively into the gloom behind the camp. "You don't suppose that chap would be waiting around here for you, Stranion? If so, I hope he won't mistake me for you!"

"Let Sam give us something cheerful now!" demanded Magnus.

"Well," said Sam, "I'll give you a story of the lumber-camps. I'll call it—

"With the next Thrust I slid like Lightning down the Middle Channel." — Page 78.

'BRUIN AND THE COOK.'

"As the O. M. is going to dress up our yarns for the cold light of print, I must be allowed to preface the story with a few introductory remarks on the life of the lumbermen in winter. Stranion and the O. M. know all about that; but the rest of you fellows never go to the lumber-camps, you know.

"To one who visits the winter camps here in our backwoods, the life led by the loggers is likely to seem monotonous after the strangeness of it has worn off. The sounds of the chopping, the shouting, the clanking of the teams, afford ample warning to all the wild creatures of the woods, who thereupon generally agree in giving a wide berth to a neighborhood which has suddenly grown so populous and noisy.

"In chopping and hauling logs the lumbermen are at work unremittingly from dawn until sun-down, and at night they have little energy to expend on the hunting of bears or panthers. The bunks and the blankets exert an overwhelming attraction; and by the time the men have concluded their after-supper smoke, and the sound of a few rough songs has died away, the wild beasts may creep near enough to smell the pork and beans, and may prowl about the camp until dawn, with small fear of molestation from the sleepers within.

" At intervals, however, the monotony of camp-life is broken. Something occurs to remind the careless woodsmen that, though in the wilderness, indeed, they are yet not truly of it. They are made suddenly aware of those shy but savage forces which, regarding them ever as trespassers, have been keeping them under an angry and eager surveillance. The spirit of the violated forest makes a swift and sometimes effectual, but always unexpected, stroke for vengeance.

" A yoke of oxen are straining at their load: a great branch reaching down catches the nearest ox by the horn, and the poor brute falls in its track with its neck broken. A stout sapling is bent to the ground by a weight of ice and snow: some thaw or the shock of a passing team releases it, and by the fierce recoil a horse's leg is shattered.

"A lumberman has strayed off into the woods by himself, perchance to gather spruce-gum for his friends in the settlements, and he is found, days afterwards, half-eaten by bears and foxes. A solitary chopper throws down his axe and leans against a tree to rest and dream, and a panther drops from the branches above and tears him.

" Yet such vengeance is accomplished but seldom, and makes no permanent impression on the heedless woodsman. His onward march is inexorable.

" The cook, it must be borne in mind, is a most

important personage in the lumber-camp. This I say of camp-cooks in general, and I assert it in particular of the cook who figures as one of the heroes in my story. The other hero is the bear.

" It was a bright March morning at Nicholson's camp over on Salmon River. There had been a heavy thaw for some days, and the snowbanks under the eaves of the camp were shrinking rapidly. The bright chips about the door, the trampled straw and fodder around the stable, were steaming and soaking under the steady sun. Such winds as were stirring abroad that day were quite shut off from the camp by the dark surrounding woods.

" From the protruding stovepipe, which did duty as a chimney, a faint blue wreath of smoke curled lazily. The cook had the camp all to himself for a while ; for the teams and choppers were at work a mile away, and the ' cookee,' as the cook's assistant is called, had betaken himself to a neighboring pond to fish for trout through the ice.

" The dishes were washed, the camp was in order, and in a little while it would be time to get the dinner ready. The inevitable pork and beans were slowly boiling, and an appetizing fragrance was abroad on the quiet air. The cook decided to snatch a wink of sleep in his bunk beneath the eaves. He had a spare half-hour before him, and under his present circumstances he knew no better way of spending it.

"The weather being mild, he left the camp-door wide open, and, swinging up to his berth, soon had himself luxuriously bedded in blankets, — his own and as many other fellows' blankets as he liked. He began to doze and dream. He dreamed of summer fields, and then of a lively Sunday-school picnic, and at last of the music of a band which he heard crashing in his ears. Then the cymbals and the big drum grew unbearably loud, and, waking with a start, he remembered where he was, and thrust his head in astonishment over the edge of the bunk. The sight that met his eyes filled him with alarm and indignation.

"The prolonged thaw had brought out the bears from their snug winter quarters; and now, in a very bad humor from having been waked up too soon, they were prowling through the forest in unusual numbers. Food was scarce; in fact, times were very hard with them, and they were not only bad-humored, but lean and hungry withal.

"To one particularly hungry bear the smell of our cook's simmering pork had come that morning like the invitation to a feast. The supposed invitation had been accepted with a rapturous alacrity. Bruin had found the door open, the coast clear, the quarters very inviting. With the utmost good faith he had entered upon his fortune. To find the source of that entrancing fragrance had been to his trained nose a simple matter.

BRUIN AND THE COOK.   Page 83.

" While cook slept sweetly, Bruin had rooted off the cover of the pot, and this was the beginning of cook's dream.

" But the pot was hot, and the first mouthful of the savory mess made him yell with rage and pain. At this point the trumpets and clarions grew shrill in cook's dreaming ears.

" Then an angry sweep of the great paw had dashed pot and kettle off the stove in a thunder of crashing iron and clattering tins. This was the point at which cook's dream had attained overwhelming reality.

" What met his round-eyed gaze, as he sat up in his blankets, was an angry bear, dancing about in a confusion of steam and smoke and beans and kettles, making ineffectual snatches at a lump of scalding pork upon the floor.

" After a moment of suspense, cook rose softly and crept to the other end of the bunks, where a gun was kept. To his disgust the weapon was unloaded. But the click of the lock had caught the bear's attention. Glancing up at the bunk above him, the brute's eye detected the shrinking cook, and straightway he overflowed with wrath. Here, evidently, was the author of his discomfort.

" With smarting jaws and vengeful paws he made a dash for the bunk. Its edge was nearly seven feet from the floor, so Bruin had to do some clambering. As his head appeared over the edge, and his great paws took firm hold upon the clapboard rim of the bunk, cook, now grown desperate, struck at him wildly with the heavy butt of the gun. But Bruin is always a skilful boxer. With an upward stroke he warded off the blow, and sent the weapon spinning across the camp. At the same time, however, his weight proved too much for the frail clapboard to which he was .holding, and back he fell on the floor with a shock like an earthquake.

"This repulse — which, of course, he credited to the cook — only filled him with tenfold greater fury, and at once he sprang back to the assault; but the delay, however brief, had given poor cook time to grasp an idea, which he proceeded to act upon with eagerness. He saw that the hole in the roof through which the stovepipe protruded was large enough to give his body passage. Snatching at a light rafter above his head, he swung himself out of the bunk, and kicked the stovepipe from its place. The sections fell with loud clatter upon the stove and the bear, for a moment disconcerting Bruin's plans. From the rafter it was an easy reach to the opening in the roof, and as Bruin gained the empty bunk and stretched his paw eagerly up toward his intended victim on the rafter, the intended victim slipped with the greatest promptitude through the hole.

"At this point the cook drew a long breath, and persuaded his heart to go down out of his throat, where it had been since he waked, and resume its proper functions.

"His first thought was to drop from the roof and run for help, but fortunately he changed his mind. The bear was no fool. No sooner had the cook got safely out upon the roof than Bruin rushed forth from the camp-door, expecting to catch him as he came down.

"Had cook acted upon his first impulse, he would have been overtaken before he had gone a hundred yards, and would have perished hideously in the snow. As it was. however. — evidently to Bruin's deep chagrin. — he stuck close to the chimney-hole. like a prairie-dog sitting by his burrow, ready at a moment's notice to plunge within, while the bear stalked deliberately twice around the camp, eying him, and evidently laying plans, as it were, for his capture.

"At last the bear appeared to make up his mind. At one corner of the shanty, piled up nearly to the eaves, was a store of firewood which 'cookee' had gathered in. Upon this pile Bruin mounted, and then made a dash up the creaking roof.

"Cook prayed most fervently that it might give way beneath the great weight of the bear, and to see if it would do so he waited almost too long; but it did not. As he scurried. belated. through the hole, the bear's paw reached its edge, and the huge claws tore nearly all the flesh from the back of the poor fellow's hand. Bleeding and trembling he crouched upon the friendly rafter, not daring to swing down into the bunk.

" The agility of that great animal was marvellous. Scarcely had cook got under shelter when Bruin rushed in again at the door, and was up on the bunk again in a twinkling, and again cook vanished by the chimney-place. A moment later the bear was again on the roof, while cook once more crouched back faintly on his rafter. This performance was repeated several times, till for cook it had quite ceased to be interesting.

" At last the chase grew monotonous even to the indefatigable Bruin, who then resolved upon a change of tactics. After driving cook out through the chimney, he decided to try the same mode of exit for himself, or at least to thrust his head through the opening, and see what it was like. Embracing the woodwork with his powerful forepaws, he swung himself up on the rafter, as he had seen cook do so gracefully. The attempt was quite successful; but the rafter was not prepared for the strain, and Bruin and beam came thundering to the floor.

" As cook gazed down through the hole, and marked what had happened, his heart sank utterly within him. His one safe retreat was gone. But Bruin did not perceive his advantage, or else was in no hurry to follow it up. The shock had greatly dampened his zeal. He sat on his haunches by the stove, and gazed up sullenly at cook, while cook gazed back despairingly at him.

" Then the bear noticed that the precious pork had got deliciously cool, and in the charms of that rare morsel cook was soon quite forgotten. All cook had to do was to lie on the roof, nursing his lacerated hand, and watching Bruin as he made away with the lumbermen's dinner, — a labor of love in which he lost no time.

" At this junction a noise was heard in the woods, and hope came back to the cook's heart. The men were returning for dinner. Bruin heard it too, and made haste to gulp down the remnant of the beans. Just as teams and choppers emerged into the little cleared space in front of the camp, Bruin, having swallowed his last mouthful, rushed out of the camp-door, to the breathless and immeasurable amazement of the lumbermen.

" Finding himself to all appearances surrounded, Bruin paused a moment irresolutely. Then charging upon the nearest team, he dealt the teamster a terrific cuff, bowling him over in the snow and breaking his arm, while the maddened horses plunged, reared, and fell over backward in a tangle of sleds and traces and lashing heels.

" This episode brought the woodsmen to their senses. Axe in hand, they closed in upon the bear, who rose on his hind-quarters to meet them. The first few blows that were delivered at him, with all the force of practised arms and vindictive energy, he warded off as if they were so many feathers; but he could not guard himself on all sides at once. A well-directed blow from the rear sank the axe-head deep between his fore-shoulders, severing the spinal column, and Bruin collapsed, a furry heap, upon the crimsoned snow.

"In their indignation over the cook's torn hand, their comrade's broken arm, and — perhaps most aggravating of all — their thoroughly demolished dinner, the lumbermen undertook to make a meal of Bruin; but in this attempt Bruin found a measure of revenge, for in death he proved to be even tougher than he had been in life, and the famous luxury of a fat bear-steak was nowhere to be had from his carcass."

"And now, Magnus," continued Sam, cleaning out his pipe, "we'll have something remote and tropical from you, with your kind permission. What else has happened to that uncle of yours?"

"Lots of things," said the imperturbable Magnus. "I'll tell you one of his Mexican stories, which he calls —

'AN ENCOUNTER WITH PECCARIES.'

This is, as near as I can remember, the way he told it to me. I speak in his name.

"In my somewhat varied wanderings over the surface of this fair round world," said my uncle, "I have had adventures more or less exciting, and generally disagreeable, with wolves, bears, and tigers, with irate and undiscriminating bulls, and with at least one of those painfully unpleasant horses, who have acquired a special relish for human flesh. Some childish memories, moreover, disclose to me at times that on more than one occasion I have come off without laurels from a contest with an indignant he-goat, and that I have even been in peril at the wings of an unusually aggressive gander. But of all the unpleasant acquaintances to make when one is feeling solitary and unprotected, I think a herd of irritated peccaries will carry off the palm. Let these sturdy little animals once conceive that their rights have been ever so little menaced, and they are tireless, implacable, and blindly fearless in their demand for vengeance. Just what they may interpret as a menace to their rights I suppose no man can say with any confidence; but my own observation has led me to believe that they think themselves entitled to possess the earth. The earth is much to be congratulated upon the fact that various climatic considerations have hitherto prevented them from entering upon their inheritance. The peccary is confined, I believe, and I state it here on the authority of reputable naturalists, to certain tropical and sub-tropical regions of the New World. My own limited acquaintance with the creature was gained in Mexico.

"Toward the end of the seventies I was engaged upon a survey of government lands in one of the interior provinces of Mexico. Our party was enjoying life, and troubled by few cares. There were no bandits in that region. The scanty inhabitants were more than well-disposed; they were ready to bow down before us in their deferential good-will. The climate, though emphatically warm, was healthful and stimulating. There were hardly enough pumas in the neighborhood to add to our content the zest of excitement. There were peccaries, as we were told in admonition, but we had seen no sign of them; and when we learned that they were only a kind of small wild pig we took little stock in the tales we heard of their unrelenting ferocity.

"On one of our numerous holidays — we could not work our peons on any saint's day be it remembered — a rumor of a remarkable waterfall adorning a tributary of the stream which meandered past our camp had taken me a longish ride into the foothills of the Sierra. My journey was along a little-frequented trail leading into the mountains, and the scenery was fascinating in its loveliness. I found the waterfall easily enough, for the trail led past its very brink, and I was more than rewarded for the trifling fatigue of my ride. A vigorous stream, rolling from a winding ravine in such a manner that it seemed to burst right out of the mountain-side, leaped sparkling and clamoring into the air from a curtain of emerald foliage, and fell a distance of nearly two hundred feet into a very valley of paradise. In this valley, down into the bosom of which I gazed from my height, the stream lingered to form a sapphire lakelet, around whose banks grew the most luxuriant of tree-ferns and mahoganies and mesquits garlanded with gorgeous-bloomed lianas. I could hear the cries of parrots rising from the splendid coverts, and I thought what a delicious retreat the valley would be but for its assortment of snakes, miasma, and a probable puma or two. I enjoyed the scene from my post, but I did not descend. Then I turned my face homeward, well content.

" The horse I rode requires more than a passing mention, for he played the most prominent and most heroic part in the adventure which befell me on my way home. He was a superb beast, a blood bay, whom I had bought in the city of Mexico from an American engineer who was leaving the country. The animal, who answered to the name of Diaz, had seen plenty of service in the interior of Mexico, and his trained instincts had kept me out of many dangers. I loved Diaz as a faithful friend and servant.

" As I descended from the foothills the trail grew heavy and soft, making our progress slow. The land was open, — a succession of rank meadows, with clumps of trees dotted here and there, and pools on either side of the trail. Suddenly, some distance in my rear, there arose a shrill, menacing chorus of grunts and squeals, at which I would fain have paused to listen. But Diaz recognized the sounds, and bounded forward instantly with every sign of apprehension. Then I said to myself, 'It must be those peccaries of which I've heard so much.'

"In a moment or two I realized that it certainly was those peccaries. They swarmed out of the rank herbage and dashed after us, gnashing their jaws; and, though Diaz was doing his best, the herd gained upon us rapidly. They galloped lightly over the soft soil wherein Diaz sank far above his fetlocks. It took me but a moment to realize, when at last face to face with them, that the peccaries were just as dangerous as they had been represented. And another moment sufficed to show me than escape by my present tactics was impossible.

" I was armed with a light breech-loading rifle, — a Remington, — and a brace of Smith & Wessons were sticking in my belt. Wheeling in my saddle I took a snap shot at the pursuing herd, and one of the animals tumbled in his tracks. His fellows took no notice of this whatever. Then I marked that Diaz appreciated our plight, for he was trembling under me. I looked about me, almost despairing of escape.

" A little behind, nearly half-way between us and the peccaries, I saw a wide-spreading tree close to the trail. We had passed it at the first of the alarm. Ahead, as far as I could see, there was no such refuge. Plenty of trees there were indeed, but all standing off amid the swamps. I decided at once upon a somewhat desperate course. I turned Diaz about, and charged down upon the peccaries with a yell.

"This stratagem appeared exactly to my horse's taste. In fact, his attitude made me rather uncomfortable. He seemed suddenly distraught. He gave several short whinnying cries of challenge or defiance, and rushed on with his mouth wide open and his lips rolled back in a fashion that made him look fiendish. My design was to swing myself from the saddle into the tree that overhung the trail, and so give Diaz a chance to run away, when free of my weight. But Diaz seemed bent on carrying the war into the enemy's country.

"I took one more shot at the peccaries, who seemed no whit dismayed by the onset of Diaz. I dropped my rifle, and kicked my feet out of the stirrups. By this time we were under the tree, and the peccaries with wild squeals were leaping upon us. I had just succeeded in grasping a branch above my head, and was swinging myself up, when I saw Diaz spring into the air, and come down with his forefeet upon one of the grunting herd. The brute's back was broken. Almost in the same instant my brave steed's teeth had made short work of another peccary; but his flanks were streaming with blood, and the dauntless animals were literally climbing upon him and ripping his hide with their short, keen tusks. I emptied my revolvers rapidly, and half a dozen animals dropped; but this made no appreciable difference in their numbers. Meanwhile Diaz had gathered himself together, and then, lashing out desperately before and behind, had shaken himself free. He sprang clear of the pack, and galloped off up the trail toward the mountains.

"The peccaries pursued him but a few paces, and then returned to besiege my tree of refuge, giving me an excellent opportunity for revolver practice. As I was refilling my emptied chambers, I heard a snorting screech coming down the trail; and there to my amazement was Diaz returning to the charge. But could that terrible-looking beast be my gentle Diaz? His eyes seemed like blazing coals, and his great jaws were dripping with blood. The peccaries darted joyously into the fray, but Diaz went right through and over them like a whirlwind, mangling I know not how many in his course, and disappeared down the trail on the homeward road. His charge had been murderous, but there were still plenty of my adversaries left to make my beleaguerment all too effective. I gazed wistfully after my heroic horse, and then, perched securely astride a branch, I continued my revolver practice. The peccaries, never

"I EMPTIED MY REVOLVERS RAPIDLY, AND HALF A DOZEN ANIMALS DROPPED." — Page 94.

heeding the diminution of their ranks, and disdaining to notice their wounds, kept scrambling on one another's shoulders, and thrusting their malignant snouts high into the air in the hope of coming at me and satiating their revenge.

"In the course of half an hour my little stock of cartridges, used deliberately and effectively, was gone; but so, as I congratulated myself, were most of the peccaries. There were still half a dozen, however; and these, as far as my imprisonment was concerned, were as bad as fourscore. These were incorruptible jailers; and I feared lest their ceaseless, angry cries might summon another herd to their assistance. When a couple of hours had passed I grew deeply disgusted, and began to plan my camping arrangements for the night.

"In the act of tying some branches together to make myself a safe couch, I caught the welcome sound of voices approaching. It was my party out in search of me. The arrival of Diaz, torn, bloody-mouthed, and in a wild excitement, had, of course, given them a terrible alarm; and they had set off without delay, hardly expecting to find me alive. A few shots from their rifles broke up the siege, and the meagre remnant of the peccaries fled into the swamps. When I got back to camp I found that none of the peons dared to do anything for Diaz, or even to approach him, he was so furious and so erratic. To me he was submissive, though with an effort. I dressed his wounds, and gave him a heavy dose of aloes, and in a day or two he was himself again. But I believe he was on the verge of going mad."

When Magnus ceased I murmured, "I only hope your uncle's adventures will last right through this trip."

" And now," said Sam, " we'll call on Queerman for something of a tender and idyllic tone; eh, Queerman?"

"All right," was the reply. "And I'll show you, Sam, that I, too, know something of the lumber-camps. Listen to a gentle —

' IDYL OF LOST CAMP.'

" In the lumber-camps they still talk about the great midwinter thaw that wrought such havoc ten years back. It came on without warning about the last week in February. There had been heavy snowfalls in the early part of the winter, and all through that district the snows were deep and soft. Before the thaw came to an end these great snow masses were dwindled to almost nothing, and the ice had gone out of the rivers in a series of tremendous floods.

" For the lumber thieves the thaw was a magnificent opportunity, of which they made haste to avail themselves. Having no stumpage dues to pay, they could afford a little extra outlay for the difficult hauling. They were comparatively secure from interruption, and the opening of the streams gave them an opportunity of quickly getting their spoils out of the way.

"One of the most important camps of the district at that time was that of the Ryckert Company, on the Little St. Francis. On a Saturday morning, the fourth day of the thaw, word was brought into camp that the thieves were having a delightful time over on Lake Pecktaweekaagomic, on the Company's timber limits. Steve Doyle, the boss of the camp, immediately called for volunteers to attempt the capture of the marauders. Every man at once came forward, with the exception of the cook; and the boss, in order to excite no jealousies, made his selection by lot. In half an hour the squad was ready to set out.

"'Be you agoin' along, sir?' inquired one of the hands.

"'Why, of course!' exclaimed Doyle. 'McCann will be in charge here while we're gone. There's such a thing possible as a brush with them fellows, though I don't anticipate no trouble with 'em. I reckon they're relyin' on the thaw to keep 'em from bein' interrupted.'

"'I thought,' responded the man who had just spoken, 'as how the "little feller" might come out to camp to-day, along of Mart. an' you mightn't want to miss him. He ain't been here fur more'n a month, now, an' we're all kind of expectin' him to-day. You kin depend on us to make a good job of it, ef so be's you'd like to stay by the camp. The hands all knows you too well to think you stay home on account of bein' *skeered,* anyways!'

"At this there was a general laugh; for Doyle's reckless courage was famous in all the camps.

"'No,' said the boss, after a thoughtful pause; 'it's my place to go, and not to stay. Anyways, I'm not lookin' for Arty to-day. His grandmother ain't goin' to let him come when the road's so bad. No!' he continued with renewed emphasis, 'this ain't no time for Arty in the woods.'

"Without more discussion the band picked up their dunnage and their guns, and set out for the lake of the unpronounceable name. It is needless to say the name became much shortened in their careless lingo. On state occasions they sometimes took pains to pronounce it 'Peckagomic.' For every-day use they found 'Gomic' quite sufficient.

"About the time the expedition was setting out from the Ryckert Camp, far away in Beardsley Settlement a very small boy was being tucked comfortably into the straw and bearskins of a roomy pung. As his grandmother kissed the round, expectant little face, she said to the driver, a slim youth of perhaps eighteen, —

"'Do you think, now, Mart, the goin' won't be too bad? Be you sure the pung ain't likely to slump down and upset? And then there's the

ice! This warm spell must have made it pretty
rotten! Will it be safe crossin' the streams?
Somehow or other, I do jist hate lettin' Arty go
along this mornin'!'"

"'Don't you be worryin' a mite, marm,' responded Mart Babcock, gathering up the reins.
'Ther' ain't no ice to cross, seein's ther' ain't no
rivers in our rowt, exceptin' the Siegus, an' that's
got a bridge to it. I'll look after Arty, trust me.
His pa'd be powerful disapp'inted if I didn't
bring him along this time, to say nawthin' of all
the hands!'

" 'Well, well,' said the old lady in a voice of
reluctant resignation ; 'I suppose it's all right;
but take keer of him, Mart, as if he was the apple
of your eye!'

"It was a soft, hazy, melting day when Mart and
Arty set out on their long drive. The travelling
was heavy, but the air was delicious, and our
travellers were in the highest spirits. This visit
to the camp was Arty's dearest treat, and was allowed him three or four times during the winter.

"Toward noon the hazy blue of the morning sky
changed to a thick gray, while the air grew almost
oppressively warm, and the woods were filled on
all sides with the strange, innumerable noises of
the great thaw. The dull crunchings of the settling masses of snow at first thrilled the child with
a vague alarm. Then, reassured by his companion, he grew interested in trying to distinguish

the varied sounds. The unbending of softened twigs and saplings, the dropping of loosened bark, the stealthy tricklings of unseen rillets — all these filled the forest with a sense of mysterious activity and bustle.

"Every little while Mart stopped to give the floundering horse rest and encouragement. Jerry belonged to Steve Doyle; but being a great pet with his owner, and devoted to the child, and at the same time somewhat too old to endure without injury the hardships of winter lumbering, he had been left at home in luxury the last two winters, with nothing to do but make a weekly trip to the camp on the Little St. Francis. In all cases Jerry was treated with affectionate consideration, which he amply repaid by his intelligence and willingness.

" When our weary travellers reached the top of the hill overlooking the camp, Jerry was pretty well fagged. There was the camp, however, not half a mile away in its clearing at the end of a straight bit of road. Arty clapped his hands, and stood up to see if he could catch a glimpse of his father looking out for him; and Mart chirruped cheerfully to the horse.

" Just at this moment the rain, which had been threatening for hours, came down. It came down in sheets. The horse was urged to a run; but the travellers, ere they reached the camp, were drenched as if they had fallen in the river. Arty, moreover, was drenched in tears for a few moments on learning of his father's absence; but soon, with the delighted pettings and caressings of the three or four woodsmen who had been left in the camp, the little fellow's disappointment was assuaged, and he was making himself at home. The camp, however, seemed to him lonely and deserted; and when, after supper, getting the cook to wrap him up in an oilskin coat, he went out to the stable to give Jerry a big piece of camp gingerbread and bid him good-night, his disappointment welled up again, and he gave way to a few more tears on the affectionate animal's neck.

"Around the blazing fire a little later Arty was himself again. The men sang songs for him, and told him stories, and blew little clouds of bitter smoke from their pipes into the brown thicket of his curls. He sat now on one rough fellow's knee, now on another's, and absorbed all the attention of the camp, and was allowed by the cook to eat all the gingerbread he wanted. When he got sleepy he was put into his father's bunk; and, since he was determined to have it so, Mart was allowed to sleep beside him. Arty having gone to bed, there was nothing for his admirers to do but follow his example. Their hearts filled with tender memories and generous thoughts, stirred up by the presence of the child among them, the backwoodsmen turned into their bunks, and soon were fast asleep.

"That night the floods came. The torrents rushing down every hillside speedily burst the already rotten ice. Some miles above the camp a jam formed itself early in the evening, — a mixed mass of ice-cakes, logs, and rubbish; and this kept the water below from rising rapidly enough to warn the camp of its danger. Just as the gray of dawn was beginning to struggle dimly through the forest aisles, the jam broke, and the mighty avalanche of ice and water swept down on the slumbering camp.

"There was no warning. Men perished in their sleep, crushed or drowned, without knowing what had happened. The camp was simply wiped out of existence.

"The bunk in which Arty lay asleep with his young protector was not built into the wall like the other bunks. It was a separate structure, and stood across the end of the building close by the fireplace. When the flood struck the camp, the stout building went down like a house of cards.

"With a choking cry of terror Arty awoke to find himself drifting in a tumult of icy waters. Great dark waves kept whirling, eddying, and crashing about him. An arm was around him, holding him firmly, and he realized that Mart was taking care of him. Presently a fragment of wreck plunged against them and he heard Mart groan; but the young man caught the timbers, and bade Arty lay hold of them. The child bravely did as he was told, and climbed actively upon the floating mass. Hardly had he done so when Mart disappeared under the dark surface.

"A shrill cry broke from Arty's lips at the sight, but in a moment the young man reappeared. He was close against the timbers — dashing against them, in fact; but Arty saw that he was unable to hold on to them. Throwing himself flat on his face, the plucky little fellow caught hold of his friend's sleeve, and clung to it with all his tiny strength. Tiny as it was, it was enough for the purpose, however, and Mart's head was kept above water; but his eyes were closed, and he did not notice the child's voice begging him to climb up onto the wreck.

"The waters subsided almost as rapidly as they had risen, though the stream remained a torrent, raging far above its wonted bounds. In a few minutes the timbers on which Arty had his refuge were swung by an eddy into shallow water. They caught against a tree, and then grounded at one end.

"Arty began crawling toward shore, dragging Mart's body through the water without great difficulty. But when he got into the shallow part it was another matter; he could not haul Mart's weight any farther. Resting the young man's head on the edge of the timbers, he paused to take breath, and looked about him in despair. Now he began to cry again; he had been too busy for lamentations while trying to save Mart.

"Presently he heard some one approaching, at-tracted by the sound of his voice. Looking up eagerly, he saw it was old Jerry, picking his way through the shallow water. He called him by name, and the horse neighed joyfully in answer. The animal was sadly bedraggled in appearance, but evidently unhurt. He had swum ashore lower down the river, and was making his way back to where he expected to find the camp. Now, how-ever, he came to Arty, sniffed him over, and rubbed him with his soft, wet nose.

"'Jerry'll help me pull Mart out,' said the child aloud, half to himself, half to the horse; and laying hold of the young man's sleeve, he again began bravely tugging upon it. 'Pull too, Jerry,' urged the little fellow, while the animal stood wondering what it was he was required to do. In a moment, however, he understood; and seizing the young man by the collar of his shirt, he speedily dragged him to land without much help from Arty. The affectionate creature rec-ognized his driver, and stood over him with drooping head, bewildered at his helplessness and silence. Mart opened his eyes, and groaned slightly once or twice, but immediately relapsed into unconsciousness. Arty sat down by his side, his little heart overflowing with grief and fear. He kept crying for his father and his grand-mother, and for Mart to open his eyes. Jerry completed the sad group, standing over it as if on guard, and ever and anon lifting his head to send forth a shrill whinny of appeal. This was the position in which, a half-hour later, guided by Jerry's signals, Steve Doyle and his party found them.

"Doyle had not caught the lumber thieves. The march of his party had been so retarded by the thaw that they had halted before going half-way. As the storm increased, and they observed how the water was rising in the brook beside which they had encamped, they became alarmed. They realized the prospect of a big flood; and Steve Doyle led his men back in hot haste. It was full daylight when they came out upon the devastated clearing where once had stood the camp.

" The horror in the lumbermen's hearts is not to be described. In a pile of wreckage, strangely mixed up with hay and straw from the stable, they found the cook, with a leg and an arm broken, but still alive. Of no one else was there a sign, nor of the horses. From the cook, Doyle learned of Arty's presence in the camp. Without a word, but with a wild, white face, the man started down stream in a despairing search; and the whole band followed, with the exception of two that stayed to take care of the unfortunate cook.

" When the father clasped Arty in his arms he was almost beside himself with joy for a few moments; then he remembered the poor fellows who were gone. Giving the child into the arms of one of the men, he busied himself with Mart, whom, by means of rubbing, he soon brought back to consciousness. The brave fellow had been stunned by a blow on the head. and afterward half drowned; but he soon recovered so far as to be able to walk with assistance. To Arty he owed his life, even as he had himself saved Arty's.

" A little later a melancholy procession started back for Beardsley Settlement. The poor cook was placed on Jerry's back, and bore his pain like a hero. Arty trudged by the side of McCann, to whose charge he was committed by his father, and Mart was helped along by two of his comrades. With these went five or six more of the hands, to get them safely to the settlement. All the rest, under the leadership of Steve Doyle, set off down river on a search for the three missing men, or their bodies. And the site of the camp was left to its desolation.

" As for Doyle's search, it proved fruitless, and the party returned heavy-hearted. Henceforth the scene of the catastrophe became known throughout that region as 'Lost Camp,' and was sedulously avoided by the lumbermen. Next season the Ryckert Company's camp on the Little St. Francis was built on higher ground some miles farther up stream."

" That's a most depressing tale, Queerman," grumbled Ranolf. " I suppose it's my turn now;

and, thank goodness, I've got something frivolous to tell!"

"Heave ahead, then," urged Stranion.

"Your title?" I demanded.

"This is the tale of 'The Cart before the Steer,'" replied Ranolf.

THE CART BEFORE THE STEER.

"'Landry!' shouted Squire Bateman, emerging from the big red door of the barn with a pitchfork in his hand.

"Landry, an excitable little Frenchman, appeared suddenly around the woodhouse, as if he had just been waiting to be called.

"'Landry,' said the squire, 'you're goin' in to Kentville this mornin' for that feed, ain't you?'

"'Yes, sare,' responded Landry.

"The farmer considered for a moment, chewing thoughtfully on a head of wheat. Then he continued, 'You'd better take the black-an'-white steer along, and leave him at Murphy's as you pass. He's fat now as he'll ever be, an' it's jest a waste o' feed to keep on stuffin' the critter.'

"'Ow'll I take him, sare?' queried Landry.

"'Oh,' replied the squire rather impatiently, turning back into the barn, 'hitch him to the back o' the cart. He'll lead all right!'

"On this point Landry seemed doubtful. He scratched his head anxiously for a moment, and then darted off in his nervous way, so unlike the deliberateness of hired men in general, to carry out his employer's orders.

"The black-and-white steer was a raw-boned beast, about three years old, with no disposition to take on fat. There was a wild, roving expression in his eye which made Landry, who knew cattle well, and appreciated the differences in their dispositions, very doubtful as to his docility when being led to market. In Squire Bateman's eyes, however, a steer was a steer; and if one could be led so could another. Squire Bateman had a constitutional hatred of exceptions.

"When Landry was ready to start he hitched the steer to the cart-tail with a strong halter, and set out with misgivings. But the steer proved docility itself. It trotted along in indolent good humor, holding its head high, and sniffing the fresh, meadow-scented air with delight. By the time they reached the top of Barnes's Hill, a long descent about two miles this side of Kentville, Landry had made up his mind that he had done the animal an injustice. But just at this stage in the journey something took place, as things will so long as Fate remains the whimsical creature she is.

"It chanced that a party of wheelmen from Halifax, on a tour through the Cornwallis valley and the Evangeline regions, arrived at the top of the hill when Landry and his charge were about halfway down. The bicyclists were riding in a long line, single file. Their leader knew the country, and he knew that Barnes's Hill was smooth and safe for 'coasting.' Some of the riders, the leader among them, were on the old-fashioned high wheels, while others rode the less conspicuous 'Safeties,' then a new thing. Each man, as he dipped over the edge of the slope, flung his legs over the handles and luxuriously 'let her go.' They saw the team ahead, but there was abundance of room for safe passing.

"Now, Squire Bateman's black-and-white steer had been brought up behind the Gaspereau hills, where the wheelman delights not to wander. A bicycle, therefore, was in his eyes a novel and terrifying sight. As the whirling and gleaming apparition flashed past he snorted fiercely, and sprang aside with a violence that almost upset the cart. Landry sprang to his feet, grinding his teeth with excitement and wrath, and the next wheelman slipped radiantly by. This was too much for the black-and-white steer, and on the third wheel he made a desperate but ineffectual charge.

"Ineffectual did I say? Well, only so far as that wheel was concerned; but he flung himself so far across the way that the next rider could not avoid the obstacle. The tall wheel struck the animal amidships, so to speak; and the rider went right on and landed in a dismal heap. The other riders darted aside up the bank into the fence, stopping themselves gracefully or ungracefully, but at any cost avoiding the now quite demented beast that was blocking their way.

"The animal made a frantic dash at the unfortunate wheelman in the gutter, who had picked himself up with difficulty, and was feeling for broken bones. He was beyond the steer's reach, but discreetly hobbled to the fence, and placed that welcome barrier between him and the foe. The fury of the animal's charge, however, had swung the cart right across the road, and now the frightened horse began to plunge and rear. Landry held him in partial control; and the next instant the steer made a second mad rush, this time aiming at the bicycle which had struck him, and which now lay in the gutter. He reached the offending wheel, but at the same time he upset the cart. Out went Landry like a rubber ball; and the horse, kicking himself free of the traces, set out at a highly creditable pace for Kentville.

"The rage of the little Frenchman, as he picked himself up, was Homeric. He abused the bellowing and bounding brute with an eloquence which, had it been expressed in English, would have made the wheelmen on the other side of the fence depart in horror. Then he seized a fence stake and rushed into close quarters, resolved to enforce his authority.

"At the moment of Landry's attack, the steer had his horns very much engaged in the wheel of the bicycle As the fence stake came down with impressive emphasis across his haunches, he tossed the machine in air, and charged on his assailant with great nimbleness and ferocity. Landry just escaped by springing over the body of the cart; and at this juncture he congratulated himself that he had hitched the animal by so strong a halter.

" By this time the bicyclists had reunited their forces a little below. Their leader, with the dismounted wheelman, now came to rescue the suffering wheel. But there was no such thing as getting near it. The steer stood guard over his prize with an air that forbade any interference.

· " 'It isn't much good now, anyway,' grumbled the victim. 'I guess I'll have to hobble on as far as Kentville, and borrow or hire another wheel there. This ain't worth mending now.'

" 'Oh, nonsense ! ' replied the leader ; ' a few dollars will put it all right. We'll leave it at Kentville to be sent back to Halifax by the D. A. R., and McInerney'll fix it so you'd never know it had been broken ! '

" 'Well,' rejoined the discomfited one, ' I don't see how we're going to get hold of it, anyway.'

" To this sentiment the steer bellowed his adherence. The leader of the wheelmen, however, glancing around at the encouraging countenances of his party, drew a small revolver from his hip pocket.

" 'Don't you think,' he said, addressing Landry,

'we ought to shoot this beast? He is blocking the highway, and he is a menace to all passers-by.'

"The astute Landry meditated for a moment.

"'What might be your name, sare?' he inquired.

"'My name's Vroot — Walter Vroot of Halifax,' replied the wheelman.

"'Eef you shoot ze steer, sare, Squire Bateman he make you pay for 'eem, sure,' said Landry.

"At this there arose a chorus of indignation led by the discomfited one. But Mr. Vroot turned on his heel, thrusting his revolver back into his pocket.

"'Perhaps,' said he to Landry, 'you'll be so good as to bring the bicycle into Kentville with you when you come.'

"''Sare,' said Landry, ''ow is dat posseeble? I go in to Kentville right now to look after my 'orse.'

"In a few minutes the wheelmen had vanished in a slender and gleaming line, Landry and the wheelless one (whose name, by the way, was Smith) were tramping dejectedly townward, and the steer was left in absolute possession of the cart, the wheel, and a portion of the Queen's highway.

"In a short time the situation might have become monotonous for the animal, as the road was dry and dusty, and the rich, short grass of the roadside beyond his reach. But just as he had

got tired of demolishing the bicycle, there came
a diversion. A light carriage containing a lady
and gentleman appeared over the crest of the
hill. The occupants of the carriage were surprised and vexed at the obstacle before them.

"'I think it's perfectly outrageous,' said the
lady, 'the way these country people leave their
vehicles right in the middle of the road.'

"'There seems to have been some accident,'
remarked the man soothingly.

"'What business had they going away and leaving things that way?' retorted the lady sharply.
'You'll have to get out and remove that animal
before we try to pass.'

"By this time the horse, a mild livery-stable
creature, was almost within reach of the angry
steer, whose tail twitched ominously. The next
instant, with a deep, grunting bellow, he charged
at the horse, who reared and backed just in time
to save himself. The carriage came within an ace
of upsetting, and the lady shrieked hysterically.
The man sprang out, and seized the horse by the
head. The lady flung herself out desperately
over the back.

"'Don't be alarmed, my dear!' said the man.
'The animal is securely fastened to the cart, and
seems to have been placed there to guard the
way. They seem to have very strange customs
in Nova Scotia!'

"'What *shall* we do?' queried the lady tear-
fully, gazing at the pawing and roaring steer.

"'Why, there's nothing to do but take down a piece of the fence and drive around. There's no occasion for alarm!' replied the man.

"He backed the horse a little way, and then tied him to the fence while he made an opening. Then he made another opening at a safe distance below the obstacle, led the horse and carriage through, put the lady back into the seat, and continued his journey philosophically. In the course of the next hour a number of other travellers approached, and taking in the situation, followed the new route through the fields. The steer invariably bellowed, and plunged and lashed himself into mad rage in trying to get at them; but Squire Bateman's halter and rope did their duty, and all his efforts proved futile.

"But meanwhile the most astounding reports were flying about Kentville. Landry had secured the horse, and related the exact truth of the whole affair; but the various romantic and exciting embellishments of wayfarers found most favor in the eventless country town. A little squad of men with guns set forth to quell the nuisance; and hard on their heels followed Landry, bent on saving the property of his employer.

"When the party drew near, and realized how securely their antagonist was tethered, they were in no haste to complete their errand. The brute's rage was so blind and fierce that they amused themselves for a little with the sport of tantalizing him. They would approach almost within his reach, and then dart back to a safer-looking distance; and presently the animal was a mass of sweat and froth, churned with red dust of the highway. At last, just as one of the men raised his rifle with the intention of ending the play, the animal threw himself in one of his maddest charges.

"Landry had just come up. The instant the steer fell he rushed forward, threw his coat over its head, and knotted the arms under its jaws. Breathless and bewildered, the panting brute ceased its struggles and lay quite still. In a moment or two it was lifted to its feet, the halter was unhitched from the cart-tail, and Landry set out for Kentville with the blindfolded steer following as gently as a lamb."

CHAPTER IV.

MORE OF CAMP DE SQUATOOK.

On the following morning we breakfasted in a very leisurely fashion, with a delightful sense of having all day before us. We spent the day in casting our flies at the outlet, and our success was a continual repetition of that of the previous night. Only Stranion grew tired. He could not hook as many fish as the rest of us; wherefore he grew disgusted, and chose to sit on the bank deriding us. But as long as the fish were feeding we heeded him not. Our heaviest trout that day just cleared two pounds and a half.

In the evening we took tea early. Before settling down we made a little voyage of exploration to the top of a neighboring hill, and watched the moon rise over the vast and empty wilderness. Returning to the camp, we doffed our scanty garments, ran down the beach, and dashed out into the gleaming lake-waters. It was such a swim as Stranion had told us of. After this we felt royally luxurious. We lolled upon our blankets with a lordly air, and the soughing of the pines was all about us for music. Then, in a peremptory tone,

Sam cried, "Stranion!"—"Sir, to you!" was Stranion's polite response.

"Stranion," continued Sam, "to you it falls to unfold to this appreciative audience the resources of your experience or your imagination. I would recommend, now, a judicious combination of the two."

Thus irresistibly adjured, Stranion began:—

"This is the story of—

'LOU'S CLARIONET,' "

said he. "Judge ye whether I speak from experience or imagination.

"It was a Christmas Eve service in the Second Westcock Church.

"The church at Second Westcock was quaint and old-fashioned, like the village over which it presided. Its shingles were gray with the beating of many winters; its little square tower was surmounted by four spindling posts, like the legs of a table turned heavenward; its staring windows were adorned with curtains of yellow cotton; its uneven and desolate churchyard, strewn with graves and snowdrifts, occupied a bleak hillside looking out across the bay to the lonely height of Shepody Mountain.

"Down the long slope below the church straggled the village. half-lost in the snow. and whistled over by the winds of the Bay of Fundy.

"Second Westcock was an outlying corner of

the rector's expansive parish, and a Christmas Eve service there was an event almost unparalleled. To give Second Westcock this service, the rector had forsaken his prosperous congregations at Westcock, Sackville, and Dorchester, driving some eight or ten miles through the snows and solitude of the deep Dorchester woods.

"And because the choir at Second Westcock was not remarkable even for willingness, much less for strength or skill, he had brought with him his fifteen-year-old niece, Lou Allison, to swell the Christmas praises with the notes of her clarionet.

"The little church was lighted with oil-lamps ranged along the white wall between the windows. The poor, bare chancel — a red cloth-covered kitchen table in a semicircle of paintless railing — was flanked by two towering pulpits of white pine. On either side the narrow, carpetless aisle were rows of unpainted benches.

"On the left were gathered solemnly the men of the congregation, each looking straight ahead. On the right were the women, whispering and scanning each other's bonnets, till the appearance of the rector from the little vestry-room by the door should bring silence and reverent attention.

"In front of the women's row stood the melodeon; and the two benches behind it were occupied by the choir, the male members of which sat blushingly self-conscious, proud of their office, but deeply abashed at the necessity of sitting among the women.

"There was no attempt at Christmas decoration, for Second Westcock had never been awakened to the delicious excitements of the church greening.

"At last the rector appeared in his voluminous white surplice. He moved slowly up the aisle, and mounted the winding steps of the right-hand pulpit; and as he did so his five-year-old son, forsaking his place by Lou's side, marched forward and seated himself resolutely on the pulpit steps. He did not feel quite at home in Second Westcock Church.

"The sweet old carol, 'While shepherds watched their flocks by night,' rose rather doubtfully from the little choir, who looked and listened askance at the glittering clarionet, into which Lou was now blowing softly. Lou was afraid to make herself distinctly heard at first, lest she should startle the singers; but in the second verse the pure vibrant notes came out with confidence, and then for two lines the song was little more than a duet between Lou and the rector's vigorous baritone. In the third verse, however, it all came right. The choir felt and responded to the strong support and thrilling stimulus of the instrument, and at length ceased to dread their own voices. The naked little church was glorified with the sweep of triumphal song pulsating through it.

"Never before had such music been heard there.

Men, women, and children sang from their very souls; and when the hymn was ended the whole congregation stood for some seconds as in a dream, with quivering throats, till the rector's calm voice, repeating the opening words of the liturgy, brought back their self-control in some measure.

"Thereafter every hymn and chant and carol was like an inspiration, and Lou's eyes sparkled with exultation.

"When the service was over the people gathered round the stove by the door, praising Lou's clarionet, and petting little Ted, who had by this time come down from the pulpit steps. One old lady gave the child two or three brown sugar-biscuits, which she had brought in her pocket, and a pair of red mittens, which she had knitted for him as a Christmas present.

"Turning to Lou, the old lady said, 'I never heerd nothing like that trumpet of yourn, Miss. I felt like it jest drawed down the angels from heaven to sing with us to-night. Ther voices was all swimming in a smoke like, right up in the hollow of the ceiling.'

"''Tain't a trumpet!' interrupted Teddy shyly; 'it's a clar'onet. I got a trumpet home!'

"'*To* be sure!' replied the old lady indulgently. 'But, Miss, as I was a-sayin,' that music of yourn would jest soften the hardest heart as ever was.'

"The rector had just come from the vestry-room, well wrapped up in his furs, and was shaking hands and wishing every one a Merry Christmas, while the sexton brought the horse to the door. He overheard the old lady's last remark, as she was bundling Teddy up in a huge woollen muffler.

" 'It certainly did,' said he, 'make the singing go magnificently to-night, didn't it, Mrs. Tait? But I wonder, now, what sort of an effect it would produce on a hard-hearted bear if such a creature should come out at us while we are going through Dorchester woods?'

"The mild pleasantry was very delicately adapted to the rector's audience, and the group about the stove smiled with a reverent air befitting the place they were in; but the old lady exclaimed in haste, —

" 'My land sakes, Parson, a bear'd be jest scared to death!'

" 'I wonder if it *would* frighten a bear?' thought Lou to herself, as they were getting snugly bundled into the warm, deep 'pung,' as the low box-sleigh with movable seats is called.

"Soon the crest of the hill was passed, and the four-poster on the top of Second Westcock Church sank out of sight. For a mile or more the road led through half-cleared pasture lands, where the black stumps stuck up so strangely through the drifts that Teddy discovered bears on every hand. He was not at all alarmed, however, for he was sure his father was a match for a thousand bears.

"By and by the road entered the curious inverted dark of the Dorchester woods, where all the light seemed to come from the white snow under the trees rather than from the dark sky above them. At this stage of the journey Teddy retired beneath the buffalo-robes, and went to sleep in the bottom of the pung.

"The horse jogged slowly along the somewhat heavy road. The bells jingled drowsily amid the soft, pushing whisper of the runners. Lou and the rector talked in quiet voices, attuned to the solemn hush of the great forest.

"*'What's that?'*

"Lou shivered up closer to the rector as she spoke, and glanced nervously into the dark woods whence a sound had come. He did not answer at once, but seized the whip and tightened the reins, as a signal to old Jerry to move on faster.

"The horse needed no signal, but awoke into an eager trot, which would have become a gallop had the rector permitted.

"Again came the sound, this time a little nearer, and still, apparently, just abreast of the pung, but deep in the woods. It was a bitter, long, wailing cry, blended with a harshly grating undertone, like the rasping of a saw.

"'What is it?' again asked Lou, her teeth chattering.

"The rector let old Jerry out into a gallop, as he answered, 'I'm afraid it's a panther, — what they call around here an "Indian devil." But I don't think there is any real danger. It is a ferocious beast, but will probably give *us* a wide berth.'

" ' Why won't it attack *us?* " asked Lou.

" ' Oh, it prefers solitary victims,' replied the rector. 'It is ordinarily a cautious beast, and does not understand the combination of man and horse and vehicle. Only on rare occasions has it been known to attack people driving, and this one will probably keep well out of our sight. However, it's just as well to get beyond its neighborhood as quickly as possible. Steady, Jerry, old boy! Steady; don't use yourself up too fast!'

"The rector kept the horse well in hand; but in a short time it was plain that the panther was not avoiding the party. The cries came nearer and nearer, and Lou's breath came quicker and quicker, and the rector's teeth began to set themselves grimly, while his brows gathered in anxious thought.

"If it should come to a struggle, what was there in the sleigh, he was wondering, that could serve as a weapon? Nothing, absolutely nothing, but his heavy pocket-knife.

" ' A poor weapon,' thought he ruefully, ' with which to fight a panther.' But he felt in his pocket with one hand, and opened the knife, and slipped it under the edge of the cushion beside him.

"At this instant he caught sight of the panther bounding along through the low underbrush, keeping parallel with the road, and not forty yards away.

"'There it is!' came in a terrified whisper from Lou's lips; and just then Teddy lifted his head from under the robes. Frightened at the speed, and at the set look on his father's face, he began to cry. The panther heard him and turned at once toward the sleigh.

"Old Jerry stretched himself out in a burst of extra speed, while the rector grasped his poor knife fiercely; and the panther came with a long leap right into the road, not ten paces behind the flying sleigh.

"Teddy stared in amazement, then cowered down in fresh terror as there came an ear-splitting screech, wild and high and long, from Lou's clarionet. Lou had turned, and over the back of the seat was blowing this peal of desperate defiance in the brute's very face. The astonished animal shrank back in his tracks, and sprang again into the underbrush.

"Lou turned to the rector with a flushed face of triumph, and the rector exclaimed in a husky voice, 'Thank God!' But Teddy, between his sobs, complained, 'What did you do that for, Lou?'

" Lou jumped to the conclusion that her victory was complete and final ; but the rector kept Jerry at his top speed, and scrutinized the underwood apprehensively.

" The panther appeared again in four or five minutes, returning to the road, and leaping along some forty or fifty feet behind the sleigh. His pace was a very curious, disjointed, india-rubbery spring, which rapidly closed up on the fugitives.

" Then round swung Lou's long instrument again, and at its piercing cry the animal again shrank back. This time, however, he kept to the road, and the moment Lou paused for breath he resumed the chase.

" ' Save your breath, child,' exclaimed the rector, as Lou again put the slender tube to her lips. ' Save your breath, and let him have it ferociously when he begins to get too near.

" The animal came within twenty or thirty feet again, and then Lou greeted him with an ear-splitting blast, and he fell back. Again and again the tactics were repeated. Lou tried a thrilling cadenza ; it was too much for the brute's nerves. He could not comprehend a girl with such a penetrating voice, and he could not screw up his courage to a closer investigation of the marvel.

" At last the animal seemed to resolve on a change of procedure. Plunging into the woods, he made an effort to get ahead of the sleigh. Old Jerry was showing signs of exhaustion ; but the rector roused him to an extra spurt—and there, just ahead, was the opening of Fillmore's settlement.

"'Blow, Lou, blow!' shouted the rector; and as the panther made a dash to intercept the sleigh, it found itself in too close proximity to the strange-voiced phenomenon in the pung, and sprang backward with an angry snarl.

"As Lou's breath failed from her dry lips, the sleigh dashed out into the open. A dog bayed angrily from the nearest farmhouse, and the panther stopped short on the edge of the wood. The rector drove into the farmyard; and old Jerry stopped, shivering as if he would fall between the shafts.

"After the story had been told, and Jerry had been stabled and rubbed down, the rector resumed his journey with a fresh horse, having no fear that the panther would venture across the cleared lands. Three of the settlers started out forthwith, and following the tracks in the new snow, succeeded in shooting the beast after a chase of two or three hours.

"The adventure supplied the country-side all that winter with a theme for conversation; and about Lou's clarionet there gathered a halo of romance that drew rousing congregations to the parish church, where its music was to be heard every alternate Sunday evening."

"I should say," remarked Queerman, "that to

experience and imagination you combine a most tenacious memory. Who would have dreamed that the shy Teddy, with his proclivity for the pulpit-steps, would have developed into the Stranion that we see before us!"

To this there was no reply. Then suddenly Magnus said, "Sam!" And Sam began at once.

" This is all about —

'JAKE DIMBALL'S WOODEN LEG,'"

said Sam.

"One evening in the early summer, I won't say how many years ago, Jake Dimball was driving the cows home from pasture. At that time Jake, a stout youth of seventeen, had no thought of such an appendage as a wooden leg. Indeed, he had no place to put one had he possessed such a thing; for his own vigorous legs of bone and muscle, with which he had been born and with which he had grown up in entire content, seemed likely to serve him for the rest of his natural life. But that very evening, amid the safe quiet and soft colors of the upland cow-pasture, fate was making ready a lesson for him in the possibilities of the unexpected.

"In Westmoreland county that summer bears were looked upon as a drug in the market. The county, indeed, seemed to be suffering from an epidemic of bears. But, so far, these woody pastures of Second Westcock, surrounded by settlements, had apparently escaped the contagion. When, therefore, Jake was startled by an angry growl, coming from a swampy thicket on his right, the thought of a bear did not immediately occur to him. He saw that the cows were running ahead with a sudden alertness, but he paused and gazed at the thicket, wondering whether it would be wise for him to go and investigate the source of the sound. While he hesitated, the question was decided for him. A large black bear burst forth from the bushes with a crash that carried a nameless terror into Jake's very soul. The beast looked so cruelly out of place, so horribly out of place, breaking in upon the beauty and security of the familiar scene. Jake had no weapon more formidable than the hazel switch he was carrying and the pocket-knife with which he was trimming off its branches. After one long horrified look at the bear, Jake took to flight along the narrow cow-path.

"Jake was a notable runner in those days, yet the bear gained upon him rapidly. The cowpath was tortuous exceedingly, and away from the path the ground was too rough for fast running — at least Jake found it so. The bear did not seem to mind the irregularities.

"Jake envied the cows their fine head start. He wished he was with them; then, as he heard the bear getting closer, he almost wished he was one of them; and then his foot caught in a root and he fell headlong.

"As he fell a great wave of despair went over him, and a thought flashed through his mind: 'This is the end of me!' His sight was darkened for an instant, as he rolled in the moss and twigs between two hillocks. Then, turning upon his back, he saw the bear already hanging over him; and now a desperate courage came to his aid.

"Raising his heels high in the air, he brought them down with violence in the brute's face. The animal started back, astonished at this novel method of defence. When it advanced again to the attack, Jake met it desperately with his heels; and all the time he kept up a lusty shouting such as he hoped would soon bring some one to the rescue. For a few minutes, strange to say, Jake's tactics were successful in keeping his foe at bay; but presently the bear, growing more angry, or more hungry, made a fiercer assault, and, succeeded in catching the lad's foot between his jaws. The brave fellowed sickened under the cruel grip of those crunching teeth; but he kept up the fight with his free heel. Just as he was about fainting with pain and exhaustion, some farmers, who had had heard the outcry, arrived upon the scene, and the bear hastily withdrew.

"That night there was a bear-hunt at Second Westcock, but it brought no spoils. Bruin had made an effective disappearance. As for Jake, his foot and the lower part of his leg were so dreadfully mangled that the leg had to be cut off just below the knee. When the lad was entirely recovered, being a handy fellow, he made himself a new leg of white oak, around the bottom of which, to prevent wear, he hammered a stout iron ring.

" The years went by in their usual surreptitious fashion, and brought few changes to Second Westcock. One June evening, ten years after that on which my story opened, Jake was driving the cows home as usual, when once more, as he passed the swampy thicket, he heard that menacing growl. Jake looked about him as if in a dream. There was the same dewy smell in the air, mingled with the fragrance of sweet fern, that he remembered so painfully and so well. There was the same long yellow cloud over the black woods to the west. There was the same dappled sky of amber and violet over his head. As before, he saw the cows breaking into a run. In a moment there was the same dreadful crashing in the thicket. Was he dreaming? He looked down in bewilderment, and his eyes fell on the iron-shod end of his wooden leg! That settled it. Evidently he was not dreaming, and it was time for him to hurry home. He broke into a run as rapid as his wooden leg would allow.

" Now, long use and natural dexterity had made Jake almost as active in the handling of this wooden leg as most men are with the limbs which nature gave them. But with his original legs in their pristine vigor he had found himself no match for a bear. What, then, could he expect in the present instance? Jake looked over his shoulder, and beheld the bear hot on his tracks. He could have sworn it was the same bear as of old. He made up his mind to run no more, but to save his breath for what he felt might be his last fight. He gave a series of terrific yells, such as he thought might pierce even to the corner grocery under the hill, and threw himself flat on his back on a gentle hummock that might pass for a post of vantage.

"Jake was not hopeful, but he was firm. He thought it would be too much to expect to come off twice victorious from a scrape like this. He eyed the bear sternly, and it seemed to him as if the brute actually smiled on observing that its intended victim had not forgotten his ancient tactics. Jake concluded that the approaching contest was likely to be fatal to himself, but he calculated on making it at least unpleasant for the bear.

"The animal turned a little to one side, and attacked his prostrate antagonist in the flank; but Jake whirled nimbly just in time, and brought down his iron-shod heel on the brute's snout. The blow was a heavy one, but that bear was not at all surprised. If it was the bear of the previous encounter, it doubtless argued that years had brought additional weight and strength to its opponent's understanding. It was not to be daunted, but instantly seized the wooden leg in its angry jaws. Jake's yells for help continued; but the bear, the moment it discovered that the limb on which it was chewing was of good white oak, fell a prey to astonishment, if not alarm.

"It dropped the leg, backed off a few paces, sat down upon its haunches, and gazed at this strange and inedible species of man. Jake realized at once the creature's bewilderment; but the crisis was such a painful one that the humor of the situation failed to strike him.

"After a few moments of contemplation, the bear made a fresh attack. It was hungry, and perhaps thought some other portion of Jake's body might prove more delicate eating than his leg. Jake, however, gave it no chance to try. The next hold the bear got was upon the very end of the oaken member, where the iron ring proved little to its taste. It tried fiercely for another hold; but Jake in his desperate struggles, endowed with the strength of his terror, succeeded in foiling it in every attempt. At length, with the utmost force of his powerful thigh, he drove the end of the leg right into the beast's open mouth, inflicting a serious wound. Blood flowed freely from the animal's throat; and presently, after a moment of hesitation, having probably concluded that the morsel was not savory enough to justify any further struggle, the bear moved sullenly away, coughing and whining.

"Jake lay quite still till his vanquished antagonist had disappeared in the covert. Then he rose and wended his way homeward, thinking to himself how much better his wooden leg had served him than an ordinary one could have done. In a few minutes he was met by some of his fellow-townsmen, who were hastening to find out the cause of all the noise. To them Jake related the adventure with great elation, adding, as he concluded, 'You see, now, how everything turns out for the best. If I hadn't lost that ere leg of mine this night ten year ago, I'd have mebbe lost my head this very evening!'

"In spite of Jake Dimball's reputation for truthfulness, his story was not believed in the village of Second Westcock. It was voted altogether too improbable, from whatever side it was looked at. In fact, so profoundly incredulous were his fellow-villagers, that Jake could not even organize a bear-hunt. Some ten days later, however, his veracity received ample confirmation. A man out looking for strayed cattle in the woods not more than a couple of miles from Jake's pasture, found a large bear lying dead in a cedar swamp. Examining the body curiously to find the cause of death, he was puzzled till he recalled Jake's story. Then he looked at the dead brute's throat. The mystery was solved; and the community was once for all convinced of the fighting qualities of the wooden leg."

"That's a good story," said Magnus. "In a vague way it reminds me of one which is as unlike it as anything could well be. Mine is a tropical tale. Let the O. M. enter it as —

'PERIL AMONG THE PEARLS.'

I got it at first-hand when I was in Halifax last autumn.

"In the tiny office of the 'Cunarder' inn the air was thick with smoke. The white, egg-shaped stove contained a fire, though September was yet young; for a raw night fog had rolled in over Halifax, making the display of bright coals no less comforting than cheerful. From the adjacent wharves came the soft washing and whispering of the tide, with an occasional rattle of oars as a boat came to land from one of the many ships.

"The density of the atmosphere in the office was chiefly due to 'Al' Johnson, the diver, who, when he was not talking, diving, eating, or sleeping, was sure to be puffing at his pipe. We had talked little, but now I resolved to turn off the smoke flowing from Johnson's pipe by getting him to tell us a story. He could never tell a story and keep his pipe lit at the same time.

"Johnson was a college-bred man, whom a love of adventure had lured into deep-sea diving. He

and his partner were at this time engaged in recovering the cargo of the steamer Oelrich, sunk
near the entrance to Halifax harbor.

"I asked Johnson, 'Do you remember promis-
ing me a yarn about an adventure you had in
the pearl-fisheries?'

"'Which adventure? and what pearl-fisheries?'
Johnson asked. 'I've fished at Tinnevelli, and in
the Sulu waters off the Borneo coast, and also
in the Torres Strait; and wheresoever it was, there
seemed to be pretty nearly always some excitement going.'

"'Oh,' said I, 'whichever you like to give us.
I think what you spoke of was an adventure in
the Torres Strait.'

"'No,' said Johnson, 'I think I'll give you a
little yarn about a tussle I had with a turtle in
the Sulu waters. I fancy there isn't much that
grows but you'll find it somewhere in Borneo; and
the water there is just as full of life as the land.'

"'Sharks?' I queried.

"'Oh, worse than sharks!' replied Johnson.
'There's a big squid that will squirt the water
black as ink; and just then, perhaps, something
comes along and grabs you when you can't defend
yourself. And there's the devil-fish, own cousin
to the squid, and the meanest enemy you'd want
to run across anywhere. And there's a tremendous giant of a shell-fish,—a kind of scalloped
clam, that lies with its huge shells wide open, but

half hidden in the long weeds and sea-mosses. If you put your foot into *that* trap — *snap!* it closes on you, and you're fast! That clam is a good deal stronger than you are; and if you have not a hatchet or something to smash the shell with, you are likely to stay there. Of course your partner in the boat up aloft would soon know something was wrong, finding that he couldn't haul you up. Then he would go down after you, and chop you loose perhaps. But meanwhile it would be far from nice, especially if a shark came along — if another clam does not nab him, for one of these big clams has been known to catch even a shark. Many natives thereabouts do a lot of diving on their own account, and, of course, don't indulge in diving-suits. I can tell you, they are very careful not to fall afoul of those clam-shells; for when they do they're drowned before they can get clear.'

" ' You can hardly blame the clam, or whatever it is,' said I. 'It must be rather a shock to its nerves when it feels a big foot thrust down right upon its stomach ! '

" ' No,' assented Johnson; 'you can't blame the clam. But besides the clam, there is a big turtle that is a most officious creature, with a beak that will almost cut railroad iron. It is forever poking that beak into whatever it thinks it doesn't know all about; and you cannot scare it as you can a shark. You have simply got to kill it before it will acknowledge itself beaten. These same turtles, however, at the top of the water or on dry land would, in most cases, prove as timid as rabbits. And then, as you say, there are the sharks, —all kinds, big and little, forever hungry, but not half so courageous as they get the credit of being.'

" ' I suppose,' I interrupted, ' you always carried a weapon of some sort!'

" ' Well, rather!' said Johnson. 'For my own part, I took a great fancy to the ironwood stakes that the natives always use. But they didn't seem to me quite the thing for smashing those big shells with, supposing a fellow should happen to put his foot into one. So I made myself a stake with a steel top, which answered every purpose. More than one big shark have I settled with that handspike of mine ; and once I found, to my great advantage. that it was just the thing to break up a shell with.'

" ' Ha, ha!' laughed Best, who had been listening rather inattentively hitherto. 'So *you* put your foot in it, did you ?"

" ' Yes, I did,' said Johnson. ' And that is just what I'm going to tell you about. I was working that season with a good partner, a likely young fellow hailing from Auckland. He tended the line and the pump to my complete satisfaction. I've never had a better tender. Also, I was teaching him to dive, and he took to it like a loon. His name was " Larry " Scott; and if he had lived, he would have made a record. He was killed about a year after the time I'm telling you of, in a row down in New Orleans. But we won't stop to talk about that now.

"'As I was saying, Larry and I pulled together pretty well from the start, and we were so lucky with our fishing that the fellows in the other boats began to get jealous and unpleasant. You must know that all kinds go to the pearl-fisheries; and the worst kinds have rather the best of it, in point of numbers. We were ready enough to fight, but we liked best to go our own way peaceably. So, when some of the other lads got quarrelsome, we just smiled, hoisted our sail, and looked up a new ground for ourselves some little distance from the rest of the fleet. Luck being on our side just then, we chanced upon one of the finest beds in the whole neighborhood.

"'One morning, as I was poking about among the seaweed and stuff, I came across a fine-looking bunch of pearl-shells. I made a grab at them, but they were firmly rooted and refused to come away. I laid down my handspike, took hold of the cluster with both hands, and shifted my foothold so as to get a good chance to pull.

"'Up came the bunch of shells at the first wrench, much more readily than I had expected. To recover myself I took a step backward; down went my foot into a crevice, "slumped" into something soft, and *snap!* my leg was fast in a grip that almost made me yell there in the little prison of my helmet.

" 'Well, as you may imagine, just as soon as I recovered from the start this gave me, I reached out for my handspike to knock that clam-shell into flinders. But a cold shiver went over me as I found I could not reach the weapon! As I laid it down, it had slipped a little off to one side; and there it rested about a foot out of my reach, reclining on one of those twisted conch-shells such as the farmers use for dinner-horns.

" 'How I jerked on my leg trying to pull it out of the trap! That, however, only hurt the leg. All the satisfaction I could get was in the thought that my foot, with its big, twenty-pound, rubber-and-lead boot, must be making the clam's internal affairs rather uncomfortable. After I had pretty well tired myself out, stretching and tugging on my leg, and struggling to reach the handspike. I paused to recover my wind, and consider the situation.

" 'It was not very deep water I was working in, and there was any amount of light. You have no sort of idea, until you have been there yourself, what a queer world it is down where the pearl-oyster grows. The seaweeds were all sorts of colors — or rather, I should say. they were all sorts of reds and yellows and greens. The rest of the colors of the rainbow you might find in the shells which lay around under foot, or went crawling among the weeds; and away overhead darted and flashed the queerest looking fish, like birds in a yellow sky. There were lots of big anemones too, waving, stretching, and curling their many-colored tentacles.

"'I saw everything with extraordinary vividness about that time, as I know by the clear way I recollect it now; but you may be sure I wasn't thinking much just then about the beauties of nature. I was trying to think of some way of getting assistance from Larry. At length I concluded I had better give him the signal to haul me up. Finding that I was stuck, he would, I reasoned, hoist the anchor, and then pull the boat along to the place of my captivity. Then he could easily send me down a hatchet wherewith to chop my way to freedom.

"'Just as I had come to this resolve, a black shadow passed over my head, and I looked up quickly. It was a big turtle. I didn't like this, I can tell you; but I kept perfectly still, hoping the new-comer would not notice me.

"'He paddled along very slowly, with his queer little head stuck far out, and presently he noticed my air-tube. It seemed to strike him as decidedly queer. My blood fairly turned to ice in my veins as I saw him paddle up and take hold of it in a gingerly fashion with his beak. Luckily, he didn't seem to think it would be good to eat; but I knew that if he should bite it I would be

"IT SEEMED TO STRIKE HIM AS DECIDEDLY QUEER."—Page 110.

a dead man in about a minute, drowned inside
my helmet like a rat in a hole. It is in an emergency like this that a man learns to know what
real terror is.

"'In my desperation I stooped down and tore
with both hands at the shells and weeds for something I might hurl at the turtle, thinking thus
perhaps to distract his attention from my air-tube.
But what do you suppose happened? Why, I
succeeded in pulling up a great lump of shells
and stones all bedded together. The mass was
fully two feet long. My heart gave a leap of
exultation, for I knew at once just what to do
with the instrument thus providentially placed in
my hands. Instead of trying to hurl it at the
turtle, I reached out with it, and managed to
scrape that precious handspike within grasp. As I
gathered it once more into my grip, I straightened
up and was a man again.

"'Just at this juncture the turtle decided to
take a hand in. I had given the signal to be
hauled up at the very moment when I got hold
of that lump of stones, and now I could feel
Larry tugging energetically on the rope. The
turtle left off fooling with the tube, and, paddling
down to see what was making such a commotion
in the water, he tackled me at once.

"'As it happened, however, he took hold of
the big copper nut on the top of the head-piece;
and that was too tough a morsel even for *his* beak,

so that all he could do was to shake me a bit.
With him at my head, and the clam on my leg,
and Larry jerking on my waistband, you may
imagine I could hardly call my soul my own.
However, I began jabbing my handspike for all
I was worth into the unprotected parts of the
turtle's body, feeling around for some vital spot, —
which is a thing mighty hard to find in a turtle!
In a moment the water was red with blood; but
that made no great difference to me, and for a
while it didn't seem to make much difference to
the turtle either.   All I could do was to keep
on jabbing as close to the neck as I could, and
between the front flippers.   And the turtle kept
on chewing at the copper joint.

"'I believe it was the clam that helped me most
effectually in that struggle.   You see, that grip
on my leg kept me as steady as a rock.   If it
hadn't been for that, the turtle would have had
me off my feet and end over end in no time, and
would probably have soon got the best of me.
As it was, after a few moments of this desperate
stabbing with the handspike, I managed to kill
my assailant; but even in death that iron beak
of his maintained its hold on the copper nut of
my helmet.   Having no means of cutting the
brute's head off, I turned my attention to the
big clam, and with the steel point of my handspike I soon released my foot.

"'Then Larry hauled me up.   He told me after-

ward he never in all his life got such a start as
when that great turtle came to the surface hanging on to the top of my helmet. The creature
was so heavy he could not haul it and me together
into the boat; so he slashed the head off with
a hatchet, and then lifted me aboard Beyond a
black-and-blue leg, I was not much the worse for
that adventure; but I was so used up with the excitement of it all that I wouldn't go down for
any more pearls that day. We took a day off, —
Larry and I, and indulged in a little run ashore.'

" ' You had earned it,' said I."

"Now, Queerman," said Sam, "as your turn
comes round again, give us something less lugubrious than your last. Be light; be cheerful!"

"It seems to me that I remember," replied
Queerman, "a merry little adventure that befell me some years ago. If it is not hilarious
enough to suit you, Sam, you can stop me in the
middle of it. While you fellows were fishing
this afternoon, I was reading Mr. Gummere's
Handbook of Poetics. Without by any means
indorsing all that he says, I was struck by many
imaginative passages. In one place he says,
' Something dimly personal stood behind the flash
of lightning. the roaring of the wind.' That is
suggestive. I'll tell you a case in point from
my own experience in Newfoundland. Let us
call the story —

'THE DOGS OF THE DRIFT.'

"The very home of visions, and strange traditions, and mysteries, is Newfoundland, that great half-explored island in the wild North Atlantic.

"Here the iron coast, harborless for league upon league, opposes a black perpendicular front to the vast green seas, which slowly and unceasingly beneath their veil of fogs roll in, and fall in thunder amidst its pinnacles and caverns.

"At wide intervals the cliffs give way a little, forming narrow coves and havens, so limited that scarce a score of fishing-boats can find safe harborage therein. In almost every such cove may be found a tiny settlement, remote from the world, utterly shut in upon itself save during the brief months of summer, with no ideas but what spring from its people's daily toil and from the stupendous aspects of surrounding nature.

"Is it strange that to such simple and lonely souls the wild elements become instinct with strange life, and seem to dominate their thoughts and their existence?

"For them the driving mists are filled with apparitions. The gnarled and wind-beaten firs take on strange features in the dusk. Through the ravings of the gale against those towering cliffs comes to their ears a hubbub of articulate voices, mingled with the cries of the baffled seabirds.

"Men dwelling under such influences are imaginative. If left in ignorance, they grow, of necessity, superstitious. The mouths of these islanders overflow with unearthly tales, nearly all of which may be traced to the workings of some natural force.

"But their faith in these fancies is as unquestioning as our acceptance of the word that the world is round.

"What were variously known to the islanders as 'The Dogs of the Drift,' 'The White Dogs,' and 'The Gray Dogs.' I heard of all over the island.

"As went the tale generally, and ever with bated breath, these beings were a team of gigantic dogs, lean and pale in color, driven furiously by a gaunt woman in flowing garments of white.

"They were said to appear to travellers caught journeying in a storm, and to dash past with shrill howls when the storm was at its highest.

"Never closer did they come than within a stone's throw; but their coming meant death ere sunset to one or another of those met by the apparition.

"In the winter of·1888 a fire took place in the out-harbor where I was then living. and a large part of the winter's stores was destroyed. To our secluded settlement this was an overwhelming calamity; and there was nothing for it, if we would escape actual starvation. but to send some one for supplies to Harbor Briton.

"The journey was one of great difficulty and hardship, — some hundred and odd miles to be traversed through an unbroken wilderness, and the only means of conveyance a dog-team and a sledge. Being young and venturesome, and ever on the search for a new experience, I volunteered for the service, taking with me my man, Mike Conley, a keen hunter, and one well skilled in driving dogs.

"Our team was a powerful one, led by a great black-and-white fellow, whom the other dogs devotedly obeyed. With provision for ourselves and team, with blankets and the other necessaries of such a trip, our long sledge was well loaded down; and we took with us money to buy supplies, as well as pay the transportation of them back to the famishing settlement.

"We marched on snow-shoes for the most part, save over those open stretches of plain where the crust had hardened like ice, and where the dogs were able, at a brisk gallop, to draw both ourselves and their load.

"At such times, exhilarated by the swift motion in that keen air and sparkling sunshine, the hardships of our journey were forgotten, and we thrilled under the beauty of the glittering world of white. But far otherwise was it when our course lay, as it generally did, through "juniper" swamps and tangled accumulation of forest-growths.

"Then a whole day's severest toil advanced us but a few miles on our way. The dogs, floundering in the drifts and gullies, would get their traces into an almost hopeless snarl; and many a beating the poor brutes brought upon themselves by the dangerous temper they displayed under such annoyances. They were a fierce and wolfish pack, and a strong hand we were compelled to keep over them.

"Our nights, when it was fine and calm, were pleasant enough, as we lay, wrapt in many blankets, around our fire. Our custom was to dig a deep hollow in the snow, and floor it with soft boughs, leaving a space at one side for the fire.

"Such a camp, nestled in a thick grove of "var" or spruce, was snug in all ordinary weather. But sometimes the rage of the gale would make a fire impossible. The wind-gusts would fairly shatter it to bits, and, bursting in upon us from every quarter, drive the brands and coals all over the camp. There was then nothing left for us but to smother the remnants with snow, and huddled altogether in a heap — men, dogs, and blankets — to await wretchedly the coming of the stormy dawn.

"Always on such occasions would Mike, who was superstitious to the finger-tips, be looking out in fascinated expectation for the dreadful 'Gray Dogs.'

"At each yelling blast he strained his eyes through the dark, till from laughing at him I grew angry, and he was constrained to hide his fears. I represented to him that, as long as he kept his eyes beneath his blanket, these dogs of the drift need have no terrors for him, even should they come the whole night long and career about the camp; for the portent only applied to those beholding it.

"This view of the case, however, was but little relief to him, as his fears were no less on my account than on his own.

"Notwithstanding one or two such grim experiences, all went well with us till our journey was two-thirds done, and the hardest of the way lay behind us.

"Then, as we floundered one afternoon through a deadwood swamp, Mike slipped between two fallen trunks, and broke his left arm near the shoulder. This was a most unlooked-for blow, but the poor fellow bore it like a hero.

"With rude splints I set the arm and bandaged it; and after a day's halt, I fixed him a sort of bed on the sledge, so that we were enabled to continue our journey.

"But now we were forced to make long detours, in order to avoid rough country.

"On the following morning, to our satisfaction, we came out upon a chain of lakes which promised us something like fair going for a while.

"In a sheltered place on the shore we found a rude cabin occupied by two hunters, who had their traps set in the surrounding woods. Neither the faces nor the manner of these men did I find prepossessing; but they received us hospitably, fed us well, and pressed us to stay with them over night.

"Not unnaturally, they were curious as to the motives of our strange journey, and before I could give him a hint of warning, my garrulous and fearless Mike had put them in possession of the whole story.

"The greedy look of intelligence which passed furtively between them upon learning we were on the way to purchase stores aroused all my suspicions, and set me sharply on my guard.

"Their hospitality now became doubly pressing. In fact, when they saw me bent on immediate departure, they grew almost threatening in their earnestness.

"At this, assuming an angry air, I asked them why they should so concern themselves about what was entirely my own business; and I gave them plainly to understand that I wanted no interference.

"Changing their tone at once, and deprecating my warmth, they called to my notice the storm that was gathering overhead.

"They were right; the signs could hardly be mistaken. The little bursts and eddies of drift that rose fitfully from the lake's white surface; the long, whispering sob of the gusts that woke at intervals behind the forests; the heavy but vague massing of clouds all over the sky, which at a little distance was confused with the earth by a sort of pearly haze — all portended a hurricane of snow before many hours.

"With reason on their side, and the evident desire of my wounded Mike as well, our hosts urged delay till the storm should have spent its fury.

"But silencing Mike with a glance, I rejected politely, but decidedly, their proffered shelter, and made ready the team for a start.

"As soon as I had begun to tackle the dogs, the younger of our hosts suddenly took up his gun and left the cabin, saying he thought he'd better visit a few traps before the storm set in.

"He turned, I noticed, down the shore of the lake, parallel to the direction in which our own course lay.

"The older man speeded our departure with all seeming good-will, announcing that he only waited to see us safely off, and would then follow his partner to examine the traps.

"Once underway I retailed my suspicions to Mike, who, heedless as he was, had been putting this and that together during the last few minutes. Bitterly he bewailed his helplessness; and many and varied were the maledictions which from his couch in the blankets he hurled upon our prospective foes. At his suggestion we shunned the wooded shores, taking our course as nearly as possible down the middle of the lake.

"With my rifle in one hand and my long-lashed whip in the other, I urged the team to such a pace as it strained my running powers to keep up with.

"The snow was soft, and for the dogs, as for myself, the work was too severe to last; but my aim was, if possible, to settle with the first ruffian (who had, it seemed likely, undertaken to head us off) before the second could overtake and join forces with him.

"But suddenly, with a whistle and a biting blast, the storm was upon us. For a moment the dogs cowered down in their tracks, and then we were fain to hug the shore for shelter.

"The shelter was not much, for the storm seemed to rage from all quarters; yet, breathless and blinded though we were, we were able to make some headway. At a momentary lull between the gusts we rounded a sharp headland, and entered a long, narrow passage between the shore and a wooded island.

"'A likely place enough for the murderin' thief!' exclaimed Mike.

"But we plunged ahead.

"The words had scarcely left his mouth when the snow seemed to rise thinly about us in a thousand spirals and swirls.   A tremendous wind drove down the channel and smote us in the face, with a long, confused, yelping howl, which made my flesh creep with its resemblance to a cry of dogs.   Our team trembled terribly and lay down.

" ' The gray dogs!' came in a hoarse cry from Mike's lips.

" And at the same moment there swept past us, in the heart of the whirlwind, a pack of wild, huddling, and leaping drifts, followed by a tall, bent, woman-like figure of snow-cloud, which seemed to stoop over and urge on their furious flight.

" The vision vanished, the shrill clamor died away over the open reaches of the lake, and shaking off my tremor, I cheered our dogs again to the road.

"But as for Mike, he was overwhelmed with horror.   He would admit no doubt but that one of us must die before nightfall.   And for my own part, I felt that our circumstances lent only too ugly a color to his fancy.

" A succession of fitful though not violent gusts confronted us through our whole course up this defile.   The air was white with fine snow, and we made but meagre headway.

" It must have been about half a mile that we had covered since seeing the apparition, when we were startled by a sharp report just ahead of us; and instantly our dogs stopped short and fell into wild confusion.

"Springing to their heads, I found the great black-and-white leader in his death-struggle, bleeding upon the snow.

"'Cut the traces!' cried Mike.

"And though not comprehending his purpose, I stooped to do so.

"It was well for me I obeyed. As I stooped, a shot snapped behind us, and the shrill whimper of a bullet sang past my ear.

"At the same moment, the gust subsiding, I saw our first assailant step boldly out of cover just ahead of us, and raise his gun to shoulder for a second shot.

"But I had severed the traces; there was a sort of fierce hiss from Mike's tongue, and with a yell, the whole team sprang forward to avenge their leader.

"The ruffian, realizing at once his peril, discharged his gun wildly, threw it down, and fled for his life.

"But he was too late! In briefer space, I think, than it takes to tell it, the pack was upon him. He was literally torn to pieces.

"With whip and gun-stock I threw myself upon the mad brutes, who presently, as if satisfied with their dreadful revenge, followed me back in submission to their places.

"As for the second scoundrel, he had taken swift warning, and vanished.

"The dogs themselves seemed cowed by what

they had done; and for my own part, I was filled with horror.

"But no such weak sentimentality found the slightest favor with Mike. Rebuking me for having beaten them, he lavished praise and endearments upon the dogs.

"He reminded me, moreover, that they had saved the lives of both of us, or had, at the very least, saved myself from the necessity of taking blood upon my hands.

"Realizing this, I made hasty amends to the poor, shivering brutes, comforting them with a liberal feast of dried dogfish.

"My present feeling toward them, as I look back upon the episode, is one of unmitigated gratitude.

"The rest of our journey was accomplished without more than ordinary trouble.

"A good deal of my spare energy I wasted in the effort to overturn Mike's faith, which stands still unshaken in the supernatural character of the Dogs of the Drift.

"With such terrible testimony in his favor I could hardly have expected much success for my arguments; for, as he concluded triumphantly, 'if the spectral team came down that channel, as it plainly did, then the scoundrel lying in wait for us must have seen it, as well as we — and did not he meet his doom before nightfall?'"

"If that's what you call a *merry* tale," said

Ranolf, "then the one *I'm* going to tell you of Newfoundland will make your eyes drop ' weeping tears.' It concerns the fate of —

'BEN CHRISTIE'S BULL CARIBOU.'

" Ben Christie was first mate of the little coasting steamer Garnet, of the Newfoundland Coastal Service. Born in one of those narrow ' out-harbors ' that wedge themselves in somehow between the cliffs and the gray sea, his eyes had been bent seaward from the beginning. Inland all was mystery to him — alluring mystery.

" He had never been out of sight of the sea, except when the fog was too thick for him to distinguish it as he leaned over the vessel's rail. He had grown up with a codline in his hands, in his eyes the alternation of fog and flashing sunlight, in his ears the scream of the seafowl, and the shattering thunder of the surf upon the cliffs.

" Of his native island he knew little but the seaward faces of her rocky ramparts, over which he had often climbed to gather the eggs of puffin and gannet. Of towns he knew but the wharves and water-fronts of St. John's and Halifax and Harbor Grace. But he was at home in his dory as it climbed the sullen purple-green slopes of the great waves on ' the Banks,' and he knew how to follow the seal, and triumph over the perils of the Floating Fields.

" One day in Halifax, in a little inn on Water

Street, Ben Christie saw the stuffed and mounted head of a well-antlered bull caribou. It fired his fancy; and from that day forth to shoot a bull caribou became his consuming ambition.

"When he had been serving as mate of the Garnet for about two years, the boiler of that redoubtable craft refused to perform its functions, and she was laid up in St. John's harbor for repairs.

" Christie's opportunity had come. He furbished up his old muzzle-loading sealing-gun, long of barrel and huge of bore, and took passage on a little coasting-schooner bound for the West Shore and the mouth of the Codroy River.

" Arrived at the Codroy, he remained in the settlement for a few days, looking for a suitable comrade to go with him into the interior.

"When his errand became known, — which was right speedily, seeing that he could talk of nothing but bull caribou, — he found plenty of practised hunters ready to accompany him on his quest; but none of these were quite to his liking. They all knew too much. They seemed to him to be impressed with the idea that he did not know anything about caribou hunting, and they talked about 'getting him the finest pair of horns on the barrens.'

"Now just what Ben wanted was to get those horns himself. He wanted to do the shooting himself, and the hunting himself; and he did *not* want any one around to patronize him, and deride his mistakes. Ben was off on a holiday, and he felt himself entitled to make mistakes if he wanted to.

" At length he met a harum-scarum little Irishman named Mike Slohan, who said he doted on hunting, but couldn't hit anything smaller than a barn door, and wouldn't know — to use his own phrase — ' a spruce caribou from a bull pa'tridge.'

" Ben took him to his heart at once, and without delay the pair made ready for their expedition. Inextinguishable was the mirth of all the experienced hunters, and grievous were the mishaps they prophesied for our amateur Nimrods till at last Ben's keen blue eyes began to flash dangerously, and they judged it prudent to check their jibes.

" Whatever Mike Slohan's inefficiency as a hunter, he was as fearless as a grizzly, and he understood to its minutest detail the art of camping out with comfort. He armed himself only with a little muzzle-loading shotgun, but in other respects the two went well equipped.

" When Mike declared that all was ready, he and Ben embarked in a canoe they had hired in the settlement, and started gayly up the river.

" After ascending the main stream some fifty or sixty miles, they turned into a small tributary which flows into the Codroy from the northward. This stream ran between precipitous banks, often more than a hundred feet in height. Its deep and gloomy ravine was chiselled through a vast table-land without landmark or limit, scourged by every wind that blows.

"This inexpressibly bleak region Mike declared to be 'the barrens,' where they would find the caribou. Into its depths they penetrated till their way was barred by fierce rapids, at the foot of which they made their camp in a warm and windless cove.

"It was well on in the autumn, a season when the bull caribou are very pugnacious, whence it came that Ben Christie had not long to wait before finding himself face to face with the object of his desire.

"The first day's hunting, however, was fruitless. Leaving the camp after a by no means early or hasty breakfast, Ben and Mike climbed the great wall of the ravine; and no sooner were they fairly out upon the level waste than they descried three caribou feeding about half a mile away. This to Ben seemed quite a matter of course; nevertheless, he was exhilarated at the sight, and set out in hot pursuit, followed by the laughing Mike. They made no secret of their approach, but advanced in plain view, as if they were driving cattle in a pasture. And the caribou, being in a pleasant humor and willing to avoid disturbance, discreetly withdrew.

"After pursuing them for three or four miles, Ben gave up the chase, much disappointed to find the animals so wild.

" When the hunters started to return to the
river, they were astonished to find no sign of a
river, or the course of one, anywhere in the landscape. Mike at once concluded that they were
lost, but Ben was not troubled. He had the sun
to steer by, and was amply satisfied.

" Indeed, he felt much at home on the barrens,
where, as he said, ' there was plenty of sea-room,
and a chap could breathe free.' He shaped his
course confidently for the camp, and ' fetched '
the river as unerringly as if it had been a port on
the South Shore.

" The barrens, which cover so large a portion
of the interior of Newfoundland, vary somewhat
in character in different parts of the island.

" Where Ben and Mike were investigating
them, they were covered with wide patches of a
sturdy, stunted shrub called, locally, ' skronnick.'

" This skronnick played a most important part
in the experiences which presently befell the
hunters. It grows about shoulder-high at its
highest, and spreads out like a miniature banyan-
tree. Its twisted stems are bare to a height of
from two to three feet, and its top so densely
matted as almost to shut out the light. The
shrub is an evergreen, a remote cousin to the
juniper, and its stems are wide enough apart for
one to freely crawl about between them. When
one is caught in a storm on the barrens, the skronnick patches make no mean shelter.

"Scattered thinly amid the skronnick stood bald, white-granite bowlders from two or three to ten or twelve feet high; and here and there lay deep pools, — cup-shaped hollows — filled to the brim with transparent, icy water.

"'Arrah,' said Mike, as they climbed down the ravine to the camp, 'but it's a quare counthry!'

"To Ben, however, all dry land was queer. So he hardly comprehended Mike's remark.

"On the following day before they set out for the hunt a council of war was held. Said Ben, —

"'You see, the critters won't let us git nigh enough to fire at 'em afore they clear out; an' *then* where are we?'

"'Sure, an' we'll hide in the skronnick,' replied Mike, 'an' shoot thim as they go by.'

"'An' maybe they won't *go* by just to oblige us,' suggested Ben. 'I reckon we'll hev to git down, so's they can't see us, an' crawl up on 'em!'"

"These tactics decided upon, the hunters mounted to the plain, enthusiastic and sanguine. Eagerly they scanned the bleak reaches. Not a caribou was there in sight. Ben's face fell, and he heaved a mighty sigh of disappointment. But Mike was not so easily cast down.

"'Come on,' said he cheerily, 'an' we'll find the bastes 'fore ye know where ye are.'

"With their guns over their shoulders, they picked their way through the skronnick for a couple of hundred yards, till suddenly, out from behind a bowlder, not twenty paces in front of them, stepped a huge bull caribou.

"The caribou was solitary, and in a very bad humor. He shook his spreading antlers and snorted ominously.

"'You shoot! He's yourn!' shouted Mike in wild excitement, brandishing his gun at full cock over his head.

"Proudly Ben raised his long weapon to his shoulder and pulled the trigger. There was no marked result, however, as he had forgotten to cock the gun. Just as he hastily remedied this oversight, the caribou charged madly. Ben fired —and missed!

"'He'll kill ye! Dodge him in the skronnick,' yelled Mike.

"And obediently Ben dived into the nearest patch.

"Acting upon a natural instinct, he scurried from side to side to throw his pursuer off the track.

"The caribou sprang furiously upon the bushes where Ben had disappeared, and trampled them with his knife-like front hoofs. Then he turned on Mike, who had been anxiously waiting for him to keep still and give him a fair shot.

"In desperation Mike fired, just grazing the animal's flank, and then he darted, like a rabbit, under the skronnick bushes.

"When those deadly forehoofs came down on

the place where he had vanished, the little Irish-man was not there. Nimbly and noiselessly he put all the distance he could between himself and the spot where he heard his enemy tearing at the skronnick.

"Finding himself unpursued, Ben made haste to reload his gun.

"At the sound of Mike's shot he thrust his head out of his hiding-place in time to see his comrade go under cover. Very deliberately Ben rammed the bullet home and put on the cap. Then, standing up to his full height, and taking aim at the caribou's hind-quarters, which were towards him, he shouted, 'Load up, Mike!' and fired again.

"Unfortunately for the accuracy of Ben's aim, the caribou had wheeled sharp round at the sound of his voice, and charged without an instant's delay; so again the shot went wide. And again, with alacrity that did credit to his bulk, Ben scuttled under the skronnick.

"But this time the indignant bull, furious at being thus outwitted, bounded into the bush, and began thrusting about at random with horns and hoofs.

"More than once Ben narrowly escaped those terrible weapons, and his trepidation began to be mingled with fierce wrath at the idea of being 'hustled 'round' this way by a 'critter.'

"He could get no chance to load up again, and he was on the point of stepping forth and attack-

ing the animal with the butt of his gun. He felt
as if he was battened under hatches in a sinking
ship.

"Before he could put his purpose into effect,
however, there was another shot from Mike. It
evidently struck the animal somewhere, for he
bellowed with rage as he bounded over the thickets to join battle with his other assailant.

"The Irishman had not waited to mark the
result of his shot, but had plunged instantly out
of sight, and betaken himself to a position well
removed.

"The angry bull had no idea of his whereabouts,
but thrashed around wildly, while the little Irishman chuckled in his sleeve.

"As soon as Ben once more got his gun loaded,
he stuck his head up through the skronnick. He
observed that in his wanderings beneath the scrub
he had worked his way very nearly to the big
granite bowlder before mentioned.

"He did not fire, for he was resolved not to
waste his shot this time. Just as he made up his
mind to try a rush for the bowlder, from the top
of which he would be master of the situation, the
caribou looked up, and caught sight of him again.

"The animal's charge was so lightning-like in
its rapidity that Ben could do nothing but dive
once more beneath the kindly skronnick.

"As fast as he could, he worked his way toward
the bowlder, but in his haste the movement of the

bushes betrayed him.   One of the razor-edged hoofs came down within a foot or two of his face, and he shrank back swiftly, making himself very small.

" His changed course brought him to the very brink of one of the deep pools already spoken of, and he almost fell into it.   In turning aside from that obstacle, the shaking of the bushes again-gave the bull a hint of his position.   With a cough and a bellow the animal leaped to the spot, just missed Ben's retiring feet, and plunged headlong into the pool.

" This seemed to Ben just his opportunity for gaining the rock.   He sprang up and made a dash for it.   But before he reached its foot, — and a glance told him that it was not to be scaled on that side, — the caribou had picked himself nimbly out of the water and was after him, his fury by no means dampened by the ducking.

" Grinding his teeth, Ben darted yet again beneath the scrub, but this time it was the closest shave he had had.   The skronnick was thinner here, and he would hardly have succeeded in evading his antagonist for more than a minute, had not Mike come to the rescue.   The Irishman rose up with a wild yell, discharged his gun right in the caribou's face, missed with his customary facility, and dropped again into the skronnick.

" The foaming animal dashed away to hunt him; and Ben, creeping stealthily around the bowlder, found its accessible side, and scrambled to the summit as the caribou came bounding to its base.

"If the bowlder had been a very few feet lower. the adventure might have had a very different issue. But as it was, the height proved sufficient. Ben surveyed those spear-sharp prongs from his point of vantage, just three feet beyond reach of their vicious thrusts, and thought proudly how fine they would look mounted in the cabin of the Garnet.

"He was in no great hurry to end the performance, and he did not like to fire while the caribou was so close to the muzzle of the gun. But presently the animal paused and looked around for Mike.

"He turned, in fact, as if to go and hunt the little Irishman again, and Ben's heart smote him for having even for a moment forgotten the peril in which his comrade yet remained. He took careful aim at a point close behind the caribou's shoulder. At the report the animal sprang straight into the air, and fell back stone dead.

"Very triumphant, quite pardonably so, in fact, were Ben and Mike as they returned to the Codroy settlement with their spoils. They discreetly refrained from detailing at Codroy all the particulars of the hunt. But if the tourist, exploring the coasts of Newfoundland in the steamer Garnet, chances to remark upon the immense pair of caribou antlers which hang over the cabin door, he will hear the whole story from Ben Christie, who is endowed with an excellent sense of humor."

When Ranolf ended he received unusual applause. Then I stepped, so to speak, into the breach. "I cannot hope," said I, "to win the ears of this worshipful company with any such gentle humor as Ranolf has just achieved. But I have a good rousing adventure to tell you, with lots of blood though little thunder. The scene of it is not far from Newfoundland. Let this fact speak in its favor!"

"Fire away, Old Man!" said Queerman.

"I take for my narrative the simple title of —

'LABRADOR WOLVES.'

said I.

"In early June, two years ago, my friend, Jack Rollings, of the Canada Geological Survey, was occupied in exploring parts of the Labrador coast, from the mouth of the Moisic River eastward. The following adventure, one of several that befell him in that wild region, has a peculiar interest from its possible connection with a throng of terrible legends, the scenes of which are laid along those shores.

"Ever since the Gulf of St. Lawrence became known to the fishing-fleets of Brittany and the Basque Provinces, its north-eastern coast has been peopled, by the vivid imaginations of the fishermen and sailors, with supernatural beings of vari-

ous fashions, all agreeing, however, in the attributes
of malignity and noisiness. Demons and griffins
and monsters indescribable were supposed to haunt
the bleak hills and dreadful ravines. Ships driven
reluctantly inshore by stress of weather were wont
to carry away strange tales of howlings and visions to freeze the marrow of the folks at home.

"The probable origin of those myths may be
found in the fact that from time to time the
coast has been ravaged by hordes of gigantic gray
wolves, sweeping down from the unfathomed wilderness of the high interior plateau. One of these
visitations was in 1873, when many of the coast
dwellers, whose scanty settlements cling here and
there in the lonely harbors, were torn to pieces on
the shore, or shut up in their cabins till starvation stared them in the face. No great stretch of
fancy is required to metamorphose a pack of ravening wolves into a yelling concourse of demons.

"What befell Jack Rollings I will tell in his
own words."

"Our schooner," said Jack, "lay at anchor in
a little landlocked bay where never a wind could
get at her, and much of our exploration was done
by means of short boat trips in one direction or
the other. One morning Frank Jones and I made
up our minds to take a day off, and try and kill a
salmon or two.

"About five miles west of where we lay, there

was a cove where, behind a low, rocky point, a
little river came down out of the mountains.
Half a mile above the head of tide the stream
fell noisily over a shallow fall into a most enticing
pool, and we calculated thatwe would be just in
good time for the first run of the salmon.

" There was a stretch of shoals off the mouth
of the stream, and no sheltered anchorage near;
so we took the small boat for the trip, and a
fresh breeze off the gulf blew us to our destina-
tion speedily. It was high tide when we arrived;
and we hauled up the boat in the cove, under shelter of the point.

" Besides our rods, we had enough grub for a
good lunch, and our top-coats in case it should
blow up cold in the afternoon. Frank had brought
his gun along, with a few cartridges loaded with
number one and number two shot, in case he
might want to shoot some big bird for his collec-
tion, which is already one of the best private col-
lections in Ottawa.

" When we had put our rods together, we moved
up along the wet edges of the beach, which glis-
tened in the morning sun, and presently found
ourselves at the basin where we expected our
sport. Over the low, foaming barrier of the falls
we saw a salmon make way in a flashing leap, and
we knew we had struck both the right place and
the right time.

"I need not tell you the particulars of the

sport. You know what a Labrador salmon stream is when you happen to take it in a good humor. Enough to say, when we began to think of lunch it was about two o'clock; and we had six fish, ranging from ten to thirty-five pounds, lying in splendid array beneath a neighboring rock. As much of our spoils as we could carry at once we took down to the spot where the boat lay; and building a little fire of driftwood, we proceeded to fry some salmon collops for lunch.

"While enjoying our after-dinner smoke we observed that the wind had shifted a point or two to the east, and was blowing up half a gale.

"'Great Scott!' exclaimed Frank. 'If we don't get away from here right off, we're going to be storm-stayed! This wind will raise a sea presently that we won't be able to face. Let's leave right off! I'll drag the boat down to the water, while you go after the rest of those fish.'

"'No, no!' said I. 'We'll just stay where we are for the present. Don't you see that the waves are already breaking into the cove too heavy for us? If you were round on the other side of the point now, you'd see what the water is, and you'd be glad enough you're out of it, I can tell you! We're all right here, and we may as well fish till toward sundown; and if the wind has not eased off by that time, we'll just have to snug the boat up here, and foot it over the hills to the schooner. It's not more than five or six miles anyway.'

"Frank strolled across the point for a look at the sea, and came back in agreement with my views. Then we returned to the pool, and whipped it assiduously till after five o'clock, but without a repetition of the morning's success.

"Meanwhile the wind got fiercer and fiercer, so we went back to the boat and made a hearty supper as preparation for the rough tramp that lay before us. We took our time, and smoked at leisure, and cached our prizes, and resolved not to start till moonrise. By this time the tide was well out, and the cove had become an expanse of shingly flats, threaded by the shallow current of the stream, and fringed along its seaward edge with a line of angry surf.

"By and by the moon got up out of the gulf, round and white, and bringing with her an extra blow. As the shore brightened up clearly, we set out, moving along the crest of the point. Frank was just saying, 'How spectral those scarred gray hills look in this light! How suitable a place for the hobgoblins those old Frenchmen imagined to possess them!' when, as if to point his remarks, there came a ghostly clamor, high and quavering, from a dark cleft far up the mountain-side.

"We both started; and I exclaimed, 'The loons have overheard you, old fellow, and are trying to work on your nerves! They want revenge for the stuffed companions of their bygone days.'

"'That's not loons!' said Frank very seriously. 'It's no more like loons than it's like lions! Listen to that!'

"I listened, and was convinced.

"'Then it must be those old Frenchmen's friends,' I suggested; 'and I feel greatly inclined to avoid meeting them if possible.'

"'It's the wolves from the interior,' rejoined Frank. "I'd rather have the griffins and goblins. Don't you remember '73? I'm afraid we're in a box."

"'Let us get down to windward of the point, and lie low among the rocks,' I suggested. 'As likely as not the brutes won't detect us, and will keep along up the shore.'

"Instantly we dropped into concealment, keeping, through the apertures of the crest, a fearful eye upon the mountain slopes. We were fools, to be sure; for we might have known those keen eyes had spotted us from the first, silhouetted as we had been against the moonlit sea.

"Presently Frank suggested the boat, but my sufficient answer was to point to the raging surf. So we lay still, and prayed to be ignored. In a few minutes our suspense was painfully relieved by the appearance of a pack of gray forms, which swept out into the moonlight beyond the river, and came heading straight for our refuge.

"'Two dozen of 'em!' gasped Frank.

"'And they've certainly spotted us,' I whispered.

"'There's not a tree nor a hole we can get into!' muttered Frank.

"'We can get on top of this rock, and fight for it,' I groaned in desperation.

"'I have it!' exclaimed Frank. 'The boat! We'll get under it, and hold it down!'

"Leaping to our feet we broke wildly for the boat. The wolves greeted us with an exultant howl as they dashed through the shallow river.

"We had just time to do it comfortably. The boat was heavy, and we turned it over in such a way that the bow was steadied between two rocks. Once safely underneath, we lifted the craft a little and jammed her between the rocks so that the brutes would be unable to root her over.

"One side was raised about eight or ten inches by a piece of rock which Frank was going to re-move; but I stopped him. By this time the brutes were on top of the boat, and we could hear by the snarling that they had unearthed our salmon. Just then a row of long snouts and snapping jaws came under the gunwale, and we shrank as small as possible. The brutes shoved and struggled so mightily that it seemed as if they must succeed in overturning the boat, and a cold sweat broke out on my forehead.

"'Shoot,' I yelled frantically; and at the same instant my ears were almost burst by the discharge of both Frank's barrels. A terrific yelping and

howling ensued, while our crowded quarters were
filled to suffocation with the smoke.

" When the air cleared somewhat we could see
that the wolves were eating the two whose heads
Frank's shot had shattered. Our position was
very cramped and uncomfortable, half-sitting, half-
lying, between the thwarts ; but by stretching flat
we could peer beneath the gunwale, and command
a view of the situation. We had a moment's
respite.

" ' Frank,' said I, ' we might as well be eaten as
scared to death. Don't fire that gun again in here.
It nearly blew my ear-drums in. Club the brutes
over the snout. All that's necessary is to disable
them, and it seems their kind companions will do
the rest.'

" ' All right,' responded Frank; 'only you must
do your share ! ' and he passed me up the hatchet
out of the ' cuddy-hole ' in the bow.

" By this time the slaughtered wolves were re-
duced to hair and bones, and the pack once more
turned their attention to us. Once more the omi-
nous row of heads appeared, squeezed under the
boat-side, and claws tore madly at the roof that
sheltered us.

" As combatants, our positions were exceedingly
constrained ; but so, too, were those of our assailants. A wolf cannot dodge well when his head
is squeezed under a gunwale.

" Hampered as I was I smashed the skulls of

the two within easiest reach, barking my knuckles villanously as I wielded my weapon. I heard Frank, too, pounding viciously up in the bow. Then the attack drew off again, and the feasting and quarrelling recommenced.

"I turned to make some remark to my companion, but gave a yell of dismay instead, as I felt a pair of iron jaws grab me by the foot, and tear away the sole of my boot. In the excitement of the contest my foot had gone too near the gunwale.

"The wolves were now growing too wary to thrust their heads under the gunwale. For a time they merely sniffed along the edge; and though we might easily have smashed their toes or the ends of their noses, we refrained in order to gain opportunity for something more effective.

"We must have waited thus for as much as ten minutes, and the inaction was becoming intolerable, when the brutes, thinking perhaps we were dead or gone to sleep, made a sudden concerted effort to reach us. There must have been a dozen heads at once thrust in beneath the gunwale. One preternaturally lean wolf even wriggled his shoulders fairly through, so that he was within an ace of taking a mouthful out of my leg before I could have a fair blow at him with my hatchet.

"I think we either killed or disabled four at least in that assault. Thereupon the pack drew off a little, and sat down on their haunches to consider.

" They could not possibly have been still hungry, having eaten two or three wolves and a hundred pounds or so of nice fresh salmon, and we were in hopes they would go away.

"But instead of that they came back to the boat, and set up a tremendous howling, which may have been a call for re-enforcements, or a challenge to to come out and settle the trouble in a square fight.

" I asked Frank how many cartridges he had left.

" 'Oh,' said he, 'a dozen or more, at least!'

" 'Verily well,' said I; 'you'd better blaze away and kill as many as you can. I'll protect my ear-drums by stuffing my ears full of rags. Try and make every shot tell.'

" As the wolves were not more than eight or ten feet away, the heavy bird-shot had the same effect as a bullet. Two of the brutes were clean bowled over. Then the others sprang furiously upon the boat. When Frank thrust forth the muzzle of the gun, it was seized and all but wrenched from his grasp. He bagged two more; then the rest moved round to the other side of the boat.

" But very soon the survivors appeared to make up their minds to a new departure; and after a little running hither and thither with their noses down, they suddenly crystallized, as it were, into a well-ordered pack, and swept away up the shore. Their strange, terrible, wind-like ululations were soon re-echoing in the mountains.

" We came forth from our uncomfortable but effectual retreat, and counted our victims. When the last sound of the howling had long died away, we set forth in the direction of the schooner, which was *not* the direction in which the wolves were journeying.'

CHAPTER V.

SQUATOOK RIVER AND HORTON BRANCH.

THE next was a rainy day at Camp de Squatook. Of course we fished off and on all day, whenever the rain held up a little; and in a deep run, about a hundred yards below the whitefish fence, Sam had the luck to land the big trout of the trip. It weighed, fresh from the water, three pounds three ounces, and it was killed with a minnow. Sam complained, however, that it had given him no more play than one of his two-pounders of the day before. We thought him very artful, in thus concealing his elation so as to ward off our envy.

By nightfall it was raining pitchforks. In our tight tent, with wax candles beaming, and the rattle of the rain on the roof, we felt very snug. But inexpressibly lonely was the washing sound in the pine-branches; and all the rest of the world seemed ages away from us. For a while no stories were called for. Instead of that we played Mississippi euchre. When we grew tired of the game, Stranion exclaimed, "Let's have one story, and then turn in!"

"Who will hold forth?" I asked.

"Well," said ·Ranolf, "since you are all so pressing, *I* will try and rise to the occasion. It seems to be an understood thing that all these stories are animal stories; but in this one I must wander from the rule, and tell you a story of rain and wind. The noise on the tent-roof to-night reminds me of a nice scrape which I got myself into only last summer. When you hear the story you will understand just why I tell it to-night. Sam, you heard all about it two days after it happened. It's appropriate to the occasion, isn't it? I mean about how I was —

·   'WRECKED IN A BOOM-HOUSE.'"

"Highly appropriate, indeed!" said Sam.

"Well, here you have it!" continued Ranolf. "You'll excuse me, of course, if I indulge at first in a little technical description, to make the incidents clear.

"The Crock's Point sheer-boom started from the shore a few yards below the Point. It slanted out and down till it met a great pier in mid-river, to which it was secured by heavy chains. From the pier it swung free down the middle of the channel for a distance of several hundred yards, swaying toward one shore or the other according to the set of the wings and the strength of the current. It was a sturdy structure, of squared and bolted timbers, about three feet in width, and rising some three or four inches above the water.

" The boom, of course, was jointed at the pier so as to swing as on a hinge ; and at a distance of perhaps seventy yards below the pier it had a second open joint. At the head of this section stood a windlass, wound with a light wire cable. At intervals of ten or twelve feet along the right-hand side of this section, for about one hundred and fifty feet in all, were hinged stout wings of two-inch plank, ten feet long and eighteen inches wide, set edgewise in the water so as to catch the current, like a rudder or a centreboard. Through iron staples, in the outer ends of these wings, ran and was fastened the cable from the windlass. When the cable was unwound, the wings lay flat against the side of the boom. But a few turns of the windlass sufficed to draw the wings out at an angle to the boom ; whereupon the force of the current, sweeping strongly against their faces, would slowly sway the whole free length of the boom toward the opposite shore. The section of the sheer-boom thus peculiarly adorned was called the wing-boom. Just above the upper end of the wing-boom, at a place widened out a few feet to receive it, was built a little shanty known as the boom-house. To the spectator from the shore the boom-house seemed to be afloat on the wide, lonely level of the river.

" The office of the sheer-boom was to guide the run of the logs as they came floating briskly down from the lumber regions of the upper river. As long as the wings were not in use, and the boom swung with the current, the logs were allowed to continue their journey down the middle of the channel. But when the wings were set, and the boom stood over toward the far shore, then the stream of logs was diverted into the mouth of the stationary boom, whose chain of piers held them imprisoned till they were wanted at the mill below the island. In the boom-house dwelt an old lumberman named Mat Barnes, who, though his feet and ankles were crippled with rheumatism from exposure to the icy water in the spring stream drivings, was, nevertheless, still clever in the handling of boat or canoe, and very competent to manage the windlass and the wing-boom.

" On the southward slope of the line of uplands which, thrusting out boldly into the river, formed Crock's Point, stood a comfortable old farmhouse in whose seclusion I was spending the months of August and September. About four o'clock in the afternoon, it was my daily habit to stroll down to the shore and hail Mat Barnes, who would presently paddle over in his skiff, and take me out to the boom for my afternoon swim. The boom was a most convenient and delightful place ' to go in off of,' as the boys say.

" One rough afternoon, when the boom was all awash, and the wind sweeping up the river so keen with suggestions of autumn that I was glad to do my undressing and my dressing in the boom-house, just as I was about to take my plunge Mat asked if I would mind staying and watching the boom for him while he paddled up to " the Corners " to buy himself some coffee and molasses. ·

"Delighted," said I; " if you'll get back in good time, so I won't keep supper waiting at the farm."

" I'll be back inside of an hour, sure," replied Mat confidently.

" Knowing Mat's fondness for a little gossip at the grocery, I felt by no means so confident; but I could not hesitate to oblige him in the matter, a small enough return for the favors he was doing me daily.

" I stayed in the water nearly half an hour, and while I was swimming about I noticed that the wind was fast freshening. The steep and broken waves made swimming somewhat difficult, and the crests of the whitecaps that occasionally slapped me in the face made me gasp for breath. While dressing I thought, with some consternation, that this vigorous wind would prove a serious hindrance to Mat Barnes's return, as it would be blowing directly in his teeth.

" For a time I sat sulkily in the door of the boom-house, with my feet on a block to keep them out of the wet. The door opened away from the wind, and against the back of the little structure the waves were beginning to lash with sufficient violence to make me uneasy. I strained my eyes up-river to catch the first glimpse of Mat forcing his way cleverly against the tossing whitecaps. But no such welcome vision rewarded me. At last I was compelled to acknowledge that the storm had become too violent for him to return against it without assistance. I should have to wait in the boom-house either till the wind abated, or till Mat should succeed in finding a pair of stout arms and a willing heart to come with him to my rescue.

"At first my thoughts dwelt with keen regret on the smoking pancakes and luscious maple-sirup that I knew were even then awaiting me at the farmhouse under the hill, and somewhat bitterly I reviled Mat's lack of consideration. But as the sky grew rapidly dark while it wanted yet a half-hour of sundown, and the wind came shrieking more madly down from the hills, and the boom-house began to creak and groan and shudder beneath the waves that were leaping upon it, anxiety for my safety took the place of all other considerations.

"Frail as the boom-house appeared, it was well jointed and framed, or it would simply have gone to pieces under the various assaults of wind and waves, and the rolling of the boom. The floor in particular was very carefully secured, being bolted to the boom at the four corners, that it might not be torn away by any chance collision with log or icecake. At every wave, however, the water came spurting through the cracks of the wall, and I was drenched almost before I knew it. Through the open door, too, the back wash of the waves rolled heavily; and even without the increasing peril of the situation, the prospect of having to pass the night in such cold, inescapable slop was far from comforting.

" The door was made to fit snugly, so I shut it in the hope of keeping out some of the water; but in the almost total darkness that ensued my apprehensions became unbearable. The writhing roll of the boom grew more and more excessive, and produced a sickening sensation. I threw the door open again, but was greeted with such a fierce rush of wave and spray that I shut it as quickly as I could.

"I had never before been on the boom-house after dark, so I did not know what Mat was accustomed to do for light. After much difficult groping, however, I found a tin box, fortunately quite waterproof, in which were matches and a good long piece of candle. When I had succeeded in getting the candle to burn, I stuck a fork through it, and pinned it to the driest spot I could find, which was the edge of Mat's bunk, away up close to the roof. Presently a spurt of water struck the veering and smoky flame, and again I was in darkness. Of course I lost no time in relighting the candle; but within ten minutes it was out again. I repeated the process, and was prepared to keep it up as long as the matches would hold out. In fact, I was thankful for that little annoyance, as it gave me something to do, and diverted my mind somewhat from my own helplessness and from the imminent peril of the situation.

" There was absolutely nothing that I could do to help myself. To reach the shore by crawling along the boom would have been quite impossible. I should have inevitably been swept off before going three feet beyond the shelter of the boom-house. In those choppy and formless seas and in the bewildering darkness, I should have found it impossible to swim, or even to keep my mind clear as to the direction in which the shore lay. Though a strong swimmer, and accustomed to rough water, I knew very well that in that chaos I should soon be exhausted, and either drowned or dashed against the boom. There was nothing to do but wait, and pray that the boom-house might hold together till calm or daylight.

" It was a strange picture my faint candle revealed to me within the four narrow walls of my refuge. All the implements and accessories of Mat's somewhat primitive housekeeping had been shaken from their shelves or from the nails on which they hung, and were coasting about the floor with a tinny clatter, as the boom twisted and lurched from side to side. Three joints of rust-eaten stovepipe kept them in countenance, and from time to time I had to jump nimbly aside to

save my shins from being broken by the careering
little stove. Sometimes I would be thrown heavily against the wall or the door. At last I climbed
into the bunk, where I crouched, dripping and shivering, both courage and hope pretty well drenched
out of me.

"Being something of a slave to routine, when
I found myself in what resembled a sleeping-place,
— or might have resembled one under more favorable circumstances, — I took out my watch to wind
it. The hour was half-past nine. From that hour
till nearly midnight there was no change in the
situation. Finding that the matches were running
low, I occupied myself in protecting the light
with the aid of the tin box already spoken of.
And at last, strange as it may seem, I found myself growing sleepy. It was partly the result of
exhaustion caused by my anxiety and suspense,
but partly also, no doubt, a sort of semi-hypnotic
bewilderment induced by the motion and by the
monotonous clamor of the storm.

"As I sat there crouching over the candle
I must have dropped into a doze, for suddenly I
felt myself hurled out of the bunk. I fell heavily
upon the floor. The boom-house was in utter
darkness. I staggered to my feet and groped for
the candle; it was gone from the edge of the
bunk. In my fall I had evidently swept it away.

"The motion of the boom had now greatly increased in violence, and it was impossible for me

to stand up without clinging tightly to the edge of the bunk. In the thick dark the stove crashed against my legs so heavily that I thought for a moment one of them was broken. I drew myself up again into the bunk, no longer feeling in the least degree sleepy.

"Presently I realized what had happened. The boom had parted at the joint where the wings began, and my section was swinging before the wind. The waves frequently went clear over the roof, and came pouring down the vacant pipe-hole in torrents, whose volume I could guess by their sound. The pitching, rolling, tossing, and the thrashing of the waves were appalling; and I fervently blessed the sound workmanship that had put together the little boom-house so as to stand such undreamed-of assaults. But I knew it could not stand them much longer. Moment by moment I expected to find myself fighting my last battle amid a crash of mad waters and shattered timbers.

"In a little I began to realize that the boom must have parted in *two* places at least. From the unchecked violence of its movements I knew it must have broken loose at the pier. With this knowledge came a ray of hope. As my section was now nothing more than a long and very attenuated raft, it might presently be blown ashore somewhere. If the boom-house would only hold out so long I might have a fair chance of escaping; but I realized that the progress of the fragment of boom would necessarily be slow, as wind and current were at odds together over it.

"Cooped up in that horrible darkness, and clinging on to the edge of the bunk desperately with both hands, the strain soon became so intolerable that I began to wish the boom-house *would* go to pieces, and put me out of my misery. None the less, however, did my heart leap into my throat when at length there came a massive thud, a grinding crash, and the side of the boom-house opposite the bunk was stove in. At the same time the marvellously tough little structure was twisted half off its foundations, and bent over as if a giant hand had crushed it down.

"I at once concluded that we had gone ashore on the Point. I tried to get the door open that I might have some chance of saving myself; but the twisting of the frame had fastened it immovably. Madly I wrenched at it, but that very stability of structure which had hitherto been my safety proved now my gravest menace. I could not budge the door; and, meanwhile, I was being thrown into all sorts of positions, while the boom ground heavily against the obstacle with which it had come in contact. The boom-house was half full of water.

"A fierce indignation now seized me at the thought of being drowned thus like a rat in a hole. Reaching down into the water my hands

came in contact with the little stove. I raised
it aloft, and brought it down with all my strength
against the door. The stove went to pieces, bruis-
ing and cutting my hands; but the door was shattered, and a wave rushed in upon me.

"Holding my breath, I was tearing at the remnant of the door, in doubt as to whether I should
get free in time to escape suffocation, when the
boom gave a mightier heave, and the upper part of
the boom-house crashed against the obstacle with
a violence that tore it clear of its base. The next
instant I was in deep water, striking out blindly.

"When I came up, providentially I rose clear
of the shattered boom-house. I could see nothing,
and I was almost choked; but I kept my presence of mind, and battled strenuously with the
boiling seas, which tossed me about like a chip.
In a second or two I was dashed against a pile
of timbers. Half-stunned, I yet made good my
hold, and instantly drew myself higher up on the
pile. As soon as I had recovered my breath suf-
ficiently to realize anything, I perceived that I
was on one of the piers.

"The upper portion of the great structure was
open, and I speedily crawled down among the
rocks with which these piers are always ballasted.
As I crouched to escape the chill wind which
hissed between the logs, how I gloried in the
thought that *here* was something not to be tossed
about by wind and wave! Drenched, shivering,

exhausted as I was, I nevertheless felt my bed of rocks in the pier-top a most luxurious retreat. I presently fell asleep, and when I awoke the dawn was pink and amber in the eastern sky. I saw that the pier which had given me refuge was that to which the sheer-boom had been fastened. The storm had moderated somewhat; and forcing its way determinedly toward the pier came Mat's skiff, propelled by Mat himself and Jim Coxen from the Corners."

"I declare," said Stranion, "I almost feel the tent and the floor itself rocking, so vivid is the picture Ranolf has given us!"

"Well," remarked Magnus, "it can rock us all to sleep, and the sooner the better!"

In a very few minutes we were snugly rolled in our blankets. Then Stranion rose on his elbow and blew out the candle,—"doused the glim," as he was wont to say. In the thick dark we swiftly sank to sleep.

On the day after the rain, there was a wonderful exhilaration in the air. We felt like shouting and running races. The face of earth wore a clean and honest look. Queerman roamed hither and thither declaiming Miss Guiney's fine lines:—

> "Up with the banners on the height,
>   Set every matin-bell astir!
> The tree-top choirs carouse in light;
>   The dew's on phlox and lavender,"—

till at last we pulled his hat down over his mouth, and made him go fishing with us. He declared he didn't want to fish that day, so we took him to carry our captures.

This time we cut through the woods, and struck the river about half a mile below the outlet. The sparkling day had made us break bounds. At this point the Squatook River, after rushing in white-capped tumult down a gloomy channel, broadens fan-like out, and breaks over a low fall into a pool of quiet waters, out of which roars a strong rapid. The pool is wide and deep, and girt with great rocks. Over the black surface fleecy masses of froth were wheeling. How our hearts leaped at the sight! Behold us waist-deep around the margin of the pool, or braced upon the edge of the fall. The surface is lashed sometimes in three or four places at once by the struggles of the speckled prey against the slow, inexorable reel. Our excitement is intense, but quiet. Its only expression is the reel's determined click, or its thrilling, swift rattle as the taut line cuts the water, and the rod bends and bends. A smallish fish has taken Sam's "drop," and is being reeled, half spent, across the basin. The "leader" trails out behind. There is a shining swirl beside it,— a strike; and stung by the check the very monarch of the pool flashes up, and darts like lightning down stream. But Sam's fly is sticking in his jaw. Now, gallant fisherman, hold thine own! We forget our own rods. More than once Sam's reel is almost empty. For twenty minutes the result is doubtful. Then, reluctantly, victory declares herself for the lithe rod and the skilful wrist. The larger of these two prizes which our lucky fisherman thus brought to land just tipped the beam at two and three-quarters pounds. The other was a light half-pounder.

That day after a hasty lunch we bade farewell to Camp de Squatook. The morning's fishing had been so good that we resolved to keep its memory unblurred. A sudden desire seized us for "fresh fields and pastures new." We struck tent, packed the canoes, and paddled out joyously from the landing. Through the whitefish barrier we slipped smoothly and swiftly onward down the racing current. Almost before we could realize it we were in the wild sluice above the fall. There was a clear channel at one side, and we raced through the big ripples with a shout and a cheer.

But alas for high spirits and heedlessness! Sam and Ranolf were in the rear canoe. They objected to this position; and just after running the shoot and clearing the basin, they tried to pass Magnus and me. We were in the strong and twisting current, however; and the first thing our rivals knew they were thrown upon a round-backed, weedy rock. Their canoe turned over gracefully, and discharged her whole burden into the stream.

Instantly the surface of the pool was diversified

with floating paddles, poles, tent-pins, tin kettles, box-covers, etc., and Stranion and Queerman, Magnus and I, were busy capturing these estrays in the eddy below. The canoe was got ashore, righted, and found to be none the worse. Our heavy valuables, guns and the like, were lashed to the canoe, and hence got no worse than a wetting; but our axe and various spoons and forks were gone from our sight forever. The oatmeal was a part of our lading, and the tobacco as well. For this last we felt no anxiety, congratulating ourselves that it was in a waterproof tin. We did not at the time open this tin, as there was tobacco enough for a time in the other canoes. But the meal-bag was a slop. Henceforth we were to have no porridge, only beans, beans, beans, to go with our trout and canned knickknacks. And this meant nothing more nor less than dinner three times a day, instead of the old appetizing sequence of breakfast, dinner, and —dinner.

After a brief delay we continued our journey. An exciting afternoon it proved throughout, leaving us well tired at evening. Taking care to preserve a discreet distance between the canoes whenever the current grew threatening, we slipped on swiftly between ever-varying shores. Rounding a sharp turn we would see before us a long slope of angry water, with huddling waves and frequent rocks; and at the foot of the slope three or four great white "ripples" foaming and roaring in the sun. Then a brief season of stern restraint, strong checkings, strenuous thrustings, sudden bold dashes, and hair's-breadth evasions — a plunge and a cheer, and, drenched from the crest of that last "ripple," we would look back on the raging incline behind us. This sort of thing took place three times within two hours. We passed without stopping through Second Lake, and under the majestic front of Sugar Loaf Mountain, which is matchlessly reflected in the deep, still waters. The mountain towers from the water's edge, its base in a cedar swamp, its lofty conical summit, which topples towards the lake as if it had received a mighty push from behind, veiled and softened with thick bushes and shrubbery.

"Some time after sundown we reached the mouth of a tributary stream known as the Horton Branch. This was a famous trout water, and we determined to fish it thoroughly on the morrow. By the time we had the tent pitched, a few trout caught in the gathering dusk, and a mighty dinner cooked and eaten, our eyes were filled with sleep. We cared not for stories that night, but smoked brief pipes and then turned in.

In the morning after an early breakfast we poled up to the Big Jam, a distance of nearly six miles. The Big Jam is a sort of dam, formed of logs and tree-trunks and a long accumulation of *débris*. Just beneath it lies one of the finest trout pools I have ever fished — which is saying not a little.   The poling up Horton Branch was delightful, — a stiffish current, but few rocks.

Arrived at the pool we made great haste to put our rods together, so tempting were the eddies. Never, surely, shall I forget .that 'morning's fishing. All the flies in our books seemed equally killing. Those Big Jam trout were insatiable. We soon grew hard to please, and made it a rule to return at once to its native element every fish that did not approach three-quarters of a pound. This had the proper effect of limiting our take to something near what we could at once consume. A few fine fish we packed in salt, in a sort of basket of birch-bark which Stranion ingeniously constructed.   Toward noon the fish stopped rising. Then we lunched, and took a long siesta.   In the afternoon the sport was brisk, but not equal to that of the morning.   No doubt if we had stayed till sundown the morning's experience would have been amply repeated ; but we were not so greedy as to desire that.   We left in high spirits at about five o'clock, and slipped merrily down to our camp on the main Squatook.

CHAPTER VI.

THE CAMP ON SQUATOOK RIVER.

THAT night around the camp-fire stories were once more in demand. Stranion was first called upon, and he at once responded.

" I'll call this story —

'SAVED BY A SLIVER,'

and ask you to observe the neat alliteration," said Stranion.

" In the autumn of 1887 I was hunting in those wildernesses about the headwaters of that famous salmon river, the south-west Miramichi. I had old Jake Christison with me, the best woodsman on the river; and I had also my inseparable companion and most faithful follower, Jeff, a large bull-terrier. Jeff was not a hunting-dog in any accepted sense of the word. He had no inherited instinct for the chase; but he had remarkable intelligence, unconquerable pluck, unquestioning obedience, and hence a certain fitness for any emergency that might arise. In the woods he always crept noiselessly at my heels, as unembarrassing and self-effacing as my shadow.

"One morning we set out from camp soon after breakfast to follow up some fresh caribou signs which Jake had just reported. We had gone but half a mile into the thickets when the woodsman discovered that he had left his hunting-knife by the camp-fire, where he had been using it to slice the breakfast bacon. To go without his hunting-knife could not for a moment be thought of; so he turned back hurriedly to get it, while I strolled on at a leisurely pace with Jeff at my heels.

"My way led me through a little wide ravine, in the centre of which lay the fragments of a giant pine, shattered years ago by lightning, and bleached by storm and sun. A portion of the trunk remained yet upright, — a tall splinter, or 'sliver' as the woodsmen call it, split from the rest of the trunk by some electric freak, and pointing like a stern white finger toward the spot of open sky above, whence the bolt had fallen. Saturated with resins, the sliver was practically incorruptible; and time had only served to harden its lance-like point and edge. A few feet beyond this blasted pine the woods grew thick, — a dusky confusion of great gnarled trunks and twisting limbs.

"As I sauntered up to the foot of that whitened trunk, Jeff suddenly thrust himself in front of me with a low, almost inaudible growl, and stood obstinately still, as if to bar my farther advance. Instantly my glance penetrated the thicket, and fell upon a huge panther crouching flat along a fallen tree of almost the same color as the brute's hide. It was the panther's cold green eyes indeed that so promptly revealed him to me. He was in the attitude to spring; and ordering Jeff ' to heel,' I sank on one knee, cocking my rifle and taking aim at the same time, for there was not a moment to lose.

"Even as I pulled the trigger the animal dashed upon me, in the very face of the flash. The suddenness of the assault of course upset my aim; but by good chance the ball went through the animal's fore shoulder, breaking the bone. I was hurled backward into a hollow under the fallen fragments of the pine-tree, and I felt the panther's teeth go through my left arm. Thrusting myself as far as possible beneath the shelter of the log, I reached for the long knife at my belt. Just as I got it out of its sheath, the panther, with an angry cry, dropped my arm, and turned half round, while keeping his place upon my prostrate body. My faithful Jeff had come to the rescue of his master, and had sunk his terrible teeth into the root of the panther's tail.

"The snarling beast doubled back upon himself, and struggled to seize the dog between his jaws; but Jeff was too wary and active for this, and the panther would not leave his post of vantage on my body. He was a sagacious beast, and

perceived that if he should let me up he would
have two enemies to contend with instead of one.
As for me, in my restricted position, I found myself unable to use my knife with any effect. I lay
still, abiding my opportunity, and watching with
intense but curiously impersonal interest the good
fight my bull-terrier was making. I was not conscious of much pain in my arm, but the shock of
the panther's assault seemed in some way to have
weakened my vital force. Presently the panther,
finding it impossible to release himself from that
deadly grip of Jeff's, threw himself over on his
back, curling himself up like a cat, and raked the
dog severely with his dangerous hind claws. The
change in our assailant's position released my right
arm, and at once I drove the knife into his side
square to the hilt. I failed to touch a vital spot,
but the wound diverted his attention; and Jeff,
bleeding and furious, was enabled to secure a new
hold. The panther was a splendid beast, and
fought as I never before or since have seen a panther fight. Had it not been for my shot, which
broke his fore shoulder, it would have gone hard
with both Jeff and me. As it was, however, the
panther found his work cut out for him, though I
was so nearly helpless from my position that Jeff
had to bear the brunt of the battle. The brave
terrier was getting badly cut up. I could not see
very well what went on, being at the bottom of
the fight, and my breath nearly knocked out of

me; but all of a sudden a rifle-shot rang in my ears, the smoke and flame filled my eyes, and the body of the panther stiffened out convulsively. The next moment old Jake was dragging me out from beneath, and anxiously inquiring about my damages.

"Reassuring him as to my condition, I sat down rather faintly on the trunk, while Jeff, at my feet, lay licking his scratches. The old woodsman leaned upon his empty rifle, contemplatively scanning our vanquished foe, and loudly praising Jeff. Suddenly he broke off in the midst of a sentence, and glanced up into the branches ahead of him.

"'Great Jee-hoshaphat!' he exclaimed in a startled voice, springing backward, and snatching for a fresh cartridge, while Jeff jumped to his feet with a wrathful snarl. In the same breath, before I could realize what was the matter, I heard the female panther, mate of him we had killed, utter her fearful scream of rage and pain. From a giant limb overhead her long tawny body flashed out into the sunlight, descending upon our devoted party like a yellow thunderbolt.

"Weak and dazed as I was, I shut my eyes with a sense of sick disgust and weariness, and a strange feeling of infinite suspense. There was a curious sound of tearing and scratching; but no shock came, and I opened my eyes in astonishment. There was Jake calmly slipping a cartridge into his rifle. There was Jeff standing just as I had seen him when I closed my eyes. It seemed hours, but it had been merely an eyewink — the fraction of a second. But where was the panther?

" My inward query was answered on the instant. A wild and indescribable screeching, spitting, and snarling arose, mixed with a sound of claws tearing desperately at the hard wood of the pine trunk. The panther was held aloft in the air, impaled on the sliver, around which she spun madly like a frightful wheel of tawny fire. Her efforts to free herself were tremendous, but there was no escape. The sliver was hard as steel and as inexorable. Suddenly Jeff sprang at the creature, but in his impetuosity missed his hold, and got a lightning blow from one of those great claws, almost laying his side open. The brave dog carries the marks of that wound to this day. His revenge was instantaneous; for his next leap gained its object, and his jaws fixed themselves securely in the panther's haunches. The whole wild scene had thus far been like a dream to me, and the yellings and snarlings sounded far off and indistinct. The only reality seemed to me the still brown and green of the forest, the moveless tree-tops, the cheerful morning sun streaming down into the little glade, and the old woodsman standing in his contemplative attitude, watching the gyrating form of the panther. Then on a sudden my blood seemed to flow with a rush of

"FROM A GIANT LIMB OVERHEAD HER LONG TAWNY BODY FLASHED IN THE SUNLIGHT." Page 199.

new force, and a sense of reality came back to me. I jumped up, slipped a cartridge into my rifle, and with a timely bullet put the unhappy beast out of its pain.

"In order to release the panther's body we had to cut down the sliver, the blood-stained top of which, with its point sharp and spear-like, as if fashioned by the hand of man, now hangs as a treasured relic upon my library wall. Right beneath, as a foot-rug to my writing-table, and a favorite napping-place for Jeff, is the panther-skin with two holes in it, where the sliver went through. The other skin I gave to old Jake as a memorial of the adventure; but it is probable he sold it at the earliest fair opportunity, for it was a comely and valuable skin."

"Stranion," said I when he concluded, "your Jeff is one of the dogs whom I am proud to have known. I have only met, in all my career, one better dog, and that was my brave old Dan, of blessed and many-scarred memory."

"Bigger, not better, dog," interrupted Stranion sternly.

"Well, we won't argue over it. They were both of the same stock, anyway; and I fear we will not look upon their like again, eh, Stranion?"

"Now you are talking, O. M.," responded Stranion warmly. "But tell us that great yarn about Dan's battle!"

"No, not to-night," was my answer. "It would seem like making rivals of Dan and Jeff, which they never were, but always sworn chums. Jeff is enough for one night. Dan shall be commemorated on another. Let Sam give us a bear story now."

"All right," said Sam. "Here's one in which Stranion and I were both concerned. Note it down by the name of —

'SKIDDED LANDING.'

"Three winters ago, as some of you will remember, Stranion and I took a month in the lumber-woods. It was drawing on toward spring. As we were both good snow-shoers, we managed to visit several widely scattered camps. At all we were received hospitably, with unlimited pork and beans, hot bread and tea; and at each we made a stay of several days.

"For our climax we selected that camp which promised us the most picturesque and exciting experiences at the breaking up of the ice. This was Evans's Camp on Green River, where the logs were gathered in what is known as a 'rough-and-tumble landing,' — a form which entails much excitement and often grave peril to the axeman whose work is to cut the 'brow' loose.

"As it happened, however, the most stirring adventure that fell to our personal experience on that trip was one we encountered at Clarke's

Camp, on the Tobique, where we stayed but three days.

"This camp, but one of the many centres of operation of the great lumbering firm of Clarke & Co., was generally known as 'Skidded Landing.' And here let me explain the terms 'brow,' 'drive,' 'rough-and-tumble landing,' and 'skidded landing.'

"In lumbermen's parlance, the logs of the winter's chopping, hauled and piled on the river-bank where they can conveniently be launched into the water upon the breaking up of the ice, are termed collectively 'a brow of logs.'

"When once the logs have been got into the water, and, shepherded by the lumbermen with their pike-poles, are flocking wildly seaward on the swollen current, they and their guardians together constitute 'the drive.'

"The task the lumbermen are now engaged upon is termed 'stream driving;' and laborious, perilous work it is, especially on those rivers which are much obstructed by rapids, rocks, and shoals. A brow of logs is a 'landing' when the logs are piled from the water's edge. A landing may be either a 'rough-and-tumble' or a 'skidded' landing.

"The 'rough-and-tumble,' which good woodsmen generally regard as a shiftless affair, is made by driving a few heavy timbers into the mud at the water's edge, at the foot of a sloping bank.

These form a strong and lofty breastwork. Into the space behind are tumbled the logs helter-skelter from the top of the bank, as they are hauled from the woods. All through the winter the space keeps filling up, and by spring the strain on the sustaining piles is something tremendous.

"When the thaw comes and the river rises, and the ice goes out with a rush, then the accumulation of logs has to be set free. This is done by cutting away the most important of the sustaining timbers, whereupon the others snap, and the logs go roaring out in a terrific avalanche.

"It is easy to realize the perils of cutting out this kind of landing. If the landing has been unskilfully or carelessly located, the peril of the enterprise is greatly increased.

"The 'skidded' landing is a much more business-like affair. In this kind of structure the logs are placed systematically. First a layer of logs is deposited parallel with the river's edge. Across these, at right angles, are laid a few light poles, technically termed *skids*. On these another layer of logs parallel to the water, and so on to the completion of the structure.

"With this species of landing, to release the logs is a very simple matter. There is nothing to do but quietly roll them off, layer by layer, into the stream, which snatches them and hurries them away.

"From this it will be seen why we did not elect to stay long at Skidded Landing. But while we were there something happened in this fashion.

"On the second day of our stay in the camp, it chanced that Stranion was lazy. When I set forth to examine some snares which I had set the night before, he chose to snooze in his bunk rather than accompany me. As events befell, he proved to have made the wiser choice.

"Of course I took my gun with me. I was thinking of small game exclusively, — during our wanderings, hitherto, we had seen nothing larger than a fox, — and both barrels were loaded with cartridges containing No. 4 shot. But with unaccountable thoughtlessness I neglected to take any heavier ammunition in my pocket; yet that was the only time on the trip that heavier ammunition was needed.

"I visited my snares, and found in one of them a rabbit. 'The boys'll appreciate a rabbit stew,' thought I, as I hitched the frozen carcass to my belt. A little farther on I started another rabbit, which I shot, and hitched beside its fellow; and then I struck out blithely for camp. Before I had retraced my path many paces, I came face to face with an immense bear, which apparently had been dogging my steps.

"We halted and eyed each other sharply. I thought I detected a guilty uneasiness in the animal's gaze, as if he were properly ashamed of himself for his ungentlemanly conduct. Presuming upon this, I spoke in an authoritative voice, and took one or two firm steps in advance. I expected the animal to step aside deferentially and let me pass, but I had forgotten that this was a hungry season for bears. The brute lumbered forward with alacrity, as if ferociously surprised at my readiness to furnish him a much-needed luncheon.

" In my trepidation I did not let him get near enough before I fired my solitary cartridge. Had I let him come to close quarters, the heavy bird-shot would have served the full purpose of a bullet. But no, I was in too much of a hurry. The charge had room to scatter before it reached my assailant; and the pellets only served to cut him up badly about the head without in the least interfering with his fighting capacity.

"With something between a grunt and a howl of pain and fury he dashed upon me; and I, dropping my cherished weapon in a panic, made a mighty bound to one side and darted toward the open river. I wanted free play for my snow-shoes, and no risk from hidden stumps.

" In the woods the snow was soft enough to give me some advantage over my pursuer. I gained on him when doing my utmost. But being gaunt from his long fast, and very light in proportion to his prodigious strength, his progress,

with that awkward gallop of his, was terrifyingly
rapid. Moreover, I had vividly before my mind's
eye the consciousness of what would be my instant fate should I trip on a buried stump or root,
or plunge into some snow-veiled bush that would
entangle my snow-shoes.

" Once out upon the river I breathed more
freely. But the bear was hard upon my heels.
Here the snow was more firmly packed, and he
travelled faster. I ceased to increase the little
distance between us. After two piercing yells for
help, I saved my breath for the race before me.

" I was really not very far from the camp; but
the trees and a high point intercepted my cries,
and the wind blew them away, so they failed to
reach Stranion's ears. Nevertheless, it happened
that Stranion grew restless about the time of my
first meeting with the bear.

" He strolled down to the landing, which was
perhaps three hundred yards from the camp,
seated himself upon a spruce log, and began to
dig off with his pocket-knife the perfumed amber-
like globules of gum. He was engaged in this
innocent if not engrossing occcupation when he
caught sight of me racing desperately around the
jutting point immediately above the landing.

" At the sight of my terror he sprang to his
feet, and was about to rush back to camp for his
gun; but straightway the bear appeared, and so
close behind me that he knew there was no time

to get the weapon. The emergency was upon him. He knew something had to be done at once. Fortunately he was ready of resource. He dropped down, and crawled swiftly to the edge of the landing.

" The track I was following led along close under the front of the landing, then turned the corner sharply and ran straight up to the camp. The bear was now gaining on me. He was not more than thirty or forty feet behind. I was beginning to realize that he must catch me before I could reach the camp.

" Coming to this conclusion, I was just about to put forth all my remaining breath in one despairing shriek for help, then to turn and make what fight I could with my sheath-knife, which had already been used to cut away the dangling rabbits, when out of the corner of my eye I caught sight of Stranion on the top of the logs. I took one look at his face and saw its look of readiness. He grinned encouragingly, but put his finger on his lips for silence.

" At the sight of him I felt new vigor flow through all my veins. With fresh speed I raced along past the front of the landing, turned the corner, and bounded up the slope. Reaching the hard track, I kicked my feet clear of the snow-shoes, and started to climb up the logs to join Stranion.

" At this moment Stranion found his opportunity. The bear came plunging along on my tracks, immediately beneath the face of the logs. And now, with a stake which he had snatched up, Stranion pried mightily upon the two front logs of the top tier. The great timbers rolled swiftly over the edge.

"One of them, the heaviest, was just in time. It caught the animal over the hindquarters, and crushed him to the ice. When Stranion's triumphant shout proclaimed the success of his attack, I threw myself down between two logs and lay there gasping, while Stranion returned to the camp, got his gun, and put the wounded animal out of his pain.

"Later in the day, much later, Stranion and I together went over the ground I had traversed with such celerity. We recovered the rabbits, and also, after a persistent search in the snow, the gun which I had so basely abandoned."

"I think that is a pretty straight account of what happened," said Stranion; "and now we will hear something from Magnus's uncle."

"No," said Magnus; "I'll tell you something my cousin Bob Raven told me about a time he had with—

'A MAD STALLION.'

"There is perhaps no beast." said Bob, "more terrible, more awe-inspiring, than a stallion that has gone mad. Such an animal, bursting all the fetters of his inherited dread of man, seems inspired with a frightful craving to take vengeance for the immemorial servitude of his kind. As a rule, he has no quarrel with anything but humanity. Often with other horses he associates amicably, and toward the cattle and lesser animals that may be with him in the fields he displays the indifference of disdain. But let man, woman, or child come within his vision, and his homicidal mania breaks into flame.

"I have had several disagreeable encounters with vicious horses, but only once was I so unfortunate as to fall in with one possessed by this homicidal mania. My escape was so narrow, and the experience left so deep an impression upon my mind, that I have felt ever since an instinctive distrust for this most noble of domestic animals.

"One autumn, when I was about eighteen, I was taking a tramp through the eastern townships of Quebec preparatory to resuming work at college. I reached the little village of Maybury one day at noon, and dropped into the village inn for luncheon. The village was in a state of excitement over a tragedy which had taken place that very morning, and which was speedily detailed to me by every one with whom I came in contact. The most authentic account, as it appeared, was that given me by the proprietor of the inn.

"'You see,' he answered eagerly, in response

to my question as to the cause of the general excitement, 'a boy 'at old Joe Cook was bringin' up on his farm has jest been killed by a mad horse. The boy come out from Liverpool las' June two year ago, with a lot more poor little beggars like him; an' old Joe kinder took a fancy to him, an' was a-bringin' him up like he was his own son. The horses is mostly runnin' at pasture now in the back lots yonder; an' Atkinson's stallion, what has always had the name of bein' kind as a lamb, is pasturin' with the rest. But he seems somehow to've gone mad all on a suddent. This mornin' airly, as Cook's boy was comin' home from drivin' the cows out onter the uplands, he found the horses all crowdin' roun' the gate leadin' onter the meadows. He knowed some of 'em might try and shove through if he didn't take keer, so he jest kind of shooed 'em off with a stick. They all scattered away savin' only Atkinson's stallion; an' he, wheelin' round with a kind of screech as'd make the marrer freeze in your bones, grabbed the boy right by the back of the neck, an' shook him like old Tige there'd shake a rat. I guess the poor boy's neck was broke right off, for he never cried out nor nothin'. Steve Barnes was jest then a-comin' up the meadow road, an' he seen it all. He yelled, an' run up as fast as he could; but afore he could git to the fence the stallion had jumped on the boy two or three times, an' was a-standin' lookin' at him curious-like. Steve seen 'at the boy was dead, but he started to climb over an' drive off the brute ; but as soon as the stallion seen Steve he let another screech, an' run at him with his mouth wide open, an' Steve had nothin' fur it but to hop back quick over the fence. Seein' as the boy was deader'n a door-nail, Steve didn't think it'd be common-sense to resk his life jest for the dead body; but he stayed there a-stonin' the brute, which was jest spilin' to git at him. After 'bout an hour the other horses came back, an' the stallion forgot about the boy an' went off with them 'way back behind the hills; an' Steve got the body an' carried it home.'

" 'And what have they done to the brute?' I inquired, with a fierce anger stirring in my veins.

" 'Well,' answered Boniface, 'this afternoon there's a crowd goin' out to ketch him an' tie him up. If he's too bad fur that, — an' if I know anything about horses he's jest gone mad, stark mad, — why, they'll have to shoot him off-hand, to save their own necks.'

" 'I wonder if I'll run any risk of meeting him?' I queried rather anxiously. I had no weapon but my heavy walking-stick, and I had an almost sentimental regard for the integrity of my neck.

" 'Which way be you bound?' inquired Boniface.

" 'For Blissville,' I answered.

"' Oh,' said he, "you're all right then. The horses are feedin' out yonder to the no'th-east, an' Blissville lays south.'

" It was with few misgivings that I now resumed my journey. In the tonic autumn air my spirits rose exultantly, and I walked with a brisk step, whistling and knocking off the golden tops of the hawk-bit with my cane. The country about Maybury is a high, rolling plateau, for the most part open pasture-ground, with here and there a shallow, wooded ravine, and here and there a terrace of loose bowlders with bramble-thickets growing between. I was soon beyond the cultivated fields, past the last of the fences. I had climbed one of those rocky terraces, and made a couple of hundred yards across the delightful breezy down, when, behind a low knoll, I caught sight of a group of horses quietly pasturing, and remembered with a qualm the morning's tragedy. Could this, I asked myself anxiously, be the herd containing that mad stallion?

" I halted, and was about to retrace my steps unobtrusively, in the hope that I had escaped their notice. But it was too late. Two or three of the animals raised their heads and looked toward me. One in the group snorted with a peculiar half-whinny, at the sound of which my heart sank. Then I caught sight of one in the centre that seemed to be jumping up in the air off all four feet at once. The next moment this creature, a great black animal, appeared outside the group, plunging and biting at his flank. Two or three times he sprang into the air in that strange, spasmodic way I had already observed, and threw his head backward over his right shoulder with an indescribable gesture of menace and defiance. Then with a short, dreadful sound he darted toward me, open-mouthed.

" Up to this point I had stood my ground, eying the brute resolutely, with an appearance of fearlessness which I was very far from feeling. But now I saw that my only hope, and that a desperate one, lay in flight. I was accounted at college a first-rate sprinter, and now I ran my best. The two hundred yards that lay between me and the terrace I had just left must have been covered in not much more than twenty seconds. But as I reached the brow of the slope the mad brute was close on my heels.

"I had no time to check myself, and even less notion to do so. In fact, I fell, and rolled headlong down, dropping bruised and bewildered into a crevice between two bowlders. The next instant I saw the black mass of my pursuer dashing over me in a splendid leap. Before he could turn and seize me I had rolled farther into the crevice, and found that one of the rocks overhung so as to form a little narrow cave into which I could squeeze myself so far as to be quite beyond the animal's reach.

"Never before or since have I discovered so unexpected and providential a refuge. The raving
stallion came bounding and leaping up to the very
door of my burrow, but I felt safe. He would
roll back his lips, lay his ears flat to his head,
spring straight into the air, and shriek through
his wide, red nostrils his fury and his challenge.
The latter I did not think it incumbent upon me
to accept. I waived it in disdainful silence.

"For a time the brute kept up his boundings
and those strange, proud jerkings of his head; but
at length he actually tried to stretch his neck into
my burrow, and reach me with his frightful naked
teeth. This was a vain attempt; but I resented
it, and picking up a stone which lay at hand, I
struck him a heavy blow on the nose. This
brought the blood from those cruel nostrils, and
made him even, if possible, more furious in his
rage; but he returned to his former demonstra-
tions.

"It must have been for nearly an hour that I
watched the mad creature's antics from my den.
The rest of the herd had approached, and were
feeding indifferently about the foot of the terrace.
From time to time my enemy would join them,
and snatch a few restless mouthfuls of grass. But
almost immediately he would return to his post at
my door, and his vigilant watch was on me all the
time.

"I was beginning to cast about somewhat anxiously for a way of escape from this imprisonment, when I saw the pasturing herd suddenly toss up their heads, and then go scurrying away across the down. My adversary saw this, too, and turned his attention away from me. I peered forth cautiously, and to my profound relief I observed a party of men, several carrying ropes and halters, and others armed with rifles, approaching below the terrace. One man walked a little ahead of the others, and held out a peck measure, in which he shook something which I presume to have been oats.

"The stallion eyed them sombrely for an instant; and then his mane rose like a crest, and his head went back with a shrill cry. In the selfsame way as he had greeted my appearance he bounced into the air twice or thrice, and then he dashed upon the party.

"The man with the oats fell back with wonderful alacrity, and the fellows who carried halters seemed bent upon effacing themselves in the humblest manner possible. One tall, gray-shirted woodsman, however, stepped to the front, raised his rifle, and drew a bead upon the approaching fury, while two or three of the others held their shots in reserve. There was a moment of breathless suspense. Then the fine, thin note of the woodsman's rifle rang out; and the stallion sprang aside with a shriek, and stumbled forward upon his knees. Almost instantly, however, he recovered himself, and rushed upon his opponents with undiminished ferocity. I held my breath. He was almost upon the party now. Then two more rifles flashed from the marksmen standing moveless in their tracks, and the mad brute rose straight up on his hind legs, and fell over backward, dead.

"I stepped out to welcome my rescuers, and detailed to them my adventures. They had been wondering who or what it was that the brute was laying siege to. There was so much, in fact, to talk about, and I found myself for the moment so important a figure, that I returned to Maybury for that evening, and there had to retell my story at least a score of times."

"If it's my turn now—and I suppose it is," said Ranolf, "I can't pretend to give you anything so blood-curdling as this story of Magnus's; but I'll do my little best to make an angry bull moose as interesting as a mad stallion. Take this down, O. M., as —

'AN ADVENTURE WITH A BULL MOOSE.'

"I don't know much about the lumber-camps; but I got this from a Restigouche lumberman, so of course it must be true.

"One day a woodsman, who had been on a long tramp prospecting for prime birch timber, rushed into a camp on the Restigouche with news that he had discovered a 'yard' of moose.

"A 'yard' it may here be explained, is an opening in the forest where a herd of moose has trampled down the snow and made its headquarters. The yard is always surrounded by young trees, upon whose succulent shoots the moose feed. It forms a striking scene — the animals lying about the space of trampled and discolored snow, while here and there a magnificently antlered bull towers above the rest, keeping watch; and here and there on the edge of the yard an animal is reaching aloft its long, prehensile lips to tear down its meal of green branches.

"Now, the news which the inspector brought into camp created an instant interest. Fresh meat was at a premium in the Restigouche Camp; and at the thought of moose-meat, which is a sort of beef idealized, every lumberman's mouth began to water longingly. The boss was quite at one with the hands in this respect; wherefore it was not long before a hunt was organized.

"Only those men could take part who had snow-shoes, for the snow was deep that season. So there was a small muster of five; but with those five went the blessings of the camp. Upon their success hung the hopes of all their hungry comrades.

"The wind, fortunately for the hunters, was blowing from the yard to the camp, so that it was not necessary to take a roundabout course. The expedition was led by the prospector, who was an enthusiastic hunter, and skilled in woodcraft.

"It was past midday as the yard was approached. The hunters separated, and closed in on the yard from all sides save that from which the wind was directly blowing. The leader, whose name was Story, had the longest way to go, in order that by the time he could get into position all the others might be ready and waiting.

"Presently an owl was heard to hoot twice. This was Story's signal. The moose heard it too, and pricked up their ears; for the owls they were accustomed to hear hooted, as a rule, in the night-time. Then they heard the soft, hurried tramping of the snow-shoes, and the crackling of frosted twigs all about them, and huddled together, terrified, in the middle of their yard.

"The next moment five rifles blazed out upon them, and the hunters rushed in. Two of the creatures fell at the volley, and two more, fat young cows, were knifed by the nimble huntsmen; and the rest of the herd dashed wildly off, running up the wind, where they scented no danger.

"Now Story was in a great disgust. His shot had failed to kill. He had fired at the chief of the herd, a splendid bull, whose antlers he craved as a trophy. The bull was struck somewhere in the body, for he staggered; but instantly recovering, he had charged fiercely in the direction of the assault. Story had stepped behind a tree; and the mad beast, not detecting him, had continued his career through the woods, almost at right angles to the direction which was taken by the rest of the herd.

"Story gave chase at a run, loading as he went. The bull was already out of sight, but his track was ample guide. The hunter knew he had hit the animal hard, and looked for a speedy triumph.

"For an hour he continued his long trot, encouraged from time to time by the sight of blood upon the snow. The animal's path led at last through a region of gullies and copses, and low, broad beech-trees. Suddenly, as Story was skirting the crest of a little ravine, from a thicket close ahead of him the great moose dashed out with a bellow, and charged upon him like lightning.

"The hunter had not time to check himself, but whipped the gun to his shoulder and took a snap-shot. Even at the same instant the snow gave way beneath his feet, and his shot flew wide as he rolled to the foot of the ravine.

"The animal was upon him before he could recover himself, and he thought his end was come. Dropping his gun, now useless, he drew his knife, and, just escaping one keen prong, he seized the antlers with one hand, while with the other he slashed at the animal's neck. It was the depth and softness of the snow, with the confusion of bushes and roots beneath it, that saved him from being crushed at once.

"As the moose felt the knife in his neck he

"AT LAST HE LOOKED UPWARD, AND SAW THE HUNTER."   Page 221.

drew back, and threw up his head with violence, intending to trample his adversary with his terrible hoofs; but the neck of the moose has tremendous power, and as the hunter clung to his hold with desperate tenacity, knowing that his last chance depended on it, he was thrown high into the air. He came in contact violently with a beech-tree branch.

"One thinks quickly in such emergencies as these; or rather an instinct, drowsy at other times, wakes up and saves us the need of thought. Story flung both arms around the branch, and with a great sigh of thankfulness, and possibly an inward utterance of the same, swung himself out of harm's way.

"When his opponent failed to fall, the moose was astonished. He turned round and round, and tore up the snow, and bellowed hoarsely in his rage. The thing was inexplicable.

"At last he looked upward, and saw the hunter in the branches. His indignation waxed fiercer than ever, and he made desperate efforts to pull down the branches by seizing and breaking off their tips.

"How the huntsman chuckled and derided him!

"After a time the mad brute grew more calm. Then, to Story's supreme disgust, he lay down under the tree to starve his prisoner out. The hunter had no gun. The weather was severe. There was nothing to eat. There was no way of stealing off unobserved. To crown all, the wretched man recalled a number of incidents showing the implacable persistence of the wounded bulls of this species.

" For perhaps an hour the hunter waited, vainly hoping that this particular moose would prove less obstinate than his kind. or would get homesick for the rest of the herd, or would die of his inward wound.

" But nothing seemed farther from the animal's intention than any one of these things. It was growing dark, and the shivering captive began to realize that he would have to spend the night in his tree.

" He tucked his knife back safely in its sheath, and undertook to warm himself a little.

" His snow-shoes he had taken off long before, and had tied them to a limb, knowing that if they should fall to the ground the moose would at once make mince-meat of them. Then he proceeded to climb about the tree with the utmost energy and agility, while the moose, who had risen promptly to his feet, looked on with the most obvious amazement.

" By this means Story soon got rid of his chill. Before it was quite dark he selected a safe and comparatively comfortable spot where two large branches forked, and tying himself securely to the limb with his long scarf, he tried to go to sleep. It was a profitless undertaking, and after an hour or two of faithful effort he gave it up. He was stiff, miserable, hungry, and half-frozen.

"It had grown so dark that he thought perhaps he might descend the other side of the tree, and slip away without the moose being any the wiser. With what he fancied perfect noiselessness, he tried it.

"He was almost down, when there was a bellow and a rush, and the animal was almost upon him. He escaped just by a hair's-breadth, and swung nimbly back into his refuge. He had no stomach for another attempt of that sort. He began to calculate how long it would be before they would miss him in camp, and come to look for him.

"The prospect did not cheer him. Known as he was for a determined hunter, his comrades would go home without him, confident that he would turn up all right when he had bagged his game. If he was not back by morning they would perhaps think something had gone wrong, and set out to look for him.

"They would have to retrace their steps to the moose-yard, and then, picking up his trail from the yard, might be expected to rescue him about noon. By that time, he thought to himself miserably, he might be frozen stiff. He decided to do something! But what?

"At first he thought of cutting a branch, fastening his knife to the end of it, and stabbing his captor with the improvised harpoon. But the beech-branches were too thick and crooked to suit his idea. He did at last, however, succeed in splicing a sort of spear about five feet long; and when he had got the knife lashed to the end of it all his stock of twine was exhausted.

" The spear was pretty satisfactory, but he of course dared not *throw* it; and the moose showed no inclination to come where he could be effectually and neatly despatched. The hunter struck his harpoon into a limb, and set out to concoct another weapon.

" By this time the moon was up. The hunter tore a little strip from his shirt, wet it in his mouth, and rubbed it full of gunpowder. This made a fair bit of slow-match, which he folded several times longitudinally, and then inserted in the top of his powder-flask. To the short end, which he left protuding, he touched a match; and then he tossed the flask down in front of the moose.

" The sputtering of the slow-match for a moment disconcerted the animal, and he drew back. Then, as if ashamed of his weakness, he sprang upon the flask and trampled it fiercely under his feet. While he was indulging in this interesting performance the powder exploded with a bang, and the astounded animal sprang high into the air.

" But though badly startled, he was not frightened by any means. He was shocked and scorched, and a little torn in the fore legs; but this only made him the more deadly. In a paroxysm of pain and hatred he dashed under the tree, and rearing frantically struggled to reach the hunter.

"This was just what the wily woodsman desired. Lying flat on a branch almost within reach of the beast's antlers, he reached down and dealt him a blow in the neck. A second thrust went deeper, and struck a more vital part, almost under the throat. The blood gushed out in a torrent, and the hunter congratulated himself that deliverance was near at hand.

"Presently the great animal stood still, and looked about him with a puzzled, anxious air. He felt his strength going from him, and could not understand it.

"Soon he began to sway from side to side, and had to brace his feet apart to keep from falling. At last he fell. Then the hunter, stretching himself, came down out of the tree and stood beside his noble and defeated antagonist.

"Story was too weak and cold and hungry to think of waiting to cut off the animal's head and hide it from the bears. He slipped on his snow-shoes, found his gun, and started back in haste for the camp. Before daylight he had reached the 'yard'; and there, to his intense delight, he met a party of his comrades who had set out in the night to look for him."

DAN.

"And now," said I, "I'll tell you of Dan's great fight. It was fought before he came into my possession; that is, before my friend H——, going away to study in Germany, handed him over to me. It was just a few weeks before H——'s departure, and we were setting out for a farewell trip to the wilderness together.

"As for Dan, he was not much to look at cer‑ tainly; and I was prejudiced against him by the fact that he took up room in the canoe. To carry a great bulldog in a birch canoe was contrary to all my notions of the fitness of things. But H—— had protested so vehemently against the idea of leaving him behind, and the dog had behaved with such sobriety and good sense when I took him out to try him in a choppy sea, that I yielded a reluc‑ tant consent.

"Our proposed route was through the chain of the Chiputneticook Lakes, down stream all the way, with no difficult water to contend against, and no bad rapids to shoot. We had two canoes, — that which bore H—— and myself, and that in which our Indian carried the baggage; so that really it was not impossible to make room for the addition to our party, and Dan was formally en‑ rolled a member.

"He took his place in the forward mid-section of my canoe, immediately behind his master,

where he coiled himself up into a compact bun-
dle. There he calmly ignored the wildest vagaries
to which the lake waves could impel our little
craft. This good seamanship of his, with his dig-
nified manner toward myself and his adoring devotion to his master, gradually won my respect;
and before we had been many days out we were
on terms of mutual consideration. I ended with
a cordial enjoyment of his company.

" I think I began by declaring that Dan was not
much to look at. This was my first and biassed
impression. But it must be modified by the ac-
knowledgment that his splendid proportions and
great strength were apparent to the most casual
observer. In fact, he was a perfect specimen of
his breed.

" But the expression of his small eye and mighty
jaw, which certainly belied his true character, was
bloodthirsty to the last degree; and his white
coat was disfigured with a tangle of long scars
which looked as if the business of his life were
brawls. As I afterwards learned, those scars
were the ornament of a hero, no less to be honored
than if his great heart had throbbed in a human
body.

" It was one night in camp at the head of the
Big Chiputneticook that I heard how those scars
were achieved. Tent was pitched on a bit of dry
interval which fringed the base of a high rock,
a well-known landmark to trappers, and distin-

guished by the name of ‘The Devil’s Pulpit.’ The rock towered over us, naked and perpendicular, for a distance of two hundred feet, then shelved, and rose again some hundreds of feet farther to a beetling cap of mingled rock and forest.

“Our camp was flanked on each side by a thicket of cherry and vines and young water-ash, and the light of our fire filled the space between with the comfort of its cheerful radiance. In the midst of this we lay basking, each waiting for the other to begin a yarn; but no one seemed prepared.

“We had been out ten days in the wilderness; and night after night our occupation had been this one of ‘swapping’ experiences, till I had found myself compelled to fall back on my inventive faculty, and our Indian, Steve, who was communicative beyond the custom of his people, had begun to repeat himself in his stories.

“As for H——, he never spun a yarn save under some strong compulsion, yet we knew more or less vaguely that many a strange experience had fallen to his lot. We had had some stirring adventures together, he and I, since first I had initiated him into the mysteries of woodcraft. But it was rare for him to recall them in conversation, and hence I judged that there was much in his experience of which I had never heard.

“On the present occasion the long silence was

becoming almost drowsy. For me the flame from our logs was beginning to change mistily into the glow from a heaped-up grate, and to play over two small curly heads and a long-eared pup on a hearth-rug, when suddenly from far up in the moonlit rocks of the summit came the wail of the northern panther.

"I was startled wide-awake; and the little vision faded instantly into a consciousness of the open heaven, the white lake, and that lonely, haunted summit.

"But it was not altogether the panther that had startled me. It was Dan, who had sprung almost over my head toward the hillside, and now stood trembling with wrath.

"At the command of his master he stalked back and sat down again; but he faced the hillside, and never withdrew his fierce gaze from the spot whence the sound had seemed to come.

"'Never mind him, old dog,' said H—— soothingly; 'you can't get at him, you know.'

"'What makes Dan so excited?' I asked. 'I never saw him so much worked up before. See, he's fairly quivering!'

"'Oh,' replied H——, 'there's no love lost between Dan and the Indian devils. That yelling stirs up some lively reminiscences in his old pate. He thinks that Indian devil is coming right down here to tackle me. See how he keeps me in his eye! And see him turn his muzzle round now

and then to lick those scars of his. I'll venture
to say he feels them smart now, when he remem-
bers the night he got them at the head of the
Little Tobique.'

"'Let's have it, old man,' I urged. 'You've
never told me about that scrape. I've been taking those scars as a certificate of Dan's fighting
propensities.'

"'Do you suppose any *dog*,' said H —— in a
tone of disdain, 'could carve Dan up in that
style? Not by a good deal! It was a big Indian
devil that undertook the contract. He accomplished the frescoing in a very elaborate fashion,
as you see. But he didn't survive the job.'

" H —— compressed his lips, and added, ' I can
tell you, my dear boy, that was something like an
Indian devil, that fellow, and came mighty near
settling my claims for me. He measured six feet
from tip of nose to tip of tail, and you know what
a poor sort of thing they all have for a tail. It
was Dan saved my life that night.'

" Pete and I settled ourselves more comfortably
against our log cushions. Dan, having heard no
more yells from the hilltop, and having perceived
that the conversation concerned himself, curled
himself up with a gratified air, and thrust his
great head into his master's lap.

"'You remember,' resumed H ——, 'last year
I went to the Tobique all by myself, except for
Dan's company. I was gone six weeks and more.

When I got back to Fredericton you were off up Quebec way, and so I never happened to tell you about the trip.

" 'Well, I had the best fishing you can conceive of. It was far better than any we've ever had together in those streams. But as for the panthers, I never heard anything like them. They used to howl round the woods at night in a frightful way.

" 'Dan used to keep awake all night, watching for them. But they never ventured near the camp. They didn't disturb me; but if I had not had Dan with me I might have felt a little shaky, perhaps, at night. I had rather a contempt for the brutes at that time, but they were not much help to a fellow when he was feeling lonely.

" 'You know that pretty cove on the right shore of the Little Tobique, about a hundred yards from where the brook flows in? On that patch of open just on top of the bank I pitched my tent. By the time the camp was fixed, and the fish fried for supper, it was getting pretty well past sundown. It was a gorgeous moonlight night, as bright as day. There wasn't a mosquito about. I tell you I felt pretty nice as I lifted the pink flakes of fried trout onto my plate, and fixed a dish for Dan.

" 'I was getting out the hardtack, when I saw a whopping big trout jump, just by the mouth of the brook. It was bigger than any I had caught so far, and I could not bear to lose the chance of taking him while he was feeding.

"'I set down my plate, telling Dan to watch it, seized my rod, tied on a cast of white and gray millers, and struck hurriedly through the bushes toward the other side of the cove, where I thought I could get a fair cast.

"'You know what sort of a place that shore is, — all banks and bowlders, and thickets and little gullies; and some of those gullies are hidden by fallen trees, or grown over with weeds and vines. You have to keep your eyes open, or you are liable to tumble into these pitfalls. I was in a hurry, and plunged right ahead. I wanted to catch that trout and get back to my supper.

"'At last, about sixty or seventy yards from the camp, I dodged round a thick fir-bush, and saw right in front of me something that brought me up mighty short, I can tell you.

"'Not ten feet away, crouched along the top of a white bowlder, lay a huge Indian devil just ready to spring.

"'I felt queer right down to my boots, but kept my eyes fixed on those of the brute, which gleamed like two emeralds in the moonlight. My right hand reached for my belt, and I stealthily drew my old sheath-knife. At the same time I whistled sharply for Dan.

"'The brute was on the very point of springing when I whistled; but the shrill sound startled him, and deterred him for a moment. He glanced uneasily from side to side, half rising. Then he drew himself together again for his spring.

"'Before he could launch himself forth, I hurled the butt of my fishing-rod full in his face, and sprang aside. I saw the long body flash toward me, and at the same instant I crashed through a tangle of underbrush, and sank into one of those gullies.

"'Instinctively I threw out my left arm to save myself. My grasp caught a tree-root on the edge of the hole. The next instant I felt the panther's teeth sink into my arm. I didn't know how deep that hole was, but I wanted to be at the bottom of it right away.

"'At the risk of stabbing myself, I slashed desperately above my head with my free right hand. It was not a breath too soon; for at that very instant the brute had reached down with the amiable intention of clawing my head. The knife went through his paw, which he snatched back, snarling fiercely. But he kept his grip on my arm.

"'Then I heard Dan come tearing through the brush. I lunged again, blindly of course; and this time the blade went through the panther's jaw and into my own flesh. The brute let go; and I rolled to the foot of the gully, a distance of some five or six feet. Even as I fell I heard Dan's vindictive cough as he sank his teeth into his adversary's throat. There was a mad snarl from the big cat, a struggle — and the two rolled down on top of me.

"'I got out of the way in a great hurry. At first it was too dark down there to distinguish the combatants. In a moment, however, my eyes got used to the gloom. The two animals were almost inextricably mixed up. Dan's grip was right under the panther's jaw, so that he could not make any use of his teeth. The wary old dog had drawn himself up into a tight ball, so as to expose as little of himself as possible to the attack of his enemy's claws. But his back and haunches were getting terribly mangled.

"'Dan fought in silence; but the Indian devil made noise enough for both, and the yelling down in that little hole was fiendish. I felt my left arm, and found it was not broken. Then I sprang on the Indian devil, seized him by the tail, and tried to jerk his hind legs clear of Dan.

"'His back was bowed up into a half-circle, and there was no unbending that arch of steel.

"'I dug the knife twice into his side, and he paid no attention to it, so absorbed was he in the life-and-death struggle with Dan. If left to themselves I saw that the fight would end with the death of both. Dan was inexorably working through the throat of his foe, but was in a fair way to be torn to pieces before he could get this accomplished.

"'I threw myself on the panther's hindquarters, twining my left arm around his supple loins, and with my right hand I reached for his heart.

"'See the length of this blade? I drove it in to the hilt three times behind that brute's fore shoulder before I fetched him. Then he straightened out and fell over.

"'It was some time before I could persuade Dan to drop him. The poor old fellow was so torn he could hardly walk. I picked him up in my arms, — though it's no joke to carry a dog of his weight, — and lugged him back to the camp.

"'We were a sight to see when we got there, a mass of blood from head to foot.

"'I stayed at that camp four days, nursing Dan and myself, before we were able to start for home; and then we *had* to go, for fear we'd be starved out. I thanked my stars and your old-time injunctions that I had taken the little medicine-case along with me. It might have gone hard with us but for that.'

"As H —— concluded, Pete grunted in astonishment and admiration. Indeed, these expressive grunts of his had furnished a running fire of comment throughout the narrative. For myself, I fetched a deep breath, got up, and went over to embrace Dan. As I rose, I cast my eyes up the mountain, and exclaimed, —

"'Talk of angels and you'll see their wings, eh? Look there!' H —— and Pete followed my gaze.

Far up, in the whiteness of the moonlight, we saw a stealthy form creep across a surface of bare rock. Dan saw it too, and every muscle became rigid.

"The form disappeared in a thick covert, and a moment later there issued again upon the stillness that strange, blood-curdling cry. It sounded like a challenge to the hero of H ——'s story.

"But the challenge went unheeded. H —— ordered Dan into the tent. In a few minutes we were wrapped in our blankets, and the panthers had the wilderness all to themselves."

"What became of Dan at last?" inquired Sam.

"Poisoned three years ago; but I made the brutes that did it smart for it!" said I, shutting my teeth with a snap.

"Hanging would have been none too bad for them!" growled Stranion. From this the talk wandered to dogs in general; and each man, of course, sang the praises of his own, till presently Stranion cried, "Douse the glim!" and we rolled into our blankets.

CHAPTER VII.

THE CAMP ON THE TOLEDI.

In the morning we set out at a reasonable hour, planning to camp that night at the foot of Toledi Lake. The last few miles.of the Squatook River were easy paddling, save that here and there a fallen tree was in the way. In passing these obstructions Stranion proved unlucky. His canoe led the procession, with himself standing erect, alert, pole in hand, in the stern, while Queerman sat lazily in the bow. At length we saw ahead of us a tree-trunk stretching across the channel. By ducking our heads down to the gunwales there was room to pass under it. But Stranion tried a piece of gymnastics, like a circus-rider jumping through a hoop. He attempted to step over the trunk while the canoe was passing under it. In this he partly succeeded. He got one foot over, according to calculation, and landed it safely in the canoe. But as for the other — well, a malicious little projecting branch took hold of it by the moccasin, and held on with the innate pertinacity of inanimate things. The canoe wouldn't wait, so Stranion remained behind with his captive foot. He dropped head-first into the water, whence we rescued him.

The next time we came to an obstruction of this kind Stranion didn't try to step over it. He stooped to go under it. But another malicious branch now came to the front. The branch was long, strong, and sharp. It reached down, seized the back of Stranion's shirt, and almost dragged him out of the canoe. Failing in this, — for Stranion's blood was up, — it ripped the shirt open, and ploughed a long red furrow down his back. It took an ocean of glycerine and arnica to assuage that wound.

On the upper Toledi we found a brisk wind blowing. Hoisting improvised sails, we sped down the lake without labor. On the lower lake (the two sheets of water are separated only by a short "thoroughfare") the wind failed us, and we had to resume our paddling. It was late in a golden, hazy afternoon when we drew near the outlet.

Here we overhauled an ancient Indian who had been visiting his traps up the lake. We recognized him as one "Old Martin," a well-known hunter and trapper. He was plying his paddle with philosophic deliberation in the stern of the most dilapidated old canoe I have ever seen afloat. His salutation to us was a grunt; but when we invited him to camp near us and have a bit of supper with us he, quickly became more civil.

Round the camp-fire that night, with a good supper comforting his stomach, Old Martin forgot the red man's taciturnity. Sam was busy frying tobacco, while the rest of us lounged aoout in the glow, testing the results of these culinary experiments. It will be remembered that when the upset took place at Squatook Falls, our tobacco was almost all shut up in a certain tin box which we fondly fancied to be water-proof. When the little store in the other canoes was exhausted, we turned to this tin box. Alas, that box was just so far water-proof as to let in the water and keep it from running out! We found a truly delectable mess inside. Sam had undertaken to dry this mess, out of which all the benign quality was pretty well steeped. He pressed it therefore, and rolled it tenderly, and spread it out in the frying-pan over a gentle fire, until it was quite dry. But oh, it was not good to smoke! Keeping a little to trifle with, we bestowed all the rest of it upon the poor Indian, whose untutored mind led him to accept it gratefully. Perchance he threw it away when our backs were turned.

Suddenly Sam's task was interrupted by a wailing, desolate, and terrible cry, coming apparently from the shores of the upper lake. We gazed at each other with wide eyes, and instinctively drew nearer the fire; while Sam cried, " Ugh, what's that? it must be Cerberus himself got loose!" Old Martin grunted, "Gluskâp's hunting-dog! Big storm bime-by, mebbe!" He looked awed, but not afraid. He said it would not come near us. It was heard sometimes in the night and far off, as now, but no man of the present days had ever seen the dog. It ranged up and down throughout these regions, howling for its master, whom now it would never find. For Gluskâp had been struck down in a deep valley north of the St. Lawrence, and a mountain placed upon him, so that neither could he stir nor anybody find him. So Martin explained that grim sound.

We learned afterwards that the cry was one of the rarer utterances of the loon; but had any one told us so that night we would not have believed him. We preferred to accept the weird notion of the faithful phantom hound seeking forever his vanished master, the beneficent Indian demigod.

About the time supper was done the weather had changed. While Sam was frying his tobacco, the soft summery sweetness fled from the air, and a cold wind set in, blowing down out of the north. It was a strange and unseasonable wind, and pierced our bones. We heaped the camp-fire to a threefold height, and huddled in our blankets between the blaze and the lee of the tent. Then Stranion was called on for a story.

TRACKED BY A PANTHER.

" Boys," said he, " the air bites shrewdly. It is a nipping and an eager air. In fact, it puts me forcibly in mind of one of my best adventures, which befell me that winter when I was trapping on the Little Sou'west Miramichi."

" Oh, come ! Tell us a good *summer* story, old man," interrupted Queerman. " I'm half-frozen as it is, to-night. Tell us about some place down in the tropics where they have to cool their porridge with boiling water."

" Nay," replied Stranion ; " my thoughts are wintry, and even so must my story be."

He traced in the air a few meditative circles with his pipe (which he rarely smoked, using it rather for oratorical effect), and then resumed : —

" That was a hard winter of mine on the Little Sou'west. I enjoyed it at the time, and it did me good ; but, looking back upon it now, I wonder what induced me to undertake it. I got the experience, and I indulged my hobby to the full ; but by spring I felt like a barbarian. It is a fine thing, boys, as we all agree, to be an amateur woodsman, and it brings a fellow very close to nature ; but it is much more sport in summer than in winter, and it's better when one has good company than when he's no one to talk to but a preternaturally gloomy Melicite.

" I had Noël with me that winter, — a good hunter and true, but about as companionable as a mud-turtle. Our traps were set in two great circuits, one on the south side of the stream, the other on the north. The range to the north was in my own charge, and a very big charge it was.

When I had any sort of luck, it used to take me a day and a half to make the round; for I had seventeen traps to tend, spread out over a range of about twenty miles. But when the traps were not well filled, I used to do it without sleeping away from camp. It's not much like play, I can tell you, tramping all day on snow-shoes through those woods, carrying an axe, a fowling-piece, food, ammunition, and sometimes a pack of furs. Whenever I had to sleep out, I would dig a big oblong hole in the snow, build a roaring fire at one end of the hole, bury myself in hemlock boughs at the other end, and snooze like a dormouse till morning. I relied implicitly on the fire to keep off any bears or Indian devils that might be feeling inquisitive as to whether I would be good eating.

"The snow must have been fully six feet deep that year. One morning near the last of February I had set out on my round, and had made some three miles from our shanty, when I caught sight of a covey of partridges in the distance, and turned out of my way to get a shot at them. It had occurred to me that perchance a brace of them might make savory morsels for my supper. After a considerable *détour*, I bagged my birds, and recovered my trail near the last trap I had visited. My tracks, as I had left them, had been solitary enough; but now I found they were accompanied by the footprints of a large Indian devil.

"I didn't really expect to get a shot at the beast, but I loaded both barrels with ball-cartridges. As I went on, however, it began to strike me as strange that the brute should happen to be going so far in my direction. Step for step his footprints clung to mine. When I reached the place where I had branched off in search of the partridges, I found that the panther had branched off with me. So polite a conformity of his ways to mine could have but one significance. I was being tracked!

"The idea, when it first struck me, struck me with too much force to be agreeable. It was a very unusual proceeding on the part of an Indian devil, displaying a most imperfect conception of the fitness of things. That I should hunt him was proper and customary, but that he should think of hunting me was presumptuous and most unpleasant. I resolved that he should be made to repent it before night.

"The traps were unusually successful that trip, and at last I had to stop and make a *cache* of my spoils. This unusual delay seemed to mislead my wily pursuer, who suddenly came out of a thicket while I was hidden behind a tree-trunk. As he crept stealthily along on my tracks, not fifty yards away, I was disgusted at his sleuth-hound persistence and crafty malignity. I raised my gun to my shoulder, and in another moment would have rid myself of his undesired attentions, but the animal must have caught a gleam from the shining barrels, for he turned like a flash, and buried himself in the nearest thicket.

"It was evident that he did not wish the matter forced to an immediate issue. As a consequence, I decided that it ought to be settled at once. I ran toward the thicket; but at the same time the panther stole out on the other side, and disappeared in the woods.

"Upon this I concluded that he had become scared, and given up his unhallowed purpose. For some hours I dismissed him from my mind, and tended my traps without further apprehension. But about the middle of the afternoon, or a little later, when I had reached the farthest point on my circuit, I once more became impressed with a sense that I was being followed. The impression grew so strong that it weighed upon me, and I determined to bring it to a test. Taking some luncheon from my pocket, I sat down behind a tree to nibble and wait. I suppose I must have sat there ten minutes, hearing nothing, seeing nothing, so that I was about to give it up, and continue my tramp, when — along came the panther! My gun was levelled instantly, but at that same instant the brute had disappeared. His eyes were sharper than mine. 'Ah!' said I to myself, 'I shall have to keep a big fire going to-night, or this fellow will pay me a call when I am snoring!'"

"Oh, surely not!" murmured Queerman pensively. The rest of us laughed; but Stranion only waved his pipe with a gesture that commanded silence, and went on: —

"About sundown I met with an unlucky accident, which dampened both my spirits and my powder. In crossing a swift brook, at a place where the ice was hardly thick enough to hold up its covering of snow, I broke through and was soaked. After fishing myself out with some difficulty, I found my gun was full of water which had frozen as it entered. Here was a pretty fix! The weapon was for the present utterly useless. I feared that most of my cartridges were in like condition. The prospect for the night, when the Indian devil should arrive upon the scene, was not a cheerful one. I pushed on miserably for another mile or so, and then prepared to camp.

"First of all, I built such a fire as I thought would impress upon the Indian devil a due sense of my importance and my mysterious powers. At a safe distance from the fire I spread out my cartridges to dry, in the fervent hope that the water had not penetrated far enough to render them useless. My gun I put where it would thaw as quickly as possible.

"Then I cut enough firewood to blaze all night. With my snow-shoes I dug a deep hollow at one side of the fire. The fire soon melted the snow beneath it, and brought it down to the level

whereon I was to place my couch. I may say
that the ground I had selected was a gentle slope,
and the fire was below my bed, so that the melting snow could run off freely. Over my head
I fixed a good, firm ' lean-to ' of spruce saplings,
thickly thatched with boughs. Thus I secured
myself in such a way that the Indian devil could
come at me only from the side on which the fire
was burning. Such approach, I congratulated myself, would be little to his Catship's taste.

"By the time my shelter was completed, it was
full night in the woods. My fire made a ruddy
circle about the camp, and presently I discerned
the panther gliding in and out among the tree-
trunks on the outer edges of the circle. He
stared at me with his round green eyes, and I
returned the gaze with cold indifference. I was
busy putting my gun in order. I would not
encourage him, lest he might grow too familiar
before I was ready for his reception.

"Between my gleaming walls of snow I had
worked up a temperature that was fairly tropical.
Away up overhead, among the pine-tops, a few
large stars glimmered lonesomely. How far away
seemed the world of my friends on whom these
same stars were looking down! I wondered how
those at home would feel if they could see me
there by my solitary camp-fire, watched relent-
lessly by that prowling and vindictive beast.

"Presently, finding that I made no attack upon

him, the brute slipped noiselessly up to within a dozen paces of the fire. There he crouched down in the snow and glared upon me. I hurled a flaming brand at him, and he sprang backward, snarling, into the gloom. But the brand spluttered in the snow and went out, whereupon the brute returned to his post. Then I threw another at him; but he regarded it this time with contempt, merely drawing aside to give it room. When it had gone black out, he approached, pawed it over, and sniffed in supremest contempt. Then he came much nearer, so that I thought he was about to spring upon me. I moved discreetly to the other side of the fire.

"By this time the gun was ready for action, but not so the cartridges. They were lying farther from the fire and dangerously near my unwelcome visitor. I perceived that I must make a diversion at once.

"Selecting a resinous stick into which the fire had eaten deeply, so that it held a mass of glowing coals, I launched it suddenly with such careful aim that it struck right between the brute's fore-legs. As it scorched there, he caught and bit at it angrily, dropped it with a screaming snarl, and shrank farther away. When he crouched down, biting the snow, I followed up my advantage by rushing upon him with a blazing roll of birch-bark. He did not await my onset. but bounded off among the trees, where I could hear

him grumbling in the darkness over his smarting
mouth. I left the bark blazing in the snow while
I went back to see to my precious cartridges.

" Before long the panther reappeared at the
limits of the lighted circle, but seemed not quite
so confident as before. Nevertheless, it was clear
that he had set his heart on making a meal of
me, and was not to be bluffed out of his design by
a few firebrands.

" I discovered that all my ball-cartridges were
spoiled ; but there were a few loaded with shot
which the water had not penetrated. From these
I withdrew the shot, and substituted ball and
slugs. Then, slipping a ball-cartridge into one
barrel, slugs into the other, and three or four
extra cartridges into a handy pocket, I waited
for my opponent to recover his confidence. As
he seemed content to wait a while, I set about
broiling my partridges, for I was becoming clam-
orously hungry.

" So also was the panther, as it seemed. When
the odor of those partridges stole seductively to
his nostrils, he once more approached my fire ; and
this time with an air of stern determination quite
different from his former easy insolence.

" The crisis had come. I seized my gun, and
knelt down behind the fire. I arranged a burning log in such a manner that I could grasp and
wield it with both hands in an emergency. Just
as the animal drew himself together for a spring,

"MAD WITH PAIN AND FURY, HE SPRANG." — Page 249.

I fired one barrel, — that containing the ball, — and shattered his lower jaw. Mad with pain and fury, he sprang. The contents of my second barrel, a heavy charge of slugs, met him full in the breast, and he fell in a heap at my feet.

" As he lay there, struggling and snarling and tearing up the snow, I slipped in another cartridge ; and the next moment a bullet in his brain put an end to his miseries.

" After this performance, I ate my partridges with a very grateful heart, and slept the sleep of the just and the victorious. The skin of that audacious Indian devil lies now in my study, where Sam is continually desecrating it with his irreverent shoes."

" Good story, Stranion," said Magnus with grave approval. " The only thing hard to believe is that you should make two such good shots."

" Well, you see I had to," responded Stranion. " And now let Magnus give us a hot story to satisfy Queerman."

" I don't think I know another tropical yarn," said Magnus.

" I'll give you one," said Sam, " and a bear story it is too. It's about a scrape I got into when I was down in Florida three years ago, looking after Uncle Bill's oranges. I'll call it —

'AN ADVENTURE IN THE FLORIDA HUMMOCKS.'

"I was boarding at a country house not far from the banks of the Caloosahatchee River, in a district full of game. Most of my time was spent in wandering with gun and dog through the luxuriant woods that clothed the hummocks, and along the edges of the waving savannas or interval meadows. The dog which always accompanied me was a large mongrel, half setter and half Newfoundland, belonging to my landlord. He was plucky and intelligent, but untrained; and I used to take him rather as a companion than as an assistant.

"The soil in Florida is generally very sandy; but in the hummocks, or, as they are more usually called in Florida, 'hammocks,' the sand is mixed with clay, and carries a heavy growth of timber. The trees are chiefly dogwood, pine, magnolia, and the several species of oak which grow in the South. These 'hammocks' vary in extent from one or two to a thousand or more acres, and in many places the trees are so interlaced with rankly growing vines that one can penetrate the forest only by the narrow cattle-paths leading to the water.

"One afternoon I was threading a path which led through a particularly dense hummock to the bank of a wide, shallow stream, known as Dogwood Creek, a branch of the Caloosahatchee. I carried a light double-barrelled fowling-p.ece, and was seeking no game more formidable than wild turkeys. My cartridges were loaded with No. 2 shot, but I had taken the precaution to drop a couple of ball-cartridges in among the rest.

" Presently there was a heavy crashing amid the dense undergrowth on my right; and Bruce, the dog, who had dropped a few paces behind, drew quickly up to my side with an angry growl. The hair lifted along his back and between his ears.

" As the crashing rapidly came nearer, — startlingly near, in fact. — I made haste to remove my light cartridges and replace them with ball. But, alas! to unload was one thing, to find one of those two ball-cartridges in the crowded depths of my capacious pocket was quite another. Every cartridge I brought to light was marked, with exasperating plainness, No. 2.

" In my eager haste the perspiration stood out all over my face. I knew well enough what was coming. It was unquestionably a bear. A panther would move more quietly; and a stray steer would cause no such great concern to Bruce. Whatever may have been my emotions, surprise was certainly not among them when, just as I had concluded that those two ball-cartridges must have been a dream, a huge bear, which seemed very angry about something, burst mightily forth into the pathway only three or four yards behind me.

"It was not hard to decide what to do. On either hand was the thicket, to me practically impenetrable; and behind was the bear. Straight ahead I ran at the top of my speed. At the same time I managed to slip a couple of cartridges into my gun. They were just whatever ones came to my hand; but devoutly I hoped against hope that they might prove, when tested, to be those which were loaded with ball.

"For perhaps two or three hundred yards the running was distinctly in my favor, but then the pace began to tell on me. At once I slackened speed, and my pursuer closed in upon me so swiftly that I concluded to try a snap shot.

"Facing about with a sharp yell, I expected the bear to rise on his hind legs and give me a fair chance for a shot. But I had miscalculated my own momentum. The bear, indeed, rose as I expected. But at the same instant I tripped on a root and fell headlong. The gun flew up in the air in a wonderful way, and disappeared in the undergrowth.

"To recover it was, I knew, impossible. Almost before I touched the ground I was on my feet again, and running faster than ever. But what refuge there was for me to run to I knew not, and how the affair was going to end I dared not guess.

"In the first burst of my renewed vigor, and while the bear was recovering from his natural surprise at my extraordinary manœuvre, I had regained my lost ground. All at once, as my breath was about forsaking me, the path opened before my eyes upon a grassy savanna, beyond which shone the waters of Dogwood Creek. At the water's edge was drawn up an old flat boat, with a pole sticking out over the bow. This craft was evidently used as a ferry to connect with a continuation of the path on the other side of the creek.

"I darted forward, thrust the punt off, and flung myself into it. An energetic push with the pole, and the little craft shot out into the stream. Bruce, meanwhile, ran up along the water's edge, barking furiously, and the bear pursued him.

"Calling the dog to come to me, I pushed the punt towards him. With a frightened whine, which I did not at the moment understand, he plunged into the water and swam out bravely. The bear hesitated a second or two, and then dashed in after him, raising a tremendous splash.

"When Bruce was within a couple of yards of the boat, I was enlightened as to the cause of his reluctance to take the water. An ugly black snout, not unlike the butt of a water-logged timber, was thrust into view close by; then another, a few feet below the desperately swimming animal; then another, and yet another, till the sullen, whitish surface of the creek was dotted thickly with the heads of alligators. They had evidently been attracted by the sound of Bruce's barking; and I called to mind some stories I had heard at the house as to the abundance and ferocity of the alligators in Dogwood Creek.

"A sturdy shove on the pole, and I was at Bruce's side. Reaching over, I seized him by the scruff of the neck, and jerked him into the boat, just as a tremendous swirl in the water behind him showed where an alligator had made a rush for his legs.

"The next instant the snout of the disappointed animal shot up beside the gunwale, to receive a fierce jab from my pole, which made it keep its distance.

"By this time the bear was dangerously near at hand. He was approaching with great wallowing plunges, the water not being deep enough to compel him to swim. I began to pole with all my might, thinking that even yet I was far from being out of the difficulty. With a few thrusts I put a safe distance between myself and my pursuer, but the creek was not wide·enough to enable me to gain any very great head start in this way. In a most discontented frame of mind I had almost reached the landing, when suddenly it occurred to me that really there was no necessity for me to land at once. I could pole up and down the creek, and dodge the bear until he should get tired and give up the chase. With this purpose I thrust out again boldly into mid-stream.

" The bear was now almost half-way across, but those black snouts were closing about him ominously. Indeed, the animal must have been blinded with rage, or he would never have ventured into the deadly stream. In a moment, however, it seemed to dawn upon him that he had got himself into trouble. He stopped with an uneasy sort of whine. Then he turned, and made for the shore as fast as he could.

" But it was too late for him to escape in that way. His path was blocked by several of the great reptiles, whose appetites were now thoroughly aroused. I thought to myself, 'If that bear is game, there's going to be a lively time around here just now.'

" And he *was* game. True, seeing that the odds were so overwhelmingly against him, he had at first tried to avoid the combat. But now that he was fairly in for it, he acquitted himself in a way that soon won my sympathetic admiration, and made me forget that but a moment before he had been thirsting for my own blood.

" With a huge grunt of indignant defiance, the bear hurled himself upon the nearest alligator. On the massive armor of the reptile's back even his powerful claws made slight impression; but with one paw he reached to the soft under-side of the throat, and the water was suddenly crimsoned, as the alligator, lashing the surface with his tail, made off and took refuge in a bed of reeds.

"At the same instant, however, the jaws of another assailant closed upon the animal's flank. With a roar he rose straight up in the water, shaking himself so mightily that his adversary's hold was broken. Then he threw his whole bulk on another which was advancing against him in front. The alligator was borne under and disappeared, probably forever *hors de combat*, and the bear gained several yards toward safety. Then others crowded in upon him, and his progress was stopped.

"Up to this time my sympathies had naturally been with the alligators, to whom I owed my release from an embarrassing situation. Now, however, I felt myself going over to the side of the bear. I hated to see the splendid, though to me very objectionable, brute thus at the mercy of a horde of ravening reptiles.

"Again shaking off his assailants, the bear seemed merely bent on selling his life as dearly as possible. Rising on his hindquarters, he faced toward the centre of the stream, where his foes were most numerous. What tremendous buffeting blows he dealt, and how the strong knife-edged hooks of his claws searched out the unarmored spots on his adversaries! In my excitement I pushed perilously near, and if I had had my lost gun I should certainly have taken a hand in the contest myself. I would have given a good deal at that moment to be able to help the bear.

"But the odds were too great for any strength or pluck to long contend against. Before many minutes the bear was dragged under, and there was nothing to be seen but a heaving, lashing, foaming mass of alligators. On the outskirts of the *mêlée* swam a few hungry reptiles, who could not get in to the division of the spoils. These presently turned their attention to the boat, purposing to console themselves with Bruce and me.

"Awaking to the peril of the situation, I began poling hurriedly toward the landing-place whence I had first started. But almost instantly I was surrounded with alligators. Excited and enraged from their battle with the bear, they were much more formidable than at ordinary times. I had great reason to be thankful for the skill in poling which I had acquired in the birch-bark canoes of our Northern rivers. Dodging some of my assailants, I beat off others with the pole, thrusting fiercely at their wicked little eyes, which is the surest way to daunt them.

"All at once there was a wild yelp from Bruce, and the punt reeled sharply. The gunwale went under water, and I was all but pitched out head-first into the swarm of alligators. My heart was in my mouth as, with a swift and violent motion of the pole, I recovered my balance, and steadied the boat. But with all my terror I had room for a pang of grief as I saw that poor Bruce had bee. dragged overboard.

" The capture of the dog, however, was probably my salvation. The alligators which were in front of the boat darted into the scramble which was taking place over the new victim, and I saw a clear space between me. and the safety of the shore. Desperately I surged on the pole, and the light craft shot in among the sedges. As the prow lifted onto solid ground, several of the long snouts rose over the stern, snapping greedily ; but I had bounded forward like lightning, and was beyond their reach in a second. I paused not till I was clear of the savanna and among the timber.

" Throwing myself down on the reeking mould of the path, I lay there till I had recovered my breath, and a measure of my equanimity. Then, after finding my gun in the depths of a mimosa thicket, I wended my way homeward, much depressed over the fate of Bruce."

" Talking of dogs," said Queerman, " *I'll* tell you a story with a dog in it. And it's got other things in it too. A college story, by way of a change. Come to think of it, though we are all college men, there has been very little in our stories to indicate the fact."

" By all means, Kelly Queerman," said Sam, " let's have the college story at once ! "

" Well, to give it a proper scholastic flavor, I will entitle it —

"DESPERATELY I SURGED ON THE POLE." — Page 258.

'THE JUNIOR LATIN SCHOLARSHIP.'

"The sunshine of mid-May streamed alluringly into the great stone portico of the old college of X——. The wide-winged gray edifice stood on a high terrace just under the crest of the hill, its ample windows looking down over the topmost boughs of ash and elm and maple over the roofs and spires of the little university town of X——, and out to the broad blue curve of the placid river. On the steps, lounged a group of students, members of the Senior and Junior years. Several of the loiterers stood close to the open, arched door, and from time to time glanced expectantly into the hall. A large black dog, a cross between Spitz and Newfoundland, lay in the centre of the hall, assiduously licking at a small but angry wound on his leg.

" At the farther end of the hall now appeared one of the professors. He stepped in front of the notice-board, and pinned a slip of white paper to the green baize-covered surface. In a moment the portico was cleared; and the men crowded in to read the announcement. They did not rush noisily, as Freshmen, or even Sophomores, might have done; but their eagerness was tempered with dignity. The Seniors, in particular, were careful to be properly deliberate; for announcements were expected by both classes, and this might prove to be merely a Junior list!

"It *was* a Junior list. Leaning on each other's shoulders, the Juniors clustered around the board, while the Seniors lingered on the outskirts, and inquired with polite interest about the results. They were mindful that these Juniors would very soon be Seniors, and were therefore to be treated with a good deal of consideration. Then they dropped away in twos and threes, while the Juniors remained to take down the marks.

"The marks which excited so much interest were those of the third terminal examination in Latin. A Latin scholarship, of the value of one hundred dollars, was dependent on the results of three terminals, compulsory for all the Latin students of the Junior class, and on a special examination to be held at the very end of the term. This examination was open only to those declaring themselves competitors for the scholarship. It was generally expected throughout the college that the winner would be Bert Knollys, who, without effort, had gained a slight lead in the first two terminals, and whose ability in classics was unquestioned.

"At the top of the present announcement stood Knollys's name with percentage of eighty-six. The second name on the list was that of J. S. Wright, with eighty-three to his credit.

" 'Wright's pulling up! Five more points will put him ahead!' was the remark of one man who had been figuring on his pad.

" Wright, a sharp-featured, sandy-haired fellow in the centre of the group, nodded his approval of this calculation. At the same moment, a slim youth of barely middle height, with laughing gray eyes and crisply-waving hair, ran up and peered eagerly through the throng of his comrades. Having deciphered his standing, he was turning away as abruptly as he had come, when some one said, —

" ' You'd better look out, Knollys ! Wright is after you with a sharp stick ! '

" ' I don't doubt Jack can beat me if he tries ! ' responded Knollys.

" ' Hold on a minute, Bert ; I want to talk to you a bit ! ' exclaimed a tall Junior by the name of Will Allison, extricating himself quickly from the crowd.

" ' Next hour, old man ! ' cried Knollys, darting away. ' I've got to catch Dawson in the laboratory, right off, and can't wait a second ! '

" Allison, who was Knollys's most intimate friend, crossed the hall, and joined a Senior who was lounging in a window overlooking the terrace.

" ' It's my firm belief, Jones,' said he discontentedly, ' that that cad, Jack Wright, is going to play Bert false ! '

" ' How so, pray ? ' inquired the Senior, in a tone of very moderate interest.

" ' Why, by going into the special exam., of course ! ' replied Allison.

"'And why *shouldn't* he, as well as Knollys, go into the special examination?' asked Jones.

"'Oh, I thought every one knew about that!' exclaimed Allison somewhat impatiently. 'But it's this way, since you inquire. Wright took the scholarship for our class last year—the Second Year Greek, you know. Well, Knollys was way ahead on the average of the terminals, and would have had a walk-over. As every man in the class knows, he can wipe out all the rest of us in classics without half trying. But Wright went to him, and made a poor mouth about being so hard up that he'd have to leave college if he didn't get the scholarship. Bert has none too much cash himself; but in his generous way he agreed not to go in for the special exam. So Wright, of course, got the scholarship. In return he promised Knollys that he would not go in for the Junior Latin the following year. This suited Bert very well, as he wanted to put his hard work on his readings for the science medal. Under these circumstances, you see, he has been taking it rather easy in the Latin; and I have reason to believe that Wright has been working extra hard at it. Mark my words, he'll go in at the last moment and catch Bert napping. But there's not another man in college that I would suspect of such a caddish trick.'

"'Well, for my part," said the Senior, 'I don't greatly care which gets it. I grant you that Wright's a cad; but I'm disappointed in Knollys!'

"'Indeed! Poor Knollys!' murmured Allison.

"'Yes,' continued the Senior loftily, ignoring the sarcasm; 'in my opinion Knollys funks.'

"'It seems to me, Jones,' retorted Allison, 'you forget certain incidents that took place when Bert Knollys was a Freshman, and you a Sophomore!'"

"'Oh,' said the Senior, calmly looking over Allison's head, 'the worm will turn! But what I'm thinking about is his refusal to play foot-ball last fall. He's quick, and sharp, and tough; just the man the team wanted for quarter-back, if only he had the nerve! Said he was too busy to train — indeed!' and Jones sniffed contemptuously as he turned away to join some members of his own class, leaving Allison in a fume of indignation.

"At this moment Jack Wright, chancing to stroll past the big black dog, gave the animal a careless kick. The dog sprang at his assailant with a ferocious snarl. Much startled, Wright evaded the attack by dodging into a knot of his classmates; and the dog lay down again, growling angrily.

"'Bran doesn't seem to be quite himself!' remarked a Senior, eying him narrowly.

"'He'd be an ugly customer to handle if he started to run amuck,' commented another Senior, chuckling at Wright's discomfiture. 'I wonder where he got that bite on his leg!'

"This was something which nobody knew; and the incident was promptly forgotten by all but

Jack Wright, who thenceforth gave the animal a wide berth.

"As soon as Knollys came out of the laboratory, Will Allison told him his suspicions in regard to Wright, and urged him to put his energies upon the Latin. But Knollys was always slow to believe that a comrade could be guilty of treachery.

"'I don't think Wright is really such a bad lot, old man,' said he; 'only his manner is unfortunate, and he isn't popular.'

"Just three days later appeared on the notice-board the announcement that B. Knollys and J. S. Wright were competitors for the Junior Latin scholarship! The examination was to take place on the following morning. Bert Knollys was hurt and indignant; his friends were furious; and Wright looked craftily triumphant over the prospect of so neatly getting ahead of a rival.

"Knollys was by no means prepared for such a contest as he knew Wright was capable of giving him; but his anger nerved him to the utmost effort. Returning in hot haste to his home in the outskirts of the town, he shut himself into his little study. All through the afternoon he toiled mightily over book and lexicon. About tea time he took a short walk, and then settled down for a night of solid "grind." He was bound that he would win if it was in him.

"Toward two o'clock, however, eyes and brain alike grew dim, and the meanings began to mix themselves most vexatiously. He sprang up, snatched his cap, let himself out of the house noiselessly, and set forth to wake his wits by a brisk run.

"For the sake of the freer air he took a path traversing the hilltop toward the college. The path ran through the open pastures, and reached at length a rocky ridge just back of the cottage of Doctor Adams, the professor of classics. Here Jack Wright was boarding. As Knollys swung past along the ridge he glanced downward to the professor's study window; and as he did so a light appeared therein. He halted instinctively; and the next moment his lip was curling with astonished contempt as he saw Jack Wright seat himself before the study table, and stealthily search the drawers. The top of the ridge was so near the window that Knollys, where he leaned against the fence, could see all that went on, as if he had been in the room. At last, after going through almost every drawer with frequent guilty, listening pauses, Wright found what he wanted, an examination paper! After making a hurried copy of it, he returned it to its place; and then, with his lamp turned very low, he stole out of the room.

"Bert Knollys's first thought was to go at once to Doctor Adams, lay his complaint, and have Wright's room searched before he could have time to destroy the stolen copy. Then it occurred to him that this would lead inevitably to Wright's expulsion, and not improbably to his ruin. He therefore dismissed the idea. He hastened back home ; tried to study, but found the effort vain ; went to bed, and fell asleep without having arrived at any solution of the problem. In the morning he was equally undecided. Perhaps his best course would have been to go to the professor, declare a suspicion that the paper had been tampered with, and ask that a new paper be set. But he failed to think of this way out of the difficulty ; and, at last, tired of worrying over it, he made up his mind to do nothing. He went in to the examination, wrote an unusually good paper, and came out feeling that there was yet a chance for him in spite of Wright's previous knowledge of the questions. But on the day following was posted the announcement that Wright was the winner by a lead of three marks on the average for the four examinations.

"The affair was a grievous disappointment to Bert Knollys, and meant the upsetting of all his plans for the summer. He had counted on the scholarship money to enable him to take a long vacation trip with Will Allison. This scheme he had now to abandon ; and Allison could not refrain from reproaching him for his misplaced confidence in Jack Wright. Furthermore, he was accused of petty jealousy by many students outside of his own class ; and his popularity, undermined by

Wright's skilful insinuations, rapidly dwindled away. Smarting under the injustice, and seeing no satisfactory way to remove the misunderstanding, Knollys grew moody and depressed.

"The days slipped by quickly, and Commencement was close at hand. One warm afternoon, a number of the students were in the baseball field, where a practice match was in progress. The college Nine was strenuously preparing for the great Commencement Day match. Knollys, Allison, Jones, and a few others, were lying under the fence on the farther side of the field, while most of the spectators were grouped as close as possible to the players. Jack Wright was at the bat.

"Suddenly in the gate of the college barnyard, above the ball-field, appeared Bran, the dog. The hair lifted along his back-bone and on his neck, and a light froth showed about his half-bared teeth. He was a sinister and menacing figure as he stood there, a strange trouble in his wild, red eyes. After glaring uneasily from side to side for several minutes, he gave utterance to a yelping snarl, and darted down the hillside toward the field. The group under the fence observed him at once.

"'What's the matter with the dog?' exclaimed Jones, in a tone of apprehension; and 'Look at Bran!' shouted some one else. The pitcher stopped in the very act of delivering the ball, and every eye went in the one direction. The dread truth was evident at once. On all sides arose the appalling cry, 'He's mad! Mad dog! Mad dog!' and players and spectators scattered in sickening panic.   As it were in the twinkling of an eye, the field was empty.

"But no! It was not quite empty! Turning in wild terror, and starting to run as he turned, Jack Wright tripped, fell, and snapped his ankle. He got up, and saw himself alone in the wide, sunny field.   The dog had just entered the gate, and was making straight for him with foaming, snapping jaws. He strove to flee, but the shattered ankle gave way beneath him; and, with a piercing cry of horror, he dropped in a heap, burying his face in his hands.

"Knollys, like all the rest, had sprung over the fence at the first alarm; but at that despairing cry he sprang back again. There was no hesitation, no waiting to see what the others would do. Swift as a deer he sped out across the shining and deadly expanse. As he ran, he stooped to snatch up a bat which lay in his path.   It was a question which would win in the awful race; and the crowd of fugitives, checking their flight, watched in spellbound silence.

"The dog arrived first, but only by a foot or two.   As it sprang at Wright's prostrate body Knollys reached out with a fierce lunge, and caught it between the jaws with the end of the bat. Biting madly at the wood, the animal rose on its hind legs, and in a flash Knollys had both hands clenched in a grip of steel about its throat.

"For a few seconds the struggle was a desperate one. The animal's strength was great, and Knollys had all he could do to hold him at arm's length. Then Will Allison arrived, panting, and conscience-stricken for his tardiness. He was followed by two or three others who had broken the spell of their panic. A couple of well-directed blows from the bat in Allison's hands stunned the dog, and it was then speedily despatched.

"Breathing somewhat quickly, but otherwise quite cool, Knollys looked down upon Jack Wright's gastly face.

"'Glad I was in time, Wright!' said he.

"'Bert,' cried Wright, in a shaking voice, "*you* won that scholarship! I just cribbed the whole paper!'

"To thank his rescuer, he felt, was not within the power of words; but reparation was in part possible, and his one thought was to make it.

"'We won't talk of that now,' answered Knollys. 'I know all about it, Jack! I saw the whole thing; and we just won't say anything more about it, old fellow!'

"But Wright had fainted from the pain and the shock, and did not hear the forgiveness in Bert's voice.

"The next day a letter went from Wright's sick-bed to the president of the college. Wright wanted to tell everything; but on Bert's advice he merely confessed that he had cribbed, without saying how, and resigned his claim to the scholarship. At Commencement, therefore, it was announced by the president that the Latin scholarship had been won by B. Knollys. Many conflicting rumors, of course, went abroad among the students; but to no one except Will Allison was the whole truth told. As for Wright, a new point of view seemed all at once to have opened before his eyes. The loftier standard which he now learned to set himself, he adhered to throughout the rest of his course, and then carried forth with him into what have proved very creditable and successful relations with the world."

"Queerman has grown didactic," said I. "That is surely not the tone for a canoe trip. Ranolf, it's your turn to take the platform. Let us have something that is simple, unmedicated adventure!"

"I'll tell you a bicycle story," said Ranolf; "an unromantic tale of a romantic land. It is all about a bull and a bicycle in the land of Evangeline."

A BULL AND A BICYCLE.

"It was in the autumn of 1889, while the old, high wheels were still in use, that I rode through the Evangeline land with a fellow-wheelman from Halifax. We rolled lazily along a well-kept road,

and sang the praises of Nova Scotia's scenery and
air.

" Ahead of us, across a wide, flashing water, the
storied expanse of Minas, towered the blue-black
bastion of Cape Blomidon, capped with rolling
vapors. To our left, and behind us, rose fair,
rounded hills, some thickly wooded, others with
orchards and meadows on their slopes ; while to
our right lay far unrolled those rich diked lands
which the vanished Acadian farmers of old won
back from the sea.

" Though another race now held these lovely
regions, we felt that the landscape, through whatever vicissitudes, must lie changelessly under the
spell of one enchantment, — the touch of the well-
loved poet. We felt that something more than
mere beauty of scene, however wonderful, was
needed to explain the exalted mood which had
taken possession of two hungry wheelmen like
ourselves ; and we acknowledged that additional-
something in the romance of history and song.

" Presently we came to a stretch of road which
had been treated to a generous top-dressing of
loose sand. Such ignorance of the principles of
good road-making soon brought us down both
from our lofty mood and from our laboring
wheels. We trudged toilsomely for nearly half
a mile, saying unkind things now of the Nova
Scotian road-makers, and quite forgetting the
melodious sorrows of the Acadian exiles.

" Then we came to the village of Avonport, and were much solaced by the sight of the village inn.

" In the porch of the unpretentious hostelry we found a fellow 'cycler in a sorely battered condition. Several strips of court-plaster, black and pink, distributed artistically about his forehead, nose, and chin, gave a mightily grotesque appearance to his otherwise melancholy countenance. One of his stockings was rolled down about his ankle, and he was busy applying arnica to a badly bruised shin.

" Against the bench on which he was sitting leaned a bicycle which looked as if it had been in collision with an earthquake.

" The poor fellow's woe-begone countenance brightened up as we entered, and we made ourselves acquainted. He was a solitary tourist from Eastport, Me., and a principal in the important case of Bull *versus* Bicycle, which had just been decided very much in favor of Bull. We dined together, and as our appetites diminished our curiosity increased.

" Presently Caldwell, as the woe-begone 'cyclist called himself, detailed to us his misadventure, as follows ; —

" ' It wasn't more than an hour before you fellows came that I got here myself. I was in a nice mess, I can tell you. But plenty of cold water and Mrs. Brigg's arnica and court-plaster have pulled me together a lot. I only hope we can do as much after dinner for that poor old wheel of mine.

" ' This morning I had a fine trip pretty nearly all the way from Windsor. Splendid weather, wasn't it; and a good hard road most of the way, eh? You remember that long, smooth hill about two miles back from here, and the road that crosses it at the foot, nearly at right angles? Well, as I came coasting down that hill, happy as a clam, my feet over the handles, I almost ran into a party of men, with ropes and a gun, moving along that cross-road.

" 'I stopped for a little talk with them, and asked what they were up to. It appeared that a very dangerous bull had got loose from a farm up the river, and had taken to the road. They were afraid it would gore somebody before they could recapture it. I asked them if they knew which way it had gone; and they told me the " critter ' was sure to make right for the dike lands, where it used to pasture in its earlier and more amiable days.

" ' That cross-road was the way to the dikes, and they pursued it confidently. I took it into my head that it would be a lark to go along with them, and see the capture of the obstreperous animal; but the men, who were intelligent fellows and knew what they were talking about, told me I should find the road too heavy and rough for my wheel. Rather reluctantly I bade them good-morning and continued my journey by the highway.

" 'Now, as a fact, that bull had no notion of going to the dikes. He had turned off the cross-road, and sauntered along the highway, just where he could get most fun, and see the most of life. But I'll venture to say he hadn't counted on meeting a bicycle.

" 'I hadn't gone more than half a mile, or perhaps less, when a little distance ahead of me I noticed some cattle feeding by the roadside. I thought nothing of that, of course ; but presently one of the cattle — a tremendous animal, almost pure white — stepped into the middle of the road and began to paw the mud. Certain anxious questionings arose within me.

" 'Then the animal put his great head to the earth, and uttered a mighty bellow. With much perturbation of spirit I concluded that the angry bull had not betaken himself to the dikes after all.

" 'I felt very bitter toward those men for this mistake, and for not having suffered me to go along with them on their futile errand. They wanted the bull, and wouldn't find him. I, on the other hand, had found him, and I didn't want him at all.

" 'I checked my course, pedalling very slowly, uncertain what to do. The bull stood watching

me. If I turned and made tracks he would catch
me on the hill or on the soft cross-road. If I took
to the woods there was little to gain, for there
were no fences behind. which to take refuge ; and
if I should climb a tree I knew the beast would
demolish my wheel.

" 'Straight ahead, however, as far as I could
see, the road was level and good ; and. in the distance I saw farms and fences. I decided to keep
right on.

" ' The road along there is wide and hard, as
you know, and bordered with a deep ditch. I
put on good speed ; and the bull, as he saw me
approaching, looked a little puzzled. He took
the wheel and me, I presume, for some unheard
of monster. I guessed his meditations, and concluded he was getting frightened.

" 'But there I was mistaken. He was only
getting in a rage. He suddenly concluded that
it was his mission to rid the world of monsters ;
and with a roar he charged down to meet me.

" ' " Now," thought I, "for a trick ! and then a
race, in which I'll show a pretty speedy pair of
heels ! " I rode straight at the bull, who must
have had strange misgivings, though he never
flinched. At the last possible moment I swerved
sharply aside, and swept past the baffled animal
in a fine triumphant curve. Before he could stop
himself and turn I was away down the road at
a pace that I knew would try his mettle.

"'But the brute had a most pernicious energy. He came thundering and pounding along my tracks at a rate that kept me quite busy. I stayed ahead easily enough, but I did not do much more than that for fear of getting winded.

"'There's where I made the mistake, I think. I ought to have done my utmost, in order to discourage and distance my pursuer. I didn't allow for contingencies ahead, but just pedalled along gayly and enjoyed the situation. Of course I kept a sharp lookout, in order that I shouldn't take a header over a stone; but I felt myself master of the situation.

"'At last, and in an evil hour, I came to where they had been mending the road with all that abominable sand. Let us pass over my feelings at this spot. They were indescribable. My wheel almost came to a standstill. Then I called up fresh energies, and bent forward and strained to the task. I went ahead, but it was like wading through a feather-bed; and the bull began to draw nearer.

"'A little in front the fences began. The first was a high board fence, with a gate in it, and a hay-road leading by a rough bridge into the highway. My whole effort now was to make that gate.

"'The perspiration was rolling down my face, half-blinding me. My mighty pursuer was getting closer and closer; and I was feeling pretty well pumped. It was as much as a bargain which would win the race. I dared not look behind, but my anxious ears kept me all too well informed.

"'I reached the bridge and darted across it. Immediately I heard my pursuer's feet upon it. I had no time to dismount. I rode straight at the gate, ran upon it, and shot over it head-first in a magnificent header, landing in a heap of stones and brambles.

"'In a glow of triumph, which at first prevented me feeling my wounds, I picked myself up, and beheld the furious beast in the act of trying to gore my unoffending bicycle.

"'At first he had stopped in consternation, naturally amazed at seeing the monster divided into two parts. The portion which had shot over the gate he perceived to be very like a man; but the other part remained all the more mysterious. Presently he plunged his horns tentatively into the big wheel; whereupon my brave bicycle reared and struck him in the eye with a handle, and set the little wheel crawling up his back.

"'At this the bull was astonished and alarmed —so much so that he backed off a little way. Then, seeing that the bicycle lay motionless on the ground, he charged upon it again, maltreating it shamefully, and tossing it up on his horns.

"'This was too much for me. I ran up, reached over the gate, and laid hold of my precious wheel. By strange good fortune I succeeded in detaching it from the brute's horns and hauling it over the gate. Then I pelted the animal with sticks and stones till he got disgusted and moved away.

"'As soon as he was safely off the scene I opened the gate and limped sorrowfully down to this place, dragging my wheel by my side. Do you think we can do anything with it?'

"'The first thing necessary,' said I, 'is to have an examination, and make a diagnosis of its injuries.''

"This we forthwith proceeded to do, and found the matter pretty serious. After spending an hour in tinkering at the machine we had to give up the job. Then we set forth on a visit to the village blacksmith who, after being regaled with a full account of Caldwell's misadventure, addressed himself to his task with. vast good-will.

"He was a skilful man, and before nightfall the wheel was in better travelling shape than its unlucky owner. But Caldwell was good stuff, and of a merry heart; so that when, on the following day, he became our travelling companion, we found that his scars and his lugubrious countenance only heightened the effect of his good-fellowship."

"I think," said I, "that after a cheerful narrative like Ranolf's you can stand a somewhat bloody one from me."

"All right, O. M.," answered Queerman; "pile on as much gore as you like."

"Don't expect too much," said I. "It's only another wolf story. The name thereof is —

'THE DEN OF THE GRAY WOLF.'

"Not long ago I was doing the Tobique with Joe Maxim, an old hunter whom I think none of you have met. We were dropping smoothly down with the current, approaching the Narrows.

"Maxim was a curious and interesting character. Of good old Colonial stock, and equipped in youth with an excellent education, he had found himself, in early manhood, at odds with society and the requirements of civilized life. Perhaps through some remote ancestor there had crept into his veins a streak of Indian or other wandering blood. At any rate, the wilderness had drawn him with a spell that overcame all counter attractions. He drifted to the remotest backwoods, and there devoted himself to hunting and trapping. Never entering the settlements except to purchase supplies or sell his furs, he had spent the best years of his life in an almost unbroken solitude. Yet the few sportsmen who penetrated to his haunts and sought his skilful services found that seclusion had failed to make him morose. He was kindly, and not uncompanionable; and though in appearance one of the roughest of his adopted class, he preserved to a marked degree the speech and accent of his earlier days.

"'You were speaking just now,' said he, 'of the wolves coming back to New Brunswick. Well, they're here, off and on, most of the time, I reckon. It was not far from here that I had a scrimmage with them about twenty years back.'

"At this point a murmurous roaring began to make itself heard on the still air; and before I could ask any more questions about the wolves, Maxim exclaimed,—

"'We can't go through the "Narrows" to-night. Not light enough with this head of water. Better camp right here.'

"'Agreed!' said I; and we slid gently up along side of a projecting log. Presently we had the tent pitched on a bit of dry, soft sward that sloped ever so little toward the waterside. Behind the tent was a thicket of spruce that sheltered us from the night wind; and in front laughed softly the river, as it hurried along its shining trail beneath the full moon, to bury itself in the chasms of the dark hill-range which separated it from its sovereign, the wide St. John.

"After supper, when the camp-fire was blazing cheerfully, Maxim told me about the wolves.

"'Well,' said he in a reminiscent tone, 'it was in those hills yonder, very near the Narrows, I struck the wolves. I knew there were a good many of them 'round that winter, as I'd come across lots of their tracks. There was a bounty then of fifteen dollars on a wolf's snout,— that was twenty years ago, — and I was keeping my eyes pretty well peeled. My lookout was all in vain, however, till along one afternoon I caught sight of one of the skulking vermin dodging behind some bushes, not far from here. but on the other side of the river. It was only a snap shot I got at the beast, but I wounded it; and you'd better believe I lost no time following up the trail. By the way he bled, I could see that he was hard hit.

"'He led me away up, nigh the top of the mountain, then took a sharp turn to the river; and pretty soon I came out onto a little level place, a sort of high platform, in front of a big, bare slope of rock. In the foot of that rock there was a hole, just about big enough for a man to crawl into on his hands and knees, and into that hole led the trail of my wolf.

"'"Got him, fast enough!" said I to myself; "but how to get at him — there's the rub!" As I stood there considering, *another* wolf slid by me, like a long, gray shadow, and sneaked into the den. Without putting the gun to my shoulder, I gave him a shot, which fetched him in the hind-quarters just as he disappeared. "That's good for thirty dollars," said I to myself, loading up again, and hoping some more would come along.

"'They didn't come; so pretty soon I gave them up, and went and examined the hole. I could see that it narrowed down rapidly, and I hardly knew

what to do. I wanted that thirty dollars; but I
didn't want to crawl into that little dark hole
after it, with maybe a couple of yet lively wolves
waiting at the other end to receive me.'

" ' Why didn't you leave them there and go
back for them next day? By that time, if they
were really hard-hit, you'd have found them dead
enough!' was my comment.

" ' There wouldn't have been much of them
left for me by the morrow,' said Maxim. ' I knew
well enough the other wolves would scent the
blood and come along, and help themselves to
snouts and all in the night. So by and by I
made up my mind to crawl in and risk it. Standing my gun up against the rock, and taking my
knife in my right hand, I started in!'

" ' Ugh!' said I, ' it makes me shiver to think
of it!'

" ' It *was* nasty,' assented Maxim; ' but then, I
counted on one of the vermin, at least, being
dead; and I didn't think there'd be much fight
left in the other. But that hole narrowed down
mighty sudden, and the first thing I knew, I had
to crawl flat on my stomach to get along at all;
and presently I found it tight squeezing even
that way. Of course I held my right hand, with
the knife in it, well to the front, ready to protect
my head and face.

" ' Just as the hole got so tight for me that I
was about concluding to give up the job, I heard

a terrific snarl right in my ear, and a wolf jumped
onto me. His fangs got me right in the jaw, —
you can see the scars here now, — and I thought
I was about fixed. But I slashed out desperately
with my big knife, and caught my assailant somewhere with a deadly thrust. He yelped, and
sprang out of the way.

" 'I felt the blood streaming over my face, and
knew I was badly bitten. I'd had enough of that
enterprise; but when I tried to back out the way
I had come, I found I couldn't work it. When it
dawned upon me that I was stuck in that trap, a
cold sweat broke out all over me. I *was* stuck,
and no mistake. Then I wriggled a little farther
in; and, at this, the wolf was onto me again.
This time my face escaped, and his fangs went
into my shoulder; but the next moment my knife-
edge found his throat, and down he came in a
heap. Then I lay still a bit, to get my breath and
consider the situation. The one thing clear was,
that I had got myself into a tight place, and I
began to wriggle for all I was worth in order to
get out of it.

" 'After twisting and tugging and straining for
perhaps ten solid minutes, I was forced to acknowledge to myself that I had not gained one
inch. Then I made up my mind that my only
hope lay in squeezing myself all the way in.
Once inside the cave, I thought, it would be comparatively easy work to wriggle out head-first.

In this direction I gained a few inches, — perhaps a foot, or more ; and by this time I felt so exhausted that I wanted to lie still and take a sleep, which, I knew, of course, would be madness.

"'Intending to rest but a moment, I must, nevertheless, have fallen into a doze. How long I lay thus, I don't know; but it must have been getting well along past sundown when I was awakened by a sound that brought my heart into my throat and made every hair stand on end. It was the howl of a wolf outside!'

"I interrupted the story at this point with an involuntary 'Ah — h — h!'

"'Yes,' said Maxim, acknowledging my sympathy, 'I could *face* any number of the vermin, and not lose hold of myself; but the idea of them coming along *behind*, and eating me gradually, feet first, was too much. I think that for a minute or two I must have been clean crazy. At any rate, I found strength enough, in that minute or two, to force my way right on, and into the cave, without knowing how I did it. And I found afterwards that the struggle had peeled off, not only most of my clothes, but lots of the flesh on my hips and shoulders as well.

"'As soon as I realized that I was inside the den, I felt round for the two dead wolves, and stuffed them head-first into the hole I had just come through. They filled it pretty snugly ; and then I seated myself on their hind legs to hold them solid, and hunted for a match.

"'In the rags of my clothes I had a pocket left, and fortunately there were some matches in it. Lighting one, I perceived in the sudden flare that I was in a little cave, about four feet high, and maybe seven or eight feet square. The floor of it was dry sand, and there were bones lying about.

"'Presently, in the tunnel behind me, sounded a snarl that seemed to come right against my backbone, and I jumped about a foot. Then I grabbed hold of the dead wolves, and hung onto them for all I was worth, for I could feel something dragging at one of them. You see, my experience in the hole had shaken my nerves pretty badly. If I'd been just myself, I should have cleared the way, and let my assailants in, killing them one by one, with my knife, as they crawled through. As it was, however, I gave a yell that scared the brute in the tunnel, so that he backed out in a hurry, and then I heard two or three of them howling outside. But it encouraged me a good deal to see what an effect my voice produced.

"'Pretty soon one of the wolves crept back, sniffing, sniffing, into the hole; and as soon as he discovered that it was only dead wolves that were stopping the way, he began to gnaw. It was a sickening sound he made, gnawing that way. After standing it as long as I could, I put my face down between the bodies, and gave another yell. How it echoed in that little place! and how quick that wolf backed out again ! For all the misery and anxiety I was in, I couldn't help laughing to myself there in the dark, wondering what the brute would think it was.

"'I tried this game on half a dozen times very successfully; but after that the wolves ceased to mind it. One would come and gnaw for a while, then another would give him a nip in the rear, squeeze past, and take his place. I soon began to fear my unique barricade would be all eaten away before morning, and I cast about in my mind for some other means of diverting the hungry animals' attention.

"'At length a brilliant idea struck me. I lit a match, and thrust it into the hole right under the cannibals' noses. That gave them a big surprise, I can tell you. They backed out in a great hurry, and sniffed about and howled a good deal before they ventured in again. As long as those matches held out, I had no trouble; and the wolves just kept howling outside the hole, not daring to come in after their victuals while there were such mysterious goings-on within the cave.

"'By and by, however, like all good things, the matches came to an end. Then presently in came the wolves, and soon they were gnawing away harder than ever. I was thinking that before long I would have to fight it out with the crowd after all, and then it occurred to me that I might as well begin right off. Lying flat down,

I thrust my right hand, with the knife in it, blade up, as far as I could reach out into the hole, but underneath the dead wolves. Then I gave two or three tremendous sweeping slashes.

"'One of the brutes must have caught it pretty stiff. He yelped and snarled hideously, and got outside for all he was worth. Then for a minute or two the whole lot howled and yelped in chorus. They must have been discussing the various mysteries of the cave, and concluded that these were too dangerous to be explored any further; for presently all was silent, and by an occasional yelp in the distance, I knew that the animals had betaken themselves elsewhere. I know it was a crazy thing to do; but just as soon as I'd made up my mind the wolves were gone, I dropped to sleep right across the entrance of the den.

"'When I awoke I was so stiff and my wounds pained so, that I could hardly move. But I knew I had to brace up, and get out of that before another night should come. I pulled away the bodies, and saw it was broad daylight. I took my knife, and chipped away for a long while at the walls and roof of the tunnel, finding the rock very soft and crumbly. Then I crawled out, with pain and difficulty, and pointed straight for the settlements, where I arrived more dead than alive. But I managed to lug along with me what there was left of those wolf-snouts, together with the tails; and I got the thirty dollars after all.'

"As Maxim finished his story, the roar of the Narrows, long unheeded, fell again upon my ear with a distinctness almost startling, and a loon cried mockingly from a hidden lakelet. Maxim rose, and replenished the sinking fire. Then we rolled ourselves into our blankets, as I propose that we all do now."

"Agreed!" cried several voices at once; and very soon the camp on the Toledi was sunk in slumber.

CHAPTER VIII.

THE TOLEDI AND TEMISCOUATA.

Noxe of us awoke next morning till the sun was high and the dew all gone in the open places about the camp. The air was sweet with wild perfumes, and alive with birds and butterflies. It was near noon by the time we found ourselves afloat on the Toledi River. This is a larger stream than the Squatook, and much more violent. The "Toledi Falls" are less than half a mile from the lake, and most travellers "portage" around them rather than risk the difficult passage. Indeed, the mighty, plunging swells, the succession of leaps, the roar and tumult between those rocky walls, render the passage by no means enticing when looked at in cold blood. But we knew the channels, and were resolved to " run it." It is no use attempting to tell just how we did it. I only know we all yelled with fierce delight as we darted into the gorge. and I imagine our eyes stuck out. Our muscles were like steel, and we tingled to the finger-tips. Then came a few wild moments when every man did his level best without knowing exactly how; for the white surges clashed deafeningly about us, and with cheers

we swept into the big eddy below the falls —
drenched, but safe. What cared we for a wetting
in that clear sunshine? The passion of travel
was on us, and we could not stay to fish. All
the rest of the run down to Temiscouata is like a
dream to me. Few rocks, few shoals, a straight
channel, and always that tearing current. At
four in the afternoon a last mad rapid hurled us
out into the wide expanse of Temiscouata. There
was a sharp wind on the lake, which is thirty
miles long, and at this point about three miles
wide. In the heavy seas, with our deep-laden
canoes, we had a rough and really perilous passage; and it was not far from six o'clock when
we reached the other shore. There, near the outskirts of the little village of Détour du Lac, we
pitched tent for the night.

After supper we took a run through the village,
and had a chat with some of the habitans. We
procured, moreover, some native Madawaska tobacco — which we smoked once, and never smoked
again.

Around the fire that night we felt a sense of
depression because our trip was drawing to an
end. At last Magnus cried, —

"Shake off this gloom, boys. A story, Stranion!"

"All right; here's something light and bright,"
answered Stranion promptly. "Let us call it —

'CHOPPING HIM DOWN.'

" There is nothing that so cheers the heart of
the lumberman as to play a practical joke on one
whom he calls a 'greenhorn,' or, in other words,
any one unused to the strange ways and flavor of
the lumber-camps. As may be imagined, the practical jokes in vogue in such rough company are
not remarkable for gentleness. One of the harsh-
est and most dangerous, as well as most admired,
is that known as 'chopping him down.'

"This means, in a word, that the unsophisti-
cated stranger in the camp is invited to climb a
tall tree to take observations or enjoy a remarkable view. No sooner has he reached the top,
than a couple of vigorous axemen attack the tree
at its base, while the terrified stranger makes
fierce haste to descend from his too lofty situation. Long before he can reach the ground the
tree begins to topple. The men shout to him to
get on the upper side, which he does with appalled alacrity; and with a mighty swish and
crash down comes the tree. As a general rule,
the heavy branches so break the shock that the
victim, to his intense astonishment, finds himself
uninjured; though frequently he is frightened out
of a year's growth. There are cases on record, however, where men have been crippled for
life in this outrageous play; and in some cases
the 'boss' of the camp forbids it.

"But it is not only the greenhorn who is subject to this discipline of chopping down. Even veterans sometimes like to climb a tree and take a view beyond the forest; and sometimes, on a holiday or a Sunday, some contemplative woodsman will take refuge in a tree-top to think of his sweetheart, or else to eat a sheet of stolen gingerbread. If his retreat be discovered by his comrades, he is promptly chopped down with inextinguishable jeers.

"I have mentioned stolen gingerbread. This bread is a favorite delicacy in the camps; and the cook who can make really good gingerbread is prized indeed. It is made in wide, thin, tough sheets; and while it is being served to the hands, some fellow occasionally succeeds in 'hooking' a whole sheet while the cook's back is toward him. But in that same instant every man's hand is turned against him. He darts into the woods, devouring huge mouthfuls as he runs. If he is very swift of foot he may escape, eat his spoils in retirement, and stroll back, an hour later, with a conscious air of triumph. More often he has to take to a tree. Instantly all hands rush to chop him down. He climbs no higher than is necessary, perches himself on a stout limb, and eats at his gingerbread for dear life. He knows just what position to take for safety; and often, ere the tree comes down, there is little gingerbread left to reward its captors. The meagre remnant is usually handed over with an admirable submissiveness, if it is not dropped in the fall, and annihilated in the snow and *débris.*

"At one time I knew a lumberman who succeeded in hiding his stolen gingerbread in his long boot-legs, and slept with the boots under his head for security. The camp was on the banks of a lake. The time of the capture of the gingerbread was a Saturday night in spring. Next morning the spoiler took possession of the one 'bateau' belonging to the camp, rowed out into the lake beyond the reach of stones and snowballs, and then calmly fished the gingerbread out of his boots. Sitting at ease in the bateau, he devoured his dainty with the utmost deliberation, while his chagrined comrades could only guy him from the shore.

"For myself, I was chopped down once, and once only. It happened in this way. In the mid-winter of 1879 I had occasion to visit the chief camp on the Little Madawaska. Coming from the city, and to a camp where I was a stranger to all the men, I was not unnaturally regarded as a pronounced specimen of the greenhorn. I took no pains to tell any one what the boss already well knew; that is, that I had been a frequenter of the camps from my boyhood. Many and many a neat trap was laid for my apparently 'tender' feet, but I avoided them all as if by accident. As for climbing a tree, I always laughed at the idea when it was proposed to me. I always suggested that it might spoil my clothes. Before long the men, by putting little things together, came to the conclusion that I was an old stager; and, rather sheepishly, they gave over their attempts to entrap me. Then I graciously waved my hand, as it were, and was frankly received as a veteran, cleared from every suspicion of being green.

"At last the day came when I *did* wish to climb a tree. The camp was on a high plateau, and not far off towered a magnificent pine-tree, growing out of the summit of a knoll in such a way as to command all the surrounding country. Its branches were phenomenally thick; its girth of trunk was magnificent. And this tree I resolved one day to climb, in order to get a clear idea of the lay of the land. Of course I strolled off surreptitiously, and, as I thought, unwatched. But there I was much mistaken. No sooner was I two-thirds of the way up the tree than, with shouts of laughter, the lumbermen rushed out of the surrounding cover, and proceeded to chop me down. The chance was too good for them to lose.

" I concealed my annoyance, and made no attempt to descend. On the contrary, I thanked them for the little attention, and climbed a few feet farther up, to secure a position which I saw would be a safe one for me when the tree should fall. As I did so, I perceived, with a gasp and a tremor, that I was not alone in the tree.

"There, not ten feet above me, stretched at full length along a large branch, was a huge panther, glaring with rage and terror. From the men below his form was quite concealed. Glancing restlessly from me to my pursuers, the brute seemed uncertain just what to do. As I carefully refrained from climbing any farther up, and tried to assume an air of not having observed him, he apparently concluded that I was not his worst enemy. In fact, I dare say he understood what was going on, and realized that he and I were fellow-sufferers.

"I laughed softly to myself as I thought how my tormentors would be taken aback when that panther should come down among them. I decided that, considering their numbers, there would be at least no more danger for them than that to which they were exposing me in their reckless fooling. And, already influenced by that touch of nature which makes us so wondrous kind, I began to hope that the panther would succeed in escaping.

"The trunk of the pine was so thick that I might almost have reached the ground before the choppers could cut it through. At last it gave a mighty shudder and sagged to one side. I balanced myself nimbly on the upper side, steadying myself by a convenient branch. The great mass of foliage, presenting a wide surface to the air, made the fall a comparatively slow one ; but the tremendous sweep of the draught upward, as the tree-top described its gigantic arc, gave me a sickening sensation. Then came the final dull and thunderous crash, and in an instant I found myself standing in my place, jarred but unhurt, with the snow threshed up all about me.

" The next instant there was another roar, or rather a sort of screaming yell, overwhelming the riotous laughter of the woodsmen ; and out of the confusion of pine-boughs shot the tawny form of the panther in a whirlwind of fury. One of the choppers was in his path, and was bowled over like a clumsy ninepin. The next bound brought the beast onto the backs of a yoke of oxen, and his cruel claws severely scratched their necks. As the poor animals bellowed and fell on their knees, the panther paused, with some idea, apparently, of fighting the whole assembled party. But as the men, recovered from their first amazement, rushed with their axes to the rescue of the oxen, the panther saw that the odds were all against him. He turned half round, and greeted his enemies with one terrific and strident snarl, then bounded off into the forest at a pace which made it idle to pursue him. The owner of the oxen hurled an axe after him, but the missile flew wide of its mark.

As the excitement subsided, and I saw that the chopper who had been knocked over was none the worse for his tumble, I chaffed my tormentors unmercifully. For their part they had no answer ready. They seemed almost to think that I had conjured up the panther for the occasion. I thanked them most fervently for coming to my rescue with such whole-hearted good-will, and promised them that if ever again I got into a tree with a panther I would send for them at once. Then I set myself to doctoring the unfortunate oxen, whose lacerated necks and shoulders we soon mended up with impromptu plasters. And the owner of the oxen gratefully vowed to me, 'If ever I see any of the chaps a-laying for ye agin, an' any of my critters is around, I'll tip ye the wink, shore!'"

"Here goes for another lumberman's yarn," began Sam, when Stranion ceased. "It's brief, so bear with it.

'A RUDE AWAKENING.'

"In the fir-woods of the Upper Bartibogue the snow was softening rapidly. The spring thaws had come on several weeks earlier than they were expected. consequently a great quantity of logs lay in the woods waiting to be hauled to the landing. The hands at Bober's Camp were working with feverish energy. in the effort to get all their logs out before the snow roads should go utterly to pieces. Old Paul Bober, the boss of the camp, had sent out to all the surrounding settlements for extra teams.

" The first result of his efforts was a team of
wild young steers, which seemed hardly more than
half-broken to the yoke. They were as long and
gaunt as their driver, long Jim Baizley; but they
looked equal to any amount of hard work.

" ' Them critters of yourn ain't much to look
at, Jim,' remarked the boss, as Baizley came ' gee-
ing ' and ' hawing ' them into camp toward sundown.

" The steers swung their hindquarters far apart,
and sagged restively on the yoke, as they came to
a halt. The teamster rolled a loving eye upon
them, and replied, —

" ' Jest wait till they git yankin' onto the logs,
an' then see what you think of 'em ! '

" Jim Baizley was a smart teamster ; and on the
following morning, with his heart set on showing
off his team to the best advantage, he was the first
to get to work hauling. The snow was getting
softer and softer, a warm wind having blown all
night so that there had been no chance for it to
stiffen up. This heightened the general anxiety ;
and there was no time lost in following Baizley
to ' the Ridge,' a patch of sloping forest where
a lot of fine timber lay waiting to be hauled out.

" From the Ridge to the Landing it was necessary to take a new road, which had been already
roughly chopped out. As Baizley with his lean
cattle started out for the Landing with a couple
of huge timbers chained together behind them,

one of the hands shouted to remind him that he was the first to go over the new road.

"'Look out for slumps, Jim!' cried the chopper. 'This here snow hain't got no kind of a bottom to it now!'

"Baizley rolled his eyes over the stretch of track before him, which his load was soon to plough into picturesque disorder. With a thoughtful gesture, and very deliberately, he spit a huge quantity of tobacco-juice over the dull-white, soggy surface just in front of the oxen, and then said, —

"'I'll look out. Gimme a peevy!'

"Grasping the long white pole, shod with a steel spike at the larger end, he started his team toward the Landing. Instead of walking beside his cattle, in the teamster's customary place, he travelled a few feet in front of their noses; and from time to time he thrust the pike-pole sharply into the snow.

"It must be borne in mind that the snow in these north shore woods lies anywhere from two to five feet deep. Under such a covering may lie concealed, not only the firm forest floor, but dangerous bog-holes, or steep little dry gullies. Hence the wise precaution which Baizley took of feeling the way for his oxen. The lack of such precaution has cost many a careless lumberman his team.

"In the present case, however, — so perverse a witch is chance, — Baizley's very prudence was the well-spring of disaster. His experience was such as might almost have led him to forswear precautions for the rest of his natural life — as a teamster.

" Close behind Baizley's team came another, driven by Tamin Landry, a little Frenchman from down the river. *Tamang*, as the Frenchman was called by his comrades, had great confidence in Baizley's skill as a guide. He felt it safe to take his team wherever Baizley should take his.

" Presently Baizley's pike-pole sank deeply into the snow with sudden and suspicious ease.

" ' Whoa-oa-o ! ' he yelled, rolling his eyes back upon the steers.

" The team surged forward till they were almost upon him, and he rapped them sharply across the muzzles. Then they stopped, with their heads far down.

" ' W'at ze matter ? ' inquired Tamang, skipping forward.

" ' Big hole here ! ' responded Baizley. He was prodding the snow near the trunk of a mighty tree.

" 'Solid ground furder this way, likely ! ' he continued ; and he gave a vicious prod some two feet farther out from the tree.

" The result was something to startle even a backwoodsman. The snowy surface rose up suddenly, with a spluttering, grunting noise, as if an infant volcano were about breaking into eruption.

" Almost thrown off his feet, Baizley sprang to
one side, while the excitable Tamang jumped into
the air with a yell of astonishment. The yoke of
steers swerved wildly to one side, and would have
run away but for their heavy load. Then there
emerged from the snow the hugest and hollowest
of black bears, his long fur thickly blotched with
lumps of his white covering.

" Thus painfully and unceremoniously aroused
from his winter sleep, the bear was in a thoroughly
justifiable rage. Perhaps also the pangs of un-
realized hunger added to his fury. He glanced
with small red eyes from side to side, then flung
himself clumsily but swiftly upon the nearest ox.

" With mad bellowing the team plunged in
among the trees ; and in their terror so great was
their strength, that the great timbers they were
hauling danced after them like jackstraws. But
this was not for long. Ere they had gone ten
yards from the road, the ox which the bear had
struck, blind with panic, caught his long horns in
a sapling, and fell forward on his knees. For a
moment his yoke-fellow held him up, then he
collapsed in a limp red-and-white heap, with his
neck broken. And the bear began tearing at him
savagely.

" Paralyzed and helpless, the other steer sank in
the snow. By this time, however, Baizley and the
Frenchman had recovered their scattered wits and
seized their axes. Baizley's eyes rolled wildly,

with pity for his team and wrath against the bear. With the full sweep of his long, wiry arms, he swung his heavy axe and brought it down upon the animal's head.

"At least, that was Baizley's amiable intention; but any one who has tried to hit a bear over the head with an axe knows how difficult a feat it is to accomplish, unless the bear is asleep. This bear was very wide-awake indeed; Baizley's pike-pole had seen to that!

"Though apparently engrossed with the dead steer, he had been watching his assailants out of the corner of his eye. Just as the great axe began its deadly descent, the beast half rose, and like a flash threw up his mighty forearm. On this the axe-handle struck and glanced, and the weapon flew violently off among the trees.

"With a desperate exclamation Baizley attempted to jump away; and at the same moment the bear brought down his other paw with a stroke that all Baizley's tried skill as a boxer would not have availed to parry. But fortunately for the tall lumberman, his footing gave way. He fell headlong in the snow, and the stroke of that armed paw passed harmlessly over him.

"The bear dropped forward upon him, but was at once distracted by a fierce blow on the shoulder from Landry's axe. With a snort he turned about, and gave chase to the nimble little Frenchman.

"Now, this was in all respects a most fortunate

"TAMANG CAME LEAPING PAST WITH THE BEAR AT HIS HEELS." — Page 343.

diversion. Tamang was so light of foot that the snow easily upbore him. He found himself able, without difficulty, to elude his floundering pursuer. He took a short circuit among the trees, and headed back toward the team.

" Baizley was now on his feet, and himself again. He was running to pick up his axe, when Tamang yelled, 'No! No! Spear him, spear him wid ze peevy, Jeem! Spear him wid ze peevy!'

" It was a good idea, and Baizley realized the force of it. The steel-shod pike-pole was indeed a formidable weapon. Grasping it short in both hands, Baizley sprang upon the logs of his ill-fated load, and a second later Tamang came leaping past with the bear at his heels.

" In an instant the plucky Frenchman turned and faced his pursuer. The bear rose on his hind legs to seize him, and Baizley's opportunity had arrived. With all his force he drove the point of the pike-pole into the brute's body, right under the foreshoulder.

" Down came the huge arm, snapping the tough pole like a splinter; but the steel point had gone home. The bear fell dead, close beside the dead ox.

" Whilst Tamang, with voluble excitement, examined the two victims of Baizley's wise precautions, the latter with taciturn deliberation proceeded to unyoke the trembling steer from its ill-starred mate. But from the way his eyes rolled in their lean sockets, it was easy to see that the gaunt lumberman was doing some swift and energetic thinking."

"Now, then, Magnus," cried Queerman, "we look to you.   Will it be more about the lumber-camps?"

"No," replied Magnus; "I shall introduce a beast of whom none of you have yet said a word. Yet he is an important beast, and played no small part in preparing the land of Canaan for the advent of the children of Israel.   My story is —

'SAVED BY A HORNET'S NEST.'

"I got the story just a few weeks ago, when I was out fishing on the Rushagornish with Dick Henderson.   Near the shore we came upon a huge hornets' nest suspended beneath a bush.   Swayed by the common impulse of destructiveness, I suggested that we should set fire to the nest.

"'No, indeed,' said Dick.   'If we attack the nest we deserve to get stung.   Mr. Yellow Jacket is a self-respecting citizen, and will not trouble you unless you wantonly interfere with him.   If he resents aggression fiercely, we cannot blame him for that, can we?   Besides, a hornets' nest is held sacred among us Hendersons.'

"'You don't mean to confess,' I exclaimed, 'that it symbolizes the spirit and temper of your family?'

"'Not exactly,' replied Dick. 'But it certainly preserved the connection between flesh and spirit for our family at a very critical moment. My Grandfather Henderson owed his life to a nest of hornets at a time when he, a young man of twenty-two, was the sole representative of his line.'

"The trout were not rising, and the rapidly heating air persuaded to indolence. I stood my rod up in a bush, threw myself down in a shady spot, and remarked to Dick that he might as well tell me about his grandfather. This invitation elicited the following curious story : —

"It was during the war of 1812. The battles of Chrysler's Farm and Chateauguay had not yet been fought, and the Canadians were in doubt as to the movements of the two American armies which were preparing to attack Montreal. They knew that General Wilkinson was at Sackett's Harbor, making ready to descend the St. Lawrence; but in regard to General Hampton, who was advancing by way of Lake Champlain, information was much in demand.

"My grandfather, James Henderson, who knew the country between the St. Lawrence and Lake Champlain, volunteered to get the information. He had many friends on the American side of the line, most of whom, as he knew, heartily disapproved of this unnecessary struggle between the

United States and England. On these he depended for help if he should get caught; and he really gave far too little heed to the nature of the risk he was running. Yet he took wise precautions, and played his part with discretion.

"With a ragged-looking horse and a shabby pedler's wagon, and himself skilfully made up for the *rôle* of a country hawker, he was comparatively secure from recognition. Indeed, I have heard him boast that he made sales to some of his most intimate acquaintances, who never for an instant dreamed that it was Jim Henderson whom they were haggling with.

"All went prosperously until the very end of the adventure drew near. My grandfather was returning with the important information that Hampton's objective point was the mouth of the Chateauguay River, whence he would cross the St. Lawrence, and descend upon Montreal from Lachine.

"At Smith's Corners, a little rudimentary village about ten miles from the Canadian border, my grandfather stopped for a bite of dinner.

"Jake Smith, the landlord of the little inn, was a trusted friend; and to him my grandfather revealed himself in obedience to a sudden impulse. It was the first time on the whole journey that he had given the slightest clew to his true personality. Well for him that he yielded to this impulse, else even the friendly hornets' nest, to which we are coming presently, would not have availed to save him.

"Jake Smith was a stirring fellow, who under ordinary circumstances would have liked nothing better than running a spy to earth; but when that spy was Jim Henderson, the case was different.

"My grandfather had stood his horse and wagon in on the spacious barn floor, and was having a wash in a little bedroom opening off the kitchen. The bedroom door was partly closed.

"Suddenly, through the crack of the door, he caught sight of a small party of American militiamen, at whose heels followed two huge brindled mastiffs, or part mastiffs, probably a cross between mastiff and bloodhound. Henderson, confident in his disguise, was just slipping on his coat with the idea of going out and speaking to the soldiers, when the leader's voice, addressing the landlord at the kitchen door, arrested him.

"'Where's that pedler chap that drove in here a few minutes ago?' inquired the officer, puzzled at seeing no sign of the wagon.

"'What do you want of him?' inquired the landlord with an air of interest.

"'We'll show you presently!' said the officer. 'And we'll want you, too, if we catch you trying to shelter a spy! Where is he?'

"'I don't shelter no spies,' growled Jake Smith ambiguously; 'and I'd advise you to keep your jaw for your own men!'"

"The officer was about to make an angry reply, but changed his mind.

"'That pedler,' said he firmly, 'is a spy; and it is your duty to assist in his capture. Is he in this house?'

"Now, Smith knew better than to try to persuade the soldiers that Henderson had driven away. He saw they had certain knowledge of the spy's presence. So he exclaimed:—

"'A spy, is he? Well, I reckon you've about got him, then. He's drove his team in on the barn floor, out of the sun, and most likely'— but the whole squad were off for the barn.

"'To the woods! The cave!' hissed Smith toward the little bedroom; and at the same instant my grandfather darted from the window, down behind the tall rows of pole-beans and a leafy bed of artichokes, and gained the cover of the woods which touched on the rear edge of the garden.

"He ran with desperate speed, following at first a well-beaten cattle-path that led straight into the woods. But he had small hope of escape. It was the glimpse he had got of those two great dogs that filled his soul with dismay.

"For the troops alone he would have cared little. He knew he could outrun most men, and the forest afforded innumerable hiding-places. But those dogs! With no weapon but his sheath-knife, he could hardly hope to overcome them without being himself disabled; and if he were to take refuge in a tree, they would just hold him there till their masters arrived to lead him off to an ignominious death.

"My grandfather concluded, however, that his only chance for escape lay in fighting the dogs. If he could kill them before the soldiers came up, he might possibly get away.

"But to make the most of this poor chance he must get deep into the woods, and lead the dogs a long distance ahead of the troops.

"He understood the sound tactics of dividing the enemy's forces. He tightened his belt and ran on, snatching up by the way a stout stick which some one had intended for a cane.

"The cave of which Smith had spoken lay about three miles from the village. After following the cattle-path for perhaps half a mile, my grandfather turned a little to the right and plunged into the trackless forest. His long, nimble legs carried him swiftly over the innumerable obstructions of the forest floor.

"His ears were strained anxiously to catch the first deep baying that would tell him the dogs were on his scent. Every minute that the dreadful voices delayed was an addition to his little stock of hopes. If only he could reach the cave, his chances of victory over the dogs would be much increased; for the entrance to it was so small that only one of his assailants would be able to get in at a time.

"At last, when he had run about two miles, his breath failed him. He threw himself flat on his face on a bit of mossy ground beside a brook. As he lay there gasping, his mouth open, his eyes shut, suddenly along the resonant ground were borne to his ears the voices of the dogs.

"When he sprang to his feet he could no longer hear them; but he knew he must gain more time. Jumping into the brook he ran several hundred yards up-stream; then, seizing a long, overhanging branch, he swung himself well ashore, some ten feet clear of the bank.

"As he once more headed for the cave, he flattered himself, not without reason, that the dogs would lose some time before they picked up his scent again.

"The baying of the pursuers soon came near enough to be distinctly heard, and then grew in volume rapidly. At last it stopped; and he knew the dogs had reached the brook, and were hunting for the scent. Before that sinister music rose again on the stillness of the wilderness air, Henderson came in sight of the hillside wherein the cave lay hidden.

"Just as he was congratulating himself that he had now a good chance of escape, a thought occurred to him that dashed his hopes. 'Why,' said he to himself, 'the dogs would most likely refuse to enter the cave!' Seeing the smallness of the entrance, they would no doubt stay baying outside, keeping him like a rat in a hole until the soldiers should come and smoke him out.

"However, he decided to risk it. He could, at least. block the entrance with stones, and make some sort of fight at the last; or even there might be some other exit, — some fissure in the hill which he had never explored. At any rate, he was too much exhausted to run any farther.

"As he approached the low opening in the hillside a lot of hornets darted past his ears. Having a dread of hornets he glanced about nervously, and imagined at first they were denizens of his cave. But in a moment he saw the nest.

"It was an immense gray globular structure, hanging from the branch of a small fir-tree, at a height of about two feet from the ground. It was not more than five or six feet from the cave, and almost directly in front of it.

"Henderson was a man of resources; and he appreciated the fighting prowess of a well-stirred colony of hornets. He decided to enlist the colony in his defence.

"The hornets were taking no notice of him whatever, being intent on business of their own. Henderson took a long piece of string from his trousers pocket, and in the most delicate fashion possible made one end fast to the branch which supported the nest. Then, lying down flat on his face, he squirmed softly past without getting into collision with the insects, and crawled into the cave, carrying with him the other end of the string.

"Once safely inside, his first care was to grope around for a big stone or two. These he soon procured, and with their aid the entrance was blocked. Then he took off his coat.

"He laid his ear to the crevices in his barricade. The dogs were getting so near that he could hear now the crashing of their heavy forms as they bounded through the underbrush.

"Holding his coat ready to stop up, if necessary, the small openings he had left for observation, he began jerking sharply on the string which connected him with the hornets' nest.

"He could hear the furious buzzing which instantly arose as the hornets swarmed forth to resent the disturbance. He could see how the air grew yellow all about the nest. But it did not occur to the angry iñsects to seek for their disturber in the cave.

"Henderson jerked again and yet again, and the enraged swarm grew thicker.

"At this moment the dogs came into view. Very deadly and inexorable they looked as they bounded along, heads low down, their dark, muscular bodies dashing the branches aside and bearing down the undergrowth.

"Now, realizing perhaps that they had run their prey to earth, they raised their heads and barked, in a tone very different from that of their baying.

SAVED BY A HORNETS' NEST

Unfalteringly they dashed straight upon the barricade; and one of them, as he sprang past, struck the nest a ruder shock than any that my grandfather's string had been able to give it.

"In that same instant the exasperated hornets were upon the dogs. A sharp chorus arose of angry and frightened yelpings. Yet for a few seconds the brave brutes persisted in their efforts to force an entrance to my grandfather's retreat. This gave the hornets a fair chance.

"They settled upon the animals' eyes and ears and jaws, till flesh and blood — even dog flesh and blood — could endure the fiery anguish no longer. Both dogs rolled over and over, burrowing their noses in the moss, and trying with their paws to scrape off their bitter assailants. But the contest was too unequal.

"Presently both dogs stuck their tails between their legs, and darted off in mad panic through the woods. Gradually their yelpings died away.

"My grandfather then and there registered a vow that he would never again break up a hornets' nest. He slackened the string till it lay loose and inconspicuous amid the moss, but he did not exactly care to go out and detach it from the branch.

"Then he lay down and rested, feeling pretty confident that the soldiers would not find their way to his retreat now that they were deprived of the assistance of the dogs. As for the dogs, he knew that their noses were pretty well spoiled for a day or two.

"That night, when he felt quite sure the hornets had gone to bed, my grandfather crept out of his refuge, stole softly past his little protectors without disturbing them to say farewell, and struck across the forest in the direction of the Canadian border. A little later the moon got up, and by her light he made good progress.

"Soon after daybreak he reached the banks of the Chateauguay, and about an hour later he fell in with a scouting-party of the Glengarry Fencibles, who took him to the headquarters of De Salaberry, the Canadian commander. As for the ragged old horse and the pedler's wagon, they remained at Smith's Corners, a keepsake for Jake Smith."

"I think," said Ranolf, "that's a good enough yarn to go to bed on. I'm as sleepy as a June-bug."

Upon this we all discovered that we were in the same condition as Ranolf. The exhilaration of the run down the Toledi, and the hard strain of the passage across Temiscouata, had tired us through and through. How delicious were our blankets that night at Détour du Lac!

CHAPTER IX.

THE LAST CAMP-FIRE.

WE got away from Détour du Lac in the early morning, and reached the outlet, the head of the Madawaska River, after a brisk paddle of some eight miles. The run down the Madawaska was swift and easy,—a rapid current and a clear channel. What more could canoemen wish? Late in the afternoon we pitched tent on a woody hill half a mile above Edmundston. To signalize our return to civilization we visited the hotel and post-office, and then returned to camp for tea. The fire blazed right merrily that night, and to ward off melancholy thoughts we told stories as usual.

"Boys," said Stranion, "I've saved for this last night in camp the one that I count choicest of all my yarns. The scene of it lies on those very waters which we have lately passed through!"

"Name?" demanded I, sharpening my pencil with a business air.

"Just —

'INDIAN DEVILS,'

replied Stranion.

"It was a scorching noon in mid-July of 1885. Dear old H—— and I were in camp on the upper

waters of the Squatook, not far below the mouth
of Beardsley Brook. How H—— loved to get
away from his professorial dignity and freely un-
bend in the woods! He used to swear he would
never again put on a starched collar. But his big
American university keeps him prim enough now!

"We had called a halt for dinner and siesta in
a little sandy cove, where the river eddied list-
lessly. It was a hollow between high banks, down
which drew a soft breeze as through a funnel, and
the deep grass fringing the tiny beach was densely
shadowed by a tangle of vines and branches.

"Our birch canoe was behind us, her resined
sides well shaded from the heat. At the water's
edge flickered the remnants of our fire, paled and
browbeaten by the steady downpour of sunshine.
The stream itself, for a wonder grown drowsy,
idled over its pebbly bed with a sleep-inducing
murmur.

"While we were thus half idling and dreaming,
I was startled wide awake by the grating of a
paddle on a line of gravelly shoals above the
point. A moment more and a birch canoe swept
into view, and drew up at our landing-place. The
crew, two youngish-looking Indians, having lifted
their craft out of the water, stalked silently up
the beach and paused before us, leaning on their
paddles. With a non-committal grunt they accepted some proffered tobacco, glanced over our
baggage, eyed greedily the bright nickel-plating

on our trout-rods, and murmured something in
Melicete which I failed to comprehend.

"The professor, somewhat annoyed at this intrusion, blinked sleepily at them for a while, and
then proceeded to sort and stow away his latest
acquired specimens, amongst which were some
splendid bits of pyrites, glittering richly in the
sun.

"One of our visitors was not unknown to me.
He was a certain Joe Tobin, of ill repute, hailing
from Francis Village. The other was an older
looking man, with high cheek-bones and little,
pig-like, half-shut eyes.

"The appearance of neither had any attraction
for me, but the Indian with the pig-like eyes I
found particularly distasteful.

"These eyes grew intent at once, as they caught
the yellow gleam of the pyrites; but their owner
preserved his air of stoical indifference.

"Approaching the professor's side, he sought a
closer examination; but the professor was not pro-
pitiatory. He dumped the ore into his specimen-
box before the Indian could touch it; and shifting
the box deeper into the shade, he took his seat
upon it. The box was plainly heavy, and a gleam
of interest crept into the cunning eyes of Joe.

"'Gold, mebbe?' he suggested persuasively.

"To which the professor, facetiously grumpy,
answered, 'Yes, all gold! Fools' gold!'

"At this a most greedy glance passed furtively

between the Indians, and it flashed upon me that by the barbaric ear 'Fools' gold' might be misinterpreted to 'Full of gold.'

"I gave the rash professor a warning look, which Joe intercepted. I then proceeded to explain what was meant by 'Fools' gold,' and declared that the things in the professor's box were valueless bits of rock, which we had picked up chiefly out of curiosity. This statement, however, as I could see by our visitors' faces, was at once regarded as a cunning and cautious lie to conceal the vast value of our treasure.

"'Whereabouts you get um?' queried Joe again.

"'Oh,' answered the professor, 'there's lots of it floating round Mud Lake and Beardsley Brook.' He took a lovely cluster of crystals out of his pocket, and laughed to see how the Indians' eyes stuck out with deluded avarice. I felt angry at his nonsense, for one of our visitors was an out-and-out ruffian.

"In a few moments, after a series of low grunts, which baffled my ear completely, though I was acacquainted with the Melicete tongue, the Indians turned to go, saying in explanation of their sudden departure, 'Sugar Loaf 'fore sundown, mebbe.' I took the precaution to display, at this juncture, a double-barrelled breech-loader, into which I slipped a couple of buck-shot cartridges; and as I nodded them a bland farewell, I said in Melicete, 'It'll be late when you get to Sugar Loaf.' The start they gave, on hearing me speak their own language, confirmed my suspicions, and they paddled off in haste without more words.

" No sooner were they well out of sight than I made ready with all speed for our own departure; nor did I neglect to upbraid the professor for his rashness. At first he pooh-poohed my apprehension, declaring that it was ' fun to fool the greedy Hottentots; ' but when I explained my grounds for alarm, he condescended to treat them with some respect. He warmed up, indeed, and made haste, so that we were once more darting along with the racing current before the Indians had been gone above ten minutes; but I could see that he had adopted my suspicions mainly for the sake of an added excitement. The professor's class-room afforded too little scope for such an adventurous spirit, and he was beginning to crave the relish of a spice of peril. With his dainty rifle just to his hand, he was soon plying a fervent and effective paddle, while his sharp eyes kept a lookout which I knew very little would evade.

"Our design was to press so closely upon the rascals' heels that any plot they might agree upon should not find time to mature. We knew they would never calculate upon our following them so promptly; still less would they dream of the speed that we were making. In a fair race we flattered ourselves that we could beat most Indians, and we rather counted on overtaking and passing this couple before they could accomplish aught against us. There was one point in the stream, however, which I remembered with misgivings.

"Three or four miles ahead of us were the rapids which, you remember, we had such fun with a few days ago. I suggested to H—— that there, if anywhere, those Indians would lie in wait for us, knowing that our hands would be well occupied in navigating the canoe.

"Those five miles soon slipped by. As we shot down the roaring channel we saw, in the reach beyond the last turmoil, a canoe thrust in among the alders.

"'Ah-h-h!' exclaimed the professor, in a tone of deepening conviction; and he shifted his grip upon his rifle. An instant more and we were in the surges.

"Just then I saw the professor start, half raising his rifle to the shoulder; but the canoe was taking all my attention, and I dared not follow his glance to shoreward.

"Our delicate craft seemed to wallow down the roaring trough. The stream was much heavier than we found it the other day, I can tell you. At the foot of the first *chute* a great thin-crested ripple slapped over us.

"I had understood the professor's gesture; and, as we plunged down the next leap, I chuckled to myself, 'Sold this time!'

"Like a bird, the true little craft took the plunge. One more blinding dash of spray, a shivering pause, and, darting forward arrow-like, she dipped to the last and steepest descent.

"At this instant, from the bank overhead, came a spurt of blue smoke and a report, followed by a twinge in my left shoulder. Another report, scarcely audible amid the falls' thunder, and cleaving the last great ripple, we swept into gentler currents. Crack! crack! crack! went the professor's little rifle, as he fired over his shoulder at the place where the smoke-puffs clung.

"I said, 'Push on, before they can load again.'

"Dropping my paddle, as we passed their empty canoe, I put two charges of buck-shot through her birchen sides. Then, satisfied that the mending of this breach would keep our enemy wholesomely occupied for some time, we pushed forward swiftly in grim triumph.

"A few miles farther on I stopped, and informed the professor that I was wounded. At this he turned about in such sudden concern that he barely missed upsetting the canoe; but he presently remarked, 'By the healthy vigor you've displayed in running away the last half hour, I don't imagine the wound can be serious.'

"On examination we found that a bullet had nicked the top of my shoulder, though not so deeply but that cold water and some strips of sticking-plaster went far toward giving relief from pain. But the muscular action of paddling caused the scratch to become inflamed; and so, when at about four in the afternoon we swept out on the smooth waters of the lake, I gave up the stern paddle to the professor, and played invalid a while in the bow.

" A light breeze, to which we hoisted our sail, took us pleasantly down the lake, and about half-past six we landed near the outlet. We tented just where Camp de Squatook stood a few days ago. Under the lulling influence of a supper of fresh fried trout, the savor of which mixed deliciously with the wholesome scent of the pines, we concluded that perhaps by this time our enemies would have given up the pursuit, disgusted by their past failure and the damage done to their canoe.

"Nevertheless, we resolved to take thorough precautions, lest our adversaries should cross the head of the lake and come upon us by night.

" We built a huge fire so that it shone upon the landing-place, and lighted up every way of approach by water. The tent stood out in the full glare. To the rear and a little to one side, beyond the limits of the grove, in the densest part of the thicket, we fixed ourselves a snug and secret couch, whence we could command a view of the whole surroundings.

" Close by we arranged a pile of bark, with kindlings and dry balsamic pine-chips, such as we could urge into a sudden blaze in case of any emergency. Immediately behind us was the water, and from that side we felt that we were safe so long as that glare of firelight could be maintained.

" We fixed up the camp to look natural and secure, hung our wet clothes to dry on the *cheep lahquah-gan*,[1] closed the tent-door for the night to keep out the mosquitoes, and retired, not dissatisfied, to our covert.

" It was a dark and almost starless night, with a soft, rainy wind soughing in the pine-tops, and making the 'Big Squatook' wash restlessly all down her pebbled beaches. As we drew our weapons close to us, and stretched ourselves luxuriously in our blankets. we could not forbear a low laugh at a certain relish the situation held for us. The professor, however, suddenly became serious; and he declared, · But this lark's in the soberest kind of earnest. anyway ; and we mustn't be letting ourselves tumble to sleep!'

" My shoulder gave an admonitory twinge, and I cordially acquiesced.

" Just then a far-off howl of hideous laughter, ending in a sob of distress, came down the night wind, making our flesh creep uncomfortably.

" · Is that what the Indians call Gluskâp's Hunting-dogs ? ' whispered the professor.

---

1 The green sapling stuck into the ground so as to slant across the fire. It is used to hang the kettle and pot upon.

" ' Not by any means ! ' I answered under my breath.

" ' Well, it ought to be,' returned the professor.

" I replied that the voice, in my opinion, came from the dangerous Northern panther, or ' Indian devil.'

" These animals, I went on to explain for H——'s comfort, were growing yearly more numerous in the Squatook regions, owing to the fact that the caribou, their favorite prey, were being driven hither from the south counties and from Nova Scotia.

" Just then the cry was repeated, this time a little nearer; and the professor began to inquire whether it was Indian or Indian devil about which we should have most call to concern ourselves. His hope, but half-expressed, was plainly for a ' whack at both.'

" I assured him that so long as the Indian devil kept up his serenading we had little need to be troubled; but should the scent of our fried trout be blown to his nostrils, and divert his mind from thoughts of love to war, then would it behoove us to be circumspect.

" As we talked on thus in an undertone which was half-drowned by the washing of the waves, the panther's cry was heard much nearer than before; and it was not again repeated. This put us sharply on our guard.

" Hour after hour passed, till we began to find

it hard to keep awake. Only the weirdness of the
place, the strange noises which stole towards us
from the depths of the forest, dying out within
a radius of a couple of hundred yards from the
firelight, together with our anxiety concerning
the movements of the panther, kept us from falling asleep.

"The professor told some stories of the skill
of Western Indians in creeping upon guarded
posts, and I retorted with examples of the cunning
and ferocity of these Northern Indian devils.

"Once we were started into renewed vigilance
by what seemed like a scratching or clawing on
the bark of some tree near at hand; but we heard
no more of it. When, as near as we could guess.
it must have been well past midnight, we began
to be concerned at the lowness of our fire. It had
fallen to a mere red glow, lighting up a circle
of not more than twenty yards around the camp.
As for our covert, it was now sunk in the outer
darkness.

"We considered the needs and risks of replen-
ishing the fire, and concluded that the risks were
so far greater than the needs, that our better plan
was to stay where we were till morning.

"If our enemies were upon our tracks. then for
either of us to approach the light would be to be-
tray our stratagem, besides furnishing a fair and
convenient target; while we felt tolerably sure
that the panther was in some not distant tree,

waiting to drop, according to his pleasant custom, upon any one that should come within his reach. These considerations made us once more satisfactorily wakeful, and with straining our sight through the blackness our nerves got painfully on the stretch.

" A bird stirred in the twigs above us, and the professor whispered, ' What's that ? '

" Then there was a trailing rustle of the dry leaves near our feet; and, with a sharp click and a jump of the pulse, I brought my gun to full cock.

" But two little points of green light close together, which met my eyes for an instant, told me that it was only a wood-mouse which we heard scurrying away.

" The professor whispered, ' What was it disturbed the mouse ? He seemed in a hurry about something when he ran against us that way.'

" This was a point, and we weighed it. We were just about to hazard some guess, allowing for an owl, or polecat, or other night prowler, when the professor gripped my arm sharply, and whispered, ' Look ! '

" Just on the outermost verge of the dim circle, I could detect a human figure, creeping like a snake toward the rear corner of the tent.

" ' Shall we shoot — wound him ? ' whispered the professor breathlessly.

" ' No; wait ! ' I answered. ' Look out for the

other fellow. We'll capture them both and take away their guns.'

" The words were scarce out of my mouth when there was a sort of mad rush, and a struggle, apparently close beside us, followed by an agonized shriek. We sprang to our feet in horror, and at once set our little beacon ablaze.

" There, not twenty yards off, beneath a tree, lay a twitching human form. Upon his breast crouched the Indian devil, with its jaws buried in his throat.

" With a cry we sprang to the rescue, and the beast, half-cowed by the sudden blaze, seemed at first disposed to slink off ; but, changing its purpose, it set its claws deeper into its prey, and faced us with an angry snarl.

" The grove all around was now as bright as day. The professor rushed straight upon the beast; but for myself, turning at the moment to draw my sheath-knife, I caught sight of the other Indian, whom we had forgotten, in the act of deliberately drawing a bead upon me.

" He stood erect, close by the tent, his pig-eyed countenance lighted up by the red glare. I had just time to drop flat upon the ground, ere a report rang out, and a bullet went *spat* into a tree-trunk close above me. I returned the shot at once from where I lay, and my assailant fell.

" Without pausing to notice more, I turned to my companion's assistance. He had just fired one charge into the animal, and then drawn his knife, afraid to fire a second time lest his shot should strike the Indian.

"As I reached his side the Indian devil sprang; but the ball had struck a vital spot, and snarling madly it fell together in a heap, while again and yet again went the professor's knife between its shoulders right up to the hilt.

"As the dead brute stiffened out its sinewy length, we dragged it one side and made haste to examine its victim. The poor wretch proved to be Tobin; and we found him stark dead, his throat most hideously mangled, and his neck broken.

"Sickened at the sight we turned away. The other Indian we found still lying where he had fallen, with his right arm badly shattered by my heavy charge of buck-shot. After brightening up the fire we proceeded to dress his wounds. At this work we had small skill, and dawn broke before we got it accomplished.

"Then, digging with our paddles a grave in a sandy spot on the shore, we buried the Indian devil's victim, and set out with our sullen prisoner for the settlements. Paddling almost night and day, we reached Détour du Lac, and there we delivered up our captive to the combined cares of the doctor and the village constable.

"As we afterwards learned, the doctor's care proved effectual; but that of the constable was so much less so, that the villain escaped before he could be brought to justice."

"Truly you keep your good wine for the last, Stranion," said Ranolf.

"Can Sam do as well, I wonder?" inquired Queerman.

"No, he can't!" said Sam positively. "But he can give you something humorsome, at least, to relieve this tragic strain. It's about a bear, of course. I'm very glad my bears hold out so well. This story is called, —

'BRUIN'S BOXING-MATCH.'

"It was a dreamy, sun-drenched September afternoon. The wide, shallow river was rippling with a mellow noise over its golden pebbles. Back from the river, upon both banks, the yellow grain-fields and blue-green patches of turnips slanted gently to the foot of the wooded hills. A little distance down stream stood two horses, fetlock-deep in the water, drinking.

"Near the top of the bank, where the gravel had thinned off into yellow sand, and the sand was beginning to bristle with the scrubby bushes of the sand-plum, lay the trunk of an ancient oak-tree. In the effort to split this gnarled and seasoned timber, Jake Simmons and I were expending the utmost of our energies. Our axes had proved unequal to the enterprise, so we had been at last compelled to call in the aid of a heavy mall and hardwood wedges.

"With the axes we had accomplished a slight split in one end of the prostrate giant. An axe-blade held this open while we inserted a hard-wood wedge, which we drove home with repeated blows of the mall till the crack was widened, whereupon, of course, the axe dropped out.

"The mall — a huge, long-handled mallet, so heavy as to require both hands to wield it — was made of the sawed-off end of a small oak log, and was bound around with two hoops of wrought iron to keep it from splitting. This implement was wielded by Jake, with a skill born of years in the backwoods.

"Suddenly, as Jake was delivering a tremendous blow on the head of the wedge, the mall flew off its handle, and pounded down the bank, making the sand and gravel fly in a way that bore eloquent witness to Jake's vigor. The sinewy old woodsman toppled over, and, losing his balance, sat down in a thicket of sand-plums.

"Of course I laughed, and so did Jake; but our temperate mirth quieted down, and Jake, picking himself up out of the sand-plums, went to re-capture the errant mall. As he set it down on the timber, and proceeded to refit the handle to it, he was all at once quite overcome with merriment. He laughed and laughed, not loudly, but with convulsive inward spasms, till I began to feel indignant at him. When mirth is not contagious, it is always exasperating. Presently he sat down on the log and gasped, holding his sides.

"'Don't be such an old fool, Jake,' said I rudely; at which he began to laugh again, with the intolerable relish of one who holds the monopoly of a joke.

"'I don't see anything so excruciatingly funny,' I grumbled, 'in the head flying off of an old mall, and a long-legged old idiot sitting down hard in the sand-plum patch. That mall might just as well as not have hit me on the head, and maybe you'd have called *that* the best joke of the season.'

"'Bless your sober soul!' answered Jake, 'it ain't that I'm laughing at.'

"I was not going to give him the satisfaction of asking him for his story, so I proceeded to fix a new wedge, and hammer it in with my axe. Jake was too full of his reminiscence to be chilled by my apparent lack of interest. Presently he drew out a short pipe, filled it with tobacco, and re-marked —

"'When I picked up that there mall-head, I was reminded of something I saw once up in the Madawaska woods that struck me as just about the funniest I ever heard tell of. I 'most died laughing over it at the time, and whenever I think of it even now it breaks me all up.'

"Here he paused and eyed me.

" ' But I don't believe *you'd* see anything funny in it, because you didn't see it,' he continued in his slow and drawling tones ' so I reckon I won't bother telling you.'

" Then he picked up the handle of the mall as if to resume work.

" I still kept silence, resolved not to ask for the story. Jake was full of anecdotes picked up in the lumbering-camps; and though he was a good workman, he would gladly stop any time to smoke his pipe, or to tell a story.

" But he kept chuckling over his own thoughts until I couldn't do a stroke of work. I saw I had to give in, and I surrendered.

" ' Oh, go along and let's have it ! ' said I, dropping the axe, and seating myself on the log in an attitude of most inviting attention.

" This encouragement was what Jake was waiting for.

" ' Did you ever see a bear box ? ' he inquired. I had seen some performances of that sort; but as Jake took it for granted I hadn't, and didn't wait for a reply, I refrained from saying so.

" ' Well, a bear can box *some*, now I tell you. But I've seen one clean knocked out by an old mall without a handle, just like this one here; and there wasn't any man at the end of it either.'

" Here Jake paused to indulge in a prolonged chuckle as the scene unrolled itself anew before his mind's eye.

"'It happened this way: A couple of us were splitting slabs in the Madawaska woods along in the fall, when, all of a sudden, the head of the mall flew off, as this 'ere one did. Bill, however, — Bill Goodin was the name of the fellow with me. — wasn't so lucky as you were in getting out of the way. The mall struck a tree, glanced, and took Bill on the side of the knee. It keeled him over so he couldn't do any more work that day, and I had to help him back to the camp. Before we left, I took a bit of codline out of my pocket, ran it through the eye, and strung the mall up to a branch so it would be easier to find when I wanted it.

"'It was maybe a week before I went for that mall, — a little more than a week, I should say; and then, it being of a Sunday afternoon, when there was no work to do, and Bill's leg being so much better that he could hobble alone, he and I thought we'd stroll over to where we'd been splitting, and bring the mall in to camp.

"'When we got pretty near the place, and could see through the trees the mall hanging there where we had left it, Bill all of a sudden grabbed me sharp by the arm, and whispered, "Keep still!"

"'"What is it?" said I, under my breath, looking all around.

"'"Use your eyes if you've got any," said he; and I stared through the branches in the direction he was looking. But there was a trunk in the way. As soon as I moved my head a bit, I saw what he was watching. There was a fine young bear sitting back on his haunches, and looking at the mall as if he didn't know what to make of it. Probably that bear had once been hurt in a trap, and so had grown suspicious. That there mall hanging from the limb of a tree was something different from anything he'd ever seen before. Wondering what he was going to do, we crept a little nearer, without makin' any noise, and crouched down behind a spruce bush.

" ' The bear was maybe a couple of yards from the mall, and watching it as if he thought it might get down any moment and come at him. A little gust of wind came through the trees and set the mall swinging a bit. He didn't like this, and backed off a few feet. The mall swung some more, and he drew off still farther; and as soon as it was quite still again, he sidled around it at a prudent distance, and investigated it from the other side of the tree.

" ' " The blame fool is scared of it," whispered Bill scornfully; " let's fling a rock at him ! "

" ' " No," said I, knowing bears pretty well; " let's wait and see what he's going to do."

" ' Well, when the mall had been pretty still for a minute or two, the bear appeared to make up his mind it didn't amount to much after all; he came right close up to it as bold as you like, and

BRUIN'S BOXING MATCH.   Page 55

pawed it kind of inquiringly. The mall swung away; and being hung short, it came back quick, and took the bear a smart rap on the nose.

" ' Bill and I both snickered, but the bear didn't hear us. He was mad right off, and with a snort he hit the mall a pretty good cuff; back it came like greased lightning, and took him again square on the snout with a whack that must have made him just see stars.

" ' Bill and I could hardly hold ourselves; but even if we had laughed right out I don't believe that bear would have noticed us, he was so mad. You know a bear's snout is mighty tender. Well, he grunted and snorted, and rooted around in the leaves a bit, and then went back at the mall as if he was just going to knock it into the other side of to-morrow. He stood up to it, and he did hit it so hard that it seemed to disappear for half a second. It swung right over the limb; and, while he was looking for it, it came down on the top of his head. Great Scott! how he roared! And then, scratching his head with one paw, he went at it again with the other, and hit it just the same way he'd hit it before. I tell you, Bill and I pretty near burst as we saw that mall fly over the limb again and come down on the top of his head just like the first time. You'd have thought it would have cracked his skull; but a bear's head is as hard as they make them.

" ' This time the bear, after rubbing his head

and his snout, and rooting some more in the leaves, sat back and seemed to consider. In a second or two he went up to the mall, and tried to take hold of it with one paw ; of course it slipped right away, and you'd have thought it was alive to see the sharp way it dodged back and caught him again on the nose. It wasn't much of a whack this time, but that nose was tender enough then! And the bear got desperate. He grabbed for the mall with both paws ; and that way, of course, he got it. With one pull he snapped the codline, and the victory was his.

" ' After tumbling the mall about for a while, trying to chew it and claw it to pieces, and getting nothing to show for his labor, he appeared absolutely disgusted. He sat down and glared at the bit of iron-bound oak lying so innocent in the leaves, and kept feeling at his snout in a puzzled sort of way. Then all of a sudden he gave it up as a bad job, and ambled off into the woods in a hurry as if he had just remembered something.' "

This story had called forth a running commentary of appreciative chuckling. When it ended, every one was in a merry humor.

" I think," remarked Queerman, " that I, too, have kept one of my best stories for the last. At least, it seems the best to me ; and I hope you fellows won't think it the worst, anyway."

" We'll tell you about that after we hear it," said Magnus.

" Well, here goes," continued Queerman. " My title is —

'THE RAFT RIVALS.'

" The last log of Thériault's 'drive,' not counting a few sticks hopelessly 'hung up' on far-off Squatook Shoals, had been captured in the amber eddies of the Lower Basin below Grand Falls, and had been safely pinned into the great raft which was just about to start on its leisurely voyage down the river to the shrieking saws of Fredericton.

" ' This 'ere's as purty a site fur pinnin' up a raft as ever I sot eyes on!'" remarked Ben Smithers, thrusting his hand into his gray-blue homespun breeches for his fig of 'black-jack.'

" Ben was sitting on a rock near the water's edge. No one made answer to his remark, which was perhaps regarded as too obvious to call for comment. Presently a large black dog, as if unwilling that any grain of wisdom should drop from his master's lips unheeded, thrust his head into Ben's lap, and uttered a short bark.

" For perhaps half an hour Ben Smithers and his fellows sat on the shore or lounged about the raft, smoking and whittling, and not one complained of the delay. The rafts which Thériault had already despatched down the river, each of quiring two or three hands to navigate it through the rapids, had thinned the numbers of the drive down to not more than ten men, all of whom were bound for Fredericton on this very raft.

"Presently one of the hands took the pipe from his mouth, tapped it gently on a log to remove the ashes, and remarked, 'Here they be!'

"A wagon was descending the precipitous road which led from the unseen village to the beach. An apprehensive looking horse between the shafts hung back warily upon the breeching, and a red-shirted lumberman clung doggedly to one of the wheels. At the anxious horse's head trudged a boy; and behind or beside the wagon, as pleased her fancy, there danced a five-year-old child, her long yellow hair and bright pink frock making her look like some strange kind of butterfly.

"As their eyes fell on the little creature a grin of rough tenderness flashed out on the faces of the gang. Little Mame Thériault, who came with this wagon-load of supplies for the gang, and who was to accompany the raft down the river, at once became the pet of the drive. Her father, a young widower, took her wherever it was possible, and her baby hands were dispensers of gentleness throughout the roughest gangs.

"Only Jake, the dog, refused his tribute of homage. Jake's heart was sore within him, for he was jealous of little Mame.

"Jake was a dog among ten thousand. He

possessed countless accomplishments, and was
ever athirst to learn more. His intelligence was
such that 'cute as Jake' had become a current
phrase of compliment with Ben Smithers and his
comrades. Wholly devoted to his master, he
was at the same time hail-fellow-well-met with
all hands.

"Until Mame's appearance on the scene, Jake
had reigned without a rival. Now it was quite
different. The hands, though as respectful as
ever, seemed strangely forgetful of his presence
at times; and with Ben, when Mame was by, his
place had become secondary, and all his eager affection seemed to go as a matter of course. Ordinarily Jake would have liked well to make a
playmate of Mame; but as it was—never!

"The whole party had got aboard, and the raft
was shoved off into the current. In the middle of the structure stood a rough, temporary
shanty of hemlock slabs, with an elbow of rusted
stovepipe projecting through the roof. Within
this shelter the cook presided, and two or three
bunks gave accommodation for part of the gang.
The others, including of course Mame and her
father, looked to more luxurious sleeping quarters
in the settlements along shore.

"Mame was enchanted with her surroundings,
— with the shores slipping smoothly past, with
the ripples washing up between the logs, with
the dashes of spray over the windward edges of

the raft, with the steersmen tugging on the great sweeps, and last, but by no means least, with the wide sheets of glossy gingerbread which the cook in his little house was producing for her particular gratification.

" She had never before experienced the delight of a raft voyage. She skipped from side to side on her swift but unsteady little feet, and all hands were kept anxiously alert to prevent her from falling into the water.

" Several times she made playful advances to the big dog, throwing herself down on the logs beside him, and scattering her yellow curls over his black and crinkly coat; but Jake, after a reluctant wagging of his tail, as if to indicate that his action was based on principle, and not on any ill-will toward herself, invariably got up and made a reserved withdrawal to some remoter corner of the raft. Thériault noticed this, as he had done on previous occasions, and it seemed to vex him.

" ' I *don't* see what Jake's got agin the child that he won't let her play with him,' he remarked half-crossly.

" ' Oh, I guess it's 'cause he ain't no ways used ter children, an' he's kinder afeared o' breakin' her,' Ben Smithers responded laughingly.

" Jake had caught the irritation in the boss's tone, and had vaguely comprehended it. Upon the boss his resentment was tending to concentrate itself. He could harbor no real ill-feeling toward the child, but upon Luke Thériault he seemed to lay the whole blame for his dethronement.

" Toward noon the breeze died down, and the heat grew fierce. The yellow-pink gum began to soften and trickle on the sunny sides of the logs, and great fragrant beads of balsam to ooze out from every axe-wound. The gang clustered. as far as possible, under the insufficient shade of the cook-house, in loosely sprawling attitudes. — hats off and shirt-bosoms thrown wide open. Jake got down on the lowermost tier of logs, and lay panting in a couple of inches of water, surrounded by floating bits of bark and iridescent patches of balsam scum.

" As for Mame, her pink frock by this time was pretty well bedraggled, and frock and hands alike smeared and blackened with balsam. Her sturdy little copper-toed boots were water-soaked. The heat had a suppressing effect even upon her, and she spent much of the time in Ben's lap in the shade of the cook-house; but now and then she would rouse herself to renewed excursions, and torment the raftsmen's weather-beaten breasts with fresh alarms.

" The river at this part of its course was full of shoals and cross-currents. calling for a skilful pilot: and Thériault kept sweltering about the open raft rather than trust the steering to less responsible hands.

"Just as the cook, with parboiled countenance, came to the door of his den to announce the dinner, Mame had run to Jake's retreat, and crawled down upon the panting animal's back.

" This contributed not at all to Jake's coolness, and he felt seriously disturbed by the intrusion. Slipping from under as gently as he could, he moved away in vexation, and Mame rolled in the shallow water.

" She picked herself up, wet and whimpering; and Thériault, who happened to be standing close by, spoke angrily to the dog, and gave him a sharp kick.

"For Jake this was a new and startling experience. He could hardly resist the temptation to spring upon his insulter, and pin him to the raft. Too wise for this, however, he merely stiffened himself to his full height with a sudden, deep growl, and rolled a significant side glance upon his assailant.

" The boss was astonished. At the same time he was just a little startled, which made him still more angry, and he shouted, —

" ' Don't you snarl at me, you brute, or I'll kick you off o' the raft!'

" Ben Smithers interposed. 'Don't kick him agin, boss!' he exclaimed. 'I don't mean no disrespec', but Jake ain't never had no kicks an' cuffs, an' I'd ruther he *didn't* have none, 'less he desarves 'em. He don't know now what you kicked him fur, an' he's only protestin'. He wouldn't hurt a hair o' yer head; an' ez fur Mame, howsomever he may keep outen her way in this 'ere heat, I'd jest like ter see anythin' try ter tech her onkind when Jake war 'round. You'd see then who was Mame's friend!'

"During Ben's expostulation Thériault had cooled down. He laughed a little awkwardly, and acknowledged that he 'hadn't no call, under the circumstances, to kick the dog;' but at the same time it was with no glance of affection that he eyed Jake during dinner.

"When the meal was over he cautioned Mame so severely that the child began to look upon the dog as a bloodthirsty monster, and thereafter Jake was persecuted no more with her attentions.

"The poor dog was none the happier on this account. Unheeded by his master, who through most of the afternoon kept nursing the wearied child in his lap, the poor animal lay grieving on a far-off corner of the raft.

"Late in the afternoon the raft entered the succession of rapids lying below the mouth of the Munquauk. There are few shoals here, but the steering is difficult by reason of turbulent water and cross currents. About this time, than which none could be more inopportune, little Mame woke to new life, and resumed her perilous flittings about the raft. The men who were not needed at the sweeps were kept busy in pursuit of her. The swift motion, the tremblings of the raft, the tumult of the currents, — these all enchanted and exhilarated the child. Like a golden-crowned fairy, she balanced tiptoe upon the upper logs, clapping her stained little hands, her hair blown all about her face.

"Suddenly forsaking Ben's company, she started toward her father, where he stood at the stern of the raft, directing the steersmen. The father reached out his hands to her, laughing. She was within three or four feet of him, but she chose to tantalize him a little. She darted to one side, pausing on the very edge of the raft.

"At this moment the timbers lurched under a heavy swell. Mame lost her balance, and with a shrill cry of terror she fell into the pitching current.

"A mingled groan and prayer went up all over the raft; and Thériault and one of the hands, a big woodsman named Vandine, plunged in to the rescue. Ben Smithers was not a swimmer, and he could only stand and wring his hands.

"Thériault and the other who had sprung in were both strong swimmers ; but a narrow surface current had seized Mame's small form, and whirled it far away from the raft, while the heavy bodies of the men, grasped by the under-current, were forced in a different direction.

"Thériault's face grew ghastly and drawn as he saw the distance between himself and his child

"SLOWLY BATTLING WITH THE WAVES, JAKE AND HIS
BUDDIES DREW NEAR THE RAFT   Page

slowly widening. His desperate efforts could not carry him away from the raft. and he marked that Vandine was no more successful than he. A choking spasm tightened about his throat, and he gave a keen, sobbing cry of anguish as he saw the little pink-frocked form go under for the first time.

"Then a great black body shot into the air above his head, and landed with a splash far beyond him. 'Jake!' he thought instantly; and a thankful sigh went up from his heart. Now he began to care once more about keeping his own head above water.

"Jake was late in noticing the catastrophe. He had been deep in a sullen and heavy sleep. When the cries awoke him he yawned, and then mounted a log to take a survey of the situation. In a second or two he caught sight of the pink frock tossing in the waves, and of the little hands flung up in appeal.

"His instantaneous and tremendous rush carried him far out from the raft, and then his pure Newfoundland blood made him master of the situation.

"Little he cared for the tumult and the white-capped waves! His sinewy shoulders and broad-webbed feet drove him straight through cross-current and eddy to where the child had sunk. When she came up he was within five feet of her, and with a quick plunge he caught her by the shoulder.

" And now Jake's difficulties began. In quieter waters he would have found no trouble, but here he was unable to choose his hold. • The men saw him let go of the child's shoulder, snatch a mouthful of the frock, and start for the raft.

" In this position Mame's head passed under water, and all hands were in a panic lest she should drown before Jake could get her in. But the dog dropped his burden yet again, seized the little one by the upper part of the arm, and in this position was able to hold her head clear.

" But it was a trying position. To maintain it, Jake had to swim high, and to set his teeth with pitiless firmness into the child's tender arm. The wave-crests slapped ceaselessly in his face, half-choking him, and strangling Mame's cries every instant.

" Thériault and Vandine were by this time so exhausted as to be quite powerless, and were with difficulty pulled back upon the raft. There stood all hands straining their gaze upon the gallant dog's progress. Ben Smithers waited, with a pike-pole, on the very edge of the timbers, ready to hook the steel into Mame's frock, and lift her aboard the moment Jake got within reach.

" Slowly battling with the waves, Jake and his precious burden drew near the raft. Already Ben Smithers was reaching out his pike-pole. Suddenly there was a crash, and the raft stopped short, quivering, while the waves poured over its upper edge. The timbers of the farther inshore corner had run aground and wedged fast.

" There was a moment of bewildering suspense, while Jake and his charge were swept swiftly past the hands stretched out to save them. Then the raft broke into two parts, and the larger outside portion swung out across the main current and drove straight down upon the swimmer.

" With a cry the raftsmen threw themselves flat on the logs. grasped at the dog. and succeeded in snatching the now silent child to a place of safety.

" Jake had just got his fore-paws over the logs when the mass drove down upon his body. His head went back under the water; and Ben. who had a firm grip in the long hair of his pet's fore shoulders. was himself well nigh dragged overboard. Two of his comrades, throwing themselves on the logs beside him, plunged down their arms into the boiling foam and got hold of the helpless dog. and, almost lifeless, Jake was laid upon the raft.

" Feebly wagging his tail. the noble fellow lay with his head in Ben Smithers's lap, while the strength returned to his sinews, and the breath found its way again to the depths of his laboring lungs. As the gang gathered about, and a babel arose of praise and sympathy, Jake seemed to appreciate the tribute.

" When the boss had seen his child put safely and warmly to bed in the cook's bunk, he rushed

forward and threw himself down beside Ben Smithers.   He embraced Jake's dripping body, burying
his face in the wet black ringlets, and speaking
words of gratitude as fast as he could utter them
   "All this, though passionately sincere, and to
Ben highly satisfactory and appropriate, was to
Jake a plain annoyance.   He knew nothing of the
delights of reconcilement, or of the beauty of an
effective situation, and he failed to respond.   He
simply didn't like Thériault.   He endured the endearments for a little, gazing straight into Ben's
face with a piteous appeal.   Then he staggered to
his feet, dragged himself around to the other side
of his master, and thrust his big wet head under
the shield of Ben's ample arm.
   "Thériault laughed good-naturedly and rose to
his feet.   'Poor Jake!' he murmured, 'I ain't goin' to persecute him with no more thanks, seein'
he don't greatly enjoy it.   But I can tell *you*, Ben
Smithers, what a mistake I made this morning, an'
how it sticks in my crop now to think on it.'
   "Here the boss thrust out his hand, and Ben
Smithers grasped it cordially.   It was a general
understanding that the boss thus apologized to
Jake for his behavior in the morning, and that
thus Jake duly accepted the apology.   Jake was
expected to understand the proceeding as the gang
did, and to abide by it.   No atom of surprise was
felt, therefore, when, after the lapse of a day, it
became plain that Jake and the boss were on the

best of terms. with Mame in her proper place of idolized and caressed subordination."

" That Jake was not all unworthy to sit with Jeff and Dan," said I, as Queerman ended.

"No," said Ranolf ; " he was a prince among dogs."

After this we told no more stories. I, who had all the records in charge, made my report, giving statistics as to fish caught, miles travelled. localities of camps, and so forth, as well as the names and tellers of all the stories. The report proving satisfactory, we sang " Home. Sweet Home" and " Auld Lang Syne." standing around the camp-fire. Then. somewhat soberly. we turned in.

Right after breakfast on the following morning we put our canoes on the train. and were soon whirling homeward, proud in the consciousness of sunburned skins, alarming appetites, and renovated digestions.